MY SISTER'S SECRET

DIANE SAXON

Boldwood

First published in Great Britain in 2023 by Boldwood Books Ltd.

Copyright © Diane Saxon, 2023

Cover Design by Head Design

Cover Photography: Shutterstock

A CIP catalogue record for this book is available from the British Library.

Paperback ISBN 978-1-80426-479-9

Large Print ISBN 978-1-80426-478-2

Hardback ISBN 978-1-80426-480-5

Ebook ISBN 978-1-80426-476-8

Kindle ISBN 978-1-80426-477-5

Audio CD ISBN 978-1-80426-485-0

MP3 CD ISBN 978-1-80426-484-3

Digital audio download ISBN 978-1-80426-482-9

Boldwood Books Ltd
23 Bowerdean Street
London SW6 3TN
www.boldwoodbooks.com

John, Margaret and Lynn. Because you're all so precious to me.

1

Gary Philpotts, aged fifty-nine, of Adelaide Street, Brierley Hill, was today discharged from court as Judge Marcus Delaney ruled there was insufficient evidence to convict.

Mr Philpotts, accused of inciting a child to engage in sexual activities and other charges, was allowed to go free after the court judge ruled that the CPS had presented flawed evidence.

Flawed evidence! Flawed evidence?

How in hell's name could the evidence be flawed? The man was guilty as sin, and everybody knew it. The police, the social services, the parents of yet another victim. The courts and that court judge.

Barely aware of the gentle simmer of annoyance, the explosion of unleashed terror and fury took me completely by surprise.

It was the damned newspaper article. I wish I'd never seen it.

I never read the papers these days. Stupid gossip plastered over the front page. This 'influencer' or that 'model'. Some damned foolishness that no one wants to see. We want news. Not 'he said, she said, tit for tat' from so-called reality TV stars I've never heard of and, quite frankly, never want to.

Today was different, though. There it was, roughly folded and dumped on the table next to the brown sugar and pot of thin wooden stirrers. I almost dropped my double shot caramel latte as I tried to place it on the coffee-stained worktop with trembling fingers.

Air backed up in my lungs and I could almost count the seconds in the silence as I stared at that photograph. Ice chilled my veins. A chill I couldn't attribute to the air-conditioned Costa coffee hut.

It was the cold memory of fear that trickled down my spine.

That man. That evil beast who had destroyed more than one life in my family. Not to mention the others he'd wrecked too.

My skin crawled.

I wouldn't have spotted the article if the newspaper hadn't been lying in the Costa coffee, folded, with Gary's face uppermost. It was a short article. Almost insignificant. As though it wasn't important. As if this man didn't deserve more exposure for the things he'd done. Because there was insufficient evidence, or the evidence had been botched. Not because he wasn't guilty, but because some bureaucrat decreed that he wasn't dangerous enough to warrant hanging onto and investigating further just because an 'i' hadn't got the correct dot, or a 't' wasn't crossed at the correct angle.

Well, that didn't mean to say it was justice.

Not for the things he'd done. Things he'd managed to get away with for years.

I'd lost my faith in the justice system.

Then again, I'd lost faith in my own sense of justice, if indeed I'd ever had one. It was stolen from me long before it had the chance to properly form.

The sun glared in through an enormous pane of glass to blur my vision of the small photograph of him. Just a head shot. A face.

The bright flash of sunlight on water.

The quick flick of a minnow's tail.
The swish of a child's fishing net.

He'd changed, I'd give him that, but I'd recognise him anywhere. Still, that scarred, pockmarked skin that no amount of treatments could ever put right. The hairline that had receded far enough to reveal wrinkles etched deep into his brow. A brow that hung low over eyes I could never forget. Pale, watery blue. Eyes that had haunted my life for what seemed like an eternity.

Eyes that had tormented me with evil deliberation.

The gaze that would follow me around the room, filled with a veiled threat only I could understand.

I swallowed back the hot acid sting in my throat as I reached with trembling fingers for the newspaper. To study it in more detail. Not a reassurance, hardly that. Confirmation though, that it wasn't my imagination.

Knees turned to water, I backed up, ready to read the small print of the article, and sank into the nearest plastic bucket chair, the curved edges digging into my thigh.

'Ah, hell.'

Birmingham Crown Court heard the offences happened between October 2001 and March 2002 with a victim who was then eight years old.

During a trial of the facts, a jury considered whether Philpotts had committed twelve acts of indecent assault. They found he had committed three.

Mr Philpotts was issued with an eighteen-month supervision order after the court decided he had been unfit to plead after his mother died under traumatic circumstances at the start of the trial.

The victim, who cannot be named due to their age at the time of the alleged crime, said, 'I can't believe this has happened. My life has been a complete nightmare for the past twenty years and he hasn't given it a second thought. I feel cheated. He's used his mum's death as an excuse to be found unfit to be sent to prison. How can that happen?'

The victim claims they were subjected to horrific abuse and have suffered breakdowns and anxiety ever since. 'This is not justice. He's not been punished for anything. A supervision order is a joke.'

As part of the order, Philpotts is subject to numerous conditions to limit any contact with children under the age of sixteen to 'supervised only'.

Supervised only. What kind of punishment is that? None whatsoever.

He'd got away with it. How had that happened?

I dropped the paper on the small, shiny table. I didn't need to read any more. He'd walked. Free. There would most likely be some kind of mental health order on that decision, but if there was, it wasn't evident in the newspaper article.

My face turned numb. I don't know how long I sat, staring into space, before a voice filled with irritation called over.

'Hey, hey! Is this yours?'

The man was tall, blond, possibly late thirties. Good looking, if a little puffy around the face, possibly from too much drink the night before. Eyes bloodshot. He held my latte up, which was evidently cluttering up the small counter, and gave it a slight sideways jiggle while he balanced a tray of four disposable coffee cups in his other hand.

'Do you want to move it, luv?'

His passive aggressiveness hung in the air between us. That 'luv', said with a downward tone which suggested I definitely wasn't his love.

There was no saliva in my mouth. I couldn't swallow. I sent him a jerky nod instead.

Perhaps he thought I was the ignorant one as he dropped the take-out cup none too lightly onto the small table beside me with a slight flick of his wrist, as though it offended him. As though he was doing the queue of people behind him a personal favour by ridding them of my one solitary cup that was evidently barring his way.

Froth sputtered out of the little hole in the top like one of those miniature volcano projects. It ran in foamy rivulets down the side of the cardboard cup and puddled out onto the Formica surface.

There'd been no need for it. No necessity for his attitude.

Why are some people so easily offended by nothing? Like the motorists who hurtle up behind you in a 30 mph zone, pushing, pushing for you to get a move on, go faster, break the speed limit.

Unwarranted aggression.

If I'd wanted, I could have spoken, told the impatient arse to get a life. To maybe understand that bad things happen sometimes. Shock hits people in different ways, and a little understanding goes a long way. Patience is a virtue. Any one of those clichés I could have pulled from my extensive file and launched at him.

I could have reduced him to ashes.

But I didn't. I couldn't.

My insides had crumpled, a piece of clingfilm wadded into a tight fist. Limp. Useless.

The bright flash of sunlight on water.

The quick flick of a minnow's tail.

The swish of a child's fishing net.

It's strange how memories long since buried can rear their ugly heads and knock your entire being right on its arse.

I pushed aside the newspaper and lurched to my feet. Unsteady for a moment, I held onto the back of the chair and then headed for the doorway, weaving like a drunkard.

'Oy, you've left your drink!' Why the blond guy felt a personal responsibility for my latte, I had no idea. After all, it was my bloody drink. I'd paid for it. If I wanted to bloody well leave it behind, it was up to me, wasn't it?

On a good day, I might have challenged him. Actually, on a good day, I probably would have turned around, smiled serenely and thanked him as I picked up my coffee.

Today wasn't a good day.

Without looking back, I raised my hand, showing him the middle finger as I punched through the doorway and strode to my car. There was so much I had to do. Literally, I had more than anyone else I knew on my plate right now. Normally I'd handle it.

A sliver of regret edged its way through. I shouldn't have been rude. There'd been no need. The guy, in all honesty, was probably just trying to be helpful.

I visualised the froth trickling down the side of the cup. Maybe. Maybe not.

I slipped into my car and reversed just as my stomach gave a low grumble to remind me I'd left behind my tuna melt. The machine had probably just pinged as the door closed behind me.

Now I didn't even have lunch to be grateful for. There was no way I was about to turn around and go back. Not with that queue of people. Not with my nasty show of bad temper which had been completely unnecessary. That man hadn't deserved it.

Humiliation stirred.

I drove around the corner and parked my car, window down. I needed a moment.

I glanced at the time. Fifteen minutes. That's how much I could allow myself before I needed to return to work.

I had a long day ahead of me, but I needed this.

I thumped the steering wheel with the heel of my hand as the trickle of annoyance pushed past the numbness and broke free.

Long buried dread burbled up to mutate into something far darker.

Far more dangerous.

2

My eyelids flickered, too heavy to stay open. They closed, taking me down the dark pathway I desperately wanted to avoid. A dark pathway where I remembered. Every last moment, each tiny aspect. Details I'd long ago tucked away. Oh, the guilt was there. It would always be there. But those finer elements I'd managed to bury for so long. In the name of self-preservation.

Until I saw Gary Philpotts' face in that newspaper, and it brought every memory charging to the fore.

It wasn't so much what had happened, as what might have.

Not so much what I did, as what I didn't do.

I rolled onto my side and curled into a ball, pressing my hand against a stomach that protested with the amount of pasta I'd consumed after work. Too much, but I'd been so exhausted from that long day. So hungry. Too late in the evening, but I'd piled on the cheese. The food of nightmares. Hard to digest.

That wasn't what caused the nightmares, though. I'd been so busy all day, I'd managed to block the vicious slide of thoughts, but now my defences were down.

I sighed and took the turn along that dark, winding path.

* * *

Brilliant sunshine beat down on my head as I leaned over to watch the olive and black flash of a sprightly minnow cut through the clear shallows of one of the Fens pools. Slick and fast, the small fish darted in large shoals, surfacing to snatch at a mosquito or skater bug, the red-striped bellies of the male glinting in the sunlight as they flipped and turned.

We'd recently moved and barely had a chance to make friends before we'd broken up for the summer holidays.

It didn't bother me to be alone. With a big family, I enjoyed the freedom of getting away. Not too far. Maybe I'd gone further than I should that day, but I'd seen the fish when I was out investigating with my sisters and Mum, but they wouldn't keep quiet. Fish liked the silence. They came closer to the water's edge when you didn't all chatter away like over-excited birds.

I wasn't supposed to have come this far, with my little fishing net on the end of a thin length of bamboo cane, but the temptation had been strong. Strong enough to lure me back.

We lived right next to The Cut, a smelly old canal slicing through what had once been the industrial centre for the Roundoak Steelworks. The likelihood that I'd find fish in those dark, murky waters was slim.

Mum had said, 'Don't be long.'

I wouldn't be.

I wasn't exactly disobeying, as Mum hadn't specifically said not to go there.

The Fens nestled just beyond the canal, between Pensnett and Brierley Hill. A literal step from the world of dirty industrial buildings into an oasis of four pools and unfenced fields that undulated beyond the horizon. Horses roamed, grazing freely on once lush grass that had withered into sparse, dried clumps under the fierce summer sun.

I never knew you could turn a horse loose into open land and let them wander. Some of them were tethered on thick, hairy ropes, but most ambled around without boundaries. They seemed to have more sense than to wander across the road.

The Grove Pool was the second smallest and a quick dash over The Cut and along the overgrown towpath. Dodging and diving through the thick foliage and branches, I gripped my net in one hand and an empty jam jar in the other. I stumbled down onto a small inlet. A little sandy beach. The entire waterline was made up of these secluded coves barely wide enough for two people. When we'd come with Mum, we'd not all been able to get to the water's edge together. We'd had to push our way through the trees to find a wider inlet.

It didn't matter when I was on my own.

A grin plastered across my face, I hunkered down to scoop a jar full of water, shovelling up a little of the shingly sand that wouldn't have been out of place on a foreign beach. I screwed the bottom of the jar into the hot, dry sand to keep it upright.

I watched for a long moment before I dipped the net into the water believing that was all I needed to do for them to sacrifice themselves to my net.

The shoal of fish darted away in one small wave of colour.

I yanked the pole back to check, just in case I'd managed to net one but with a stab of disappointed tugged out a slimy string of green weed that clung to the wire edging. I scooped and snatched again and again, but the fish evaded my net until my arm ached with the drag of the water.

Disappointed, I stood for a long moment, gazing into the pool until the shoal eddied with the current and drifted away to my right.

As the sun heated the back of my neck, I waited but they never returned.

I dashed through the narrow strip of thicket to the next inlet and held my breath as I watched the quiet water.

The silence was broken by the sharp snap of a twig, the thunder of stamping feet.

I whirled to face the interloper, the cane clutched tight in my fist as though I might whip him with it.

'Hi.' A big boy, fine wispy hair framing a round face, puffed out a short breath, forcing a laugh as he pinwheeled his arms, struggling to keep his feet under him. His knee grazed the ground before he staggered upright.

I recognised him. I wasn't sure where from. Maybe from the big school. He looked familiar, in any case. Cheeks and forehead ravaged and raw with yellow pus-filled spots to leave angry red crevices.

Pity stirred in me. Poor boy. That's not nice.

I touched my fingers to my own smooth cheeks.

'That's dangerous, tharris.' A thick Black Country accent rolled off his tongue.

We'd not lived in Pensnett long, Dad having traipsed us all the way from Surrey to set up a new life. A better life. The prospect had been exciting.

The accent was like a different language.

It confused me. I stared at him while I let his words process in my mind.

The boy flicked his hand to indicate the embankment behind him. The dry root of a tree snaked just above the surface of the sand. 'Watch out, yow. I nearly fell on my arse.'

He lumbered forward a step.

Trapped between him and the water's edge, I stiffened, uncomfortable, but not really knowing why. He'd used a naughty word, something we weren't allowed to say, although I'd heard it before. My mum didn't swear. Never had. Sometimes she whispered to my dad out of the side of her mouth, 'Not in front of the children,' although the misdemeanour could range from a mild swear word, to pinching a packet of crisps before dinner time, to giving Mum a sly squeeze when he thought no one was watching. Not that any of us minded. They loved each other. They were always having a cuddle.

The boy sent me the rictus of a smile. As though he'd really had to force it, and I took a cautious step back and then froze. I never spoke. I stared at him as he took another clumsy step towards me. The excitement of the small vibrant fish flashing through the water dulled.

There was something not quite right.

He tucked his hands inside the pockets of mucky shorts slung low under his stomach. and then turned away to amble down to the water's edge. The sun beat down on the top of my head as I saw a pathway open up for me to dart along.

I glanced at the lad as he rubbed a rounded tummy under an over-stretched T-shirt.

Moisture formed on his top lip, and he took one hand out of his pocket to swipe it away and then rolled his shoulders forward to peer into the clear water as though my presence had lost any interest. He leaned both hands on his knees as he watched the bright fish flit through the shallows.

'There's some lovely fish biting.' He nodded towards them and then glanced over his shoulder at me. Excitement gleamed in his eyes and tempted me to peer in the shallow, clear water lapping in gentle riffles.

'I see you've got a fishing net. That's bostin, thar is. Where d'yow gerrit?'

With a little surge of pride, I placed the end of the bamboo in the earth and gave the cane a wiggle, but the boy didn't wait for an answer and took another step closer to the edge, the toes of scuffed trainers almost dipping into the water.

Ignoring me, he studied the fish in front of him, so still I could almost believe he'd stopped breathing until he spoke.

'You know what these are? They're minnows.'

I knew they were. Mum had helped me to look them up in her ency-clopaèdia.

In the absence of any threat, I took a cautious step closer, my eyes scanning the water for movement.

A large shoal flashed through the shallows. Excitement had the boy bouncing on his toes as he pointed, his hand leaping with excitement as he tried to follow the swish of the brightly coloured fish.

'Look, oh my god, look.'

His excitement contagious, he snapped his head around, a wide grin breaking out, so nothing about his next move was contrived but came from a surge of childish enthusiasm I totally related to.

He flexed his fingers at the cane. 'Giz your net, I'll see if I can catch some for yow.'

My gaze clashed with his. Could I trust him with my fishing net? Would he run away with it? Mum would kill me if someone nabbed my new present.

He held still, his arm outstretched as he waited for a decision from me while the sun scorched us. Sweat made the back of my knees tickle like the skitter of spiders' legs running down them.

I glanced at the water. The shoal of fish flowed by in an arc again.

I thrust the bamboo stick into his hand. If he ran with it now, Mum would shout at me for trusting a stranger.

'Never trust strangers.' The words had been ingrained in us all our lives.

The boy broke into a wild grin, uneven teeth flashing as his cheeks reddened with excitement.

With a surprisingly gentle motion, he dipped the net into the shallows and held still. I edged closer, barely moving for fear of the fish sensing my presence and zipping off, never to be seen again.

The fresh smell of talcum powder and apple shampoo that our family used was overwhelmed by a warm unpleasant odour, a bit like when Dad was sweating after working really hard on his old car. Only this was sour and smelly. Like someone who doesn't wash very often.

With a sudden move, the boy dashed the net through the water, and then snatched it back with a quick flick of his wrist to catch it in one hand.

'Look!'

He shoved the net towards me, his face alight as small fish flapped

*against the net he'd palmed in his hand. I drew closer, mesmerised by the
frantic flip-flopping of the tails.*

*I stared back at him for a moment, excitement skimming through my
veins. 'I have a jar.'*

*He looked surprised when I spoke. I suppose I hadn't said anything
until then.*

*Before he could respond, I ignored his warning about the slippery tree
root, sprinted up the small incline and dashed away to where I'd left
the jar.*

* * *

'Oh.'

I rolled myself out of a bed damp with sweat and stumbled
through to the bathroom. My heart staggered around in my chest.

I didn't want to think about the past. Didn't want to re-live it. But
my mind, weak with stress and fatigue and the constant ebb and
flow of hormones, let these memories slip through.

Anger raged inside of me as I peed, a hot sting shot through,
and a soft sob caught in my throat. Cystitis. Again.

I finished up and let my nighty drop back into place while I
considered changing it. A cool breeze from the open bathroom
window teased me but did nothing to calm my mind.

I sank onto the closed toilet seat and breathed in the fresh air
reluctant to return to my overheated bed.

There was no justice in the world if that man got away with this.
With everything he'd ever done.

I hated him. Hated him with a passion.

* * *

I burst back through the thick curtain of bushes, breaking the silence. A brilliant smile I knew would show the gap of two missing teeth right in the front. Mum's voice in my head told me not to smile as wide, keep my lips over that gap. But I couldn't help it. I was so excited.

'I have it, I have it.' I thrust the water-filled jar out with desperate enthusiasm as the sun broke free from behind a scudding cloud and the big boy's fist closed around the fish, as though he was about to crush them. Panic shot through my voice. 'Quick!'

The anger that seemed to have settled on his face slid away at the sight of me as though he was surprised at my return. He grinned.

The boy seized the jar and turned the net inside out, so the small fish plopped into the water, one after the other. Five of them in total.

With heads pressed together, we leaned in, intent on watching the fish swish fast tails as they swam in tight, desperate circles. Trapped.

It never occurred to me then what it would be like to be stuck in a never-ending circle. Never able to be free.

The boy pressed his head against mine and brought his nose closer to my hair. I heard him breathe in and slanted a look at him. Maybe he liked the smell of Mum's apple shampoo.

His breathing was more rapid than mine, but I'd been the one to do the running.

His fingers trembled and the water slopped over the edge of the jar onto the back of his hand.

Uncomfortable for some odd reason, I found myself edging away from him but his next moved surprised me.

As if exhausted, he let out a puffy laugh and flopped down onto the sandy beach, taking the little jar of fish with him, the water slopping over the rim.

His tongue darted out to lick dry, cracked lips and he sent me a look through pale, watery eyes I wasn't sure of. One that made me uneasy once again.

* * *

I padded my way through to the kitchen and flicked on the kettle, knowing it was half-full of water. It was still tepid from the last one I had before I went to bed. There was no point trying to sleep. A cup of tea would be good. A distraction.

Nothing was going to distract me completely. I couldn't persuade my mind away from him. From Gary Philpotts.

3

Bobbi Channing slapped the lids on the last of the lunchboxes, clipped the sides down and shoved them into schoolbags.

'Kids,' she yelled at the ceiling, only for the third time in the hope that her children would miraculously appear instead of having to be dragged kicking and screaming from the house.

'Coming!' Shanna, her second eldest, yelled down the stairs, impatience grinding through her voice.

At fifteen, she'd moved from being a sweet little princess into a raging diva with hormones enough to fill every room in the house.

Shanna thundered down the stairs, her heavy footsteps making the whole house shudder as she stomped on each tread in her new shoes.

Ones she'd insisted her dad buy. Like all the other girls had at school instead of good, sensible, sturdy Clarks shoes Bobbi had always insisted on for her children.

'Has anyone seen my mascara?' Shanna's shrill voice echoed up the stairwell.

Bobbi sighed. It might be an idea never to let Shanna out with Craig ever again as she'd honed the skill of wrapping her dad around her little finger, it appeared. Bobbi had always considered that *her* prerogative, one she felt she'd never taken full advantage of. Because she wouldn't. It was there, though. In her arsenal of weapons should she ever need it.

Move over, Mum. It appeared the time had come when another 'woman' had finessed that talent.

A talent that went along with Shanna's teenage rebellion. Bobbi wouldn't mind so much but it seemed to be rubbing off onto her youngest daughter, Toni. At the age of five, she still needed good practical shoes with her delicate, developing feet. Unlike Shanna, who at five feet ten inches already sported a size eight. Difficult enough to find a range of footwear in that size, never mind that Shanna demanded the height of fashion. No wonder Craig had caved. It had been the easier option. Find shoes, shoes fit, buy shoes.

'Mum, Mum...' Still nowhere to be seen, Shanna's demanding voice let everyone know where she was.

'Toni.' Bobbi's voice gentled as she addressed her youngest, still at the breakfast table, shovelling as much food in her mouth as she could. Fuel to sustain her until lunchtime, because god only knew, but that child was having the growth spurt of giants.

Toni raised her head, rammed a last piece of toast slavered with blackcurrant jam into her mouth and slipped down from her chair.

She swiped the back of her hand over her lips, smearing sticky dark purple jam up to her wrist.

With a swift, natural move, Bobbi cornered her daughter and scrubbed the damp dishcloth she'd been wiping the bench down with over both hands and the child's tacky mouth before she could take a step.

Toni wrinkled her button nose. 'Euww, Muuuum.'

Hygiene be damned, Bobbi lobbed the dishcloth back into the sink. She'd averted the disaster of Toni having to change her pale blue school blouse for the second time that morning. The first was when she spilt milk all down her front.

Luckily, the milk didn't drip onto her skirt as that was the only clean one she had left until Craig did the next load of washing later that day. Thank god for her husband's mild-mannered domesticity. He never complained, or slacked, just fell in naturally. They were a team.

It was a constant round of washing these days. The kids believed it was acceptable to drop any item of clothing on the floor for Mum or Dad to pick up. No matter how short a time they'd had it on.

Of all her children, Toni was by far the least tidy, and the dirtiest. Toni, her precious mid-life surprise. When their family of five had settled into a comfortable routine, Antonia burst onto the scene with all the energy and personality of the rest of the household put together.

Shanna bustled into the kitchen and Bobbi raised her head. 'Are you ready?'

'I can't find my mascara.'

Without missing a beat, Bobbi handed her eldest her fake Michael Kors bag, which Shanna slipped over her shoulder. 'You're not allowed to wear make-up anyway.'

Shanna shrugged as she hitched the strap onto her shoulder. 'They don't notice, Mum. Nobody pays any attention.' She rummaged in the cutlery drawer as though fully expecting to find it there.

'Well, what did you do with it? When did you last have it?'

'I don't know.' Her voice turned whiny. Was she really going to have a tantrum?

Bobbi ran fingers through her short, choppy hair that she'd barely had time to brush that morning while she glanced at the kitchen clock. They needed to get a shuffle on. Really. She was going to be late for work.

'I have a mascara upstairs, if you're quick.'

Shanna poked her bottom lip out. 'Yours is no good. It'll be all dried up and crappy.' She whipped her bag off, dumping it on the countertop, hunched her shoulders and slapped her overly high heeled shoes across the kitchen to communicate peevish annoyance.

With what she considered the calmness of a saint, Bobbi slipped her youngest daughter's schoolbag from the kitchen table to hook it cross-body over Toni, still addressing her eldest. 'Do you have your homework?'

Shanna's glossy lips twisted, and she shook her head as though Bobbi had asked the most stupid question in the world. 'I always do my homework.' Yes, she did. She often left it behind, though. 'Unlike Josh.' She nodded at her older brother as he slipped through the doorway.

At seventeen, her eldest child already towered over Bobbi. Not that it would take much. She was only five feet one and he was six feet two in his bare feet and the spitting image of his dad. Eyes the colour of caramel and fine blond hair that flopped over his forehead, so he peered from beneath it.

He'd also inherited that casual gentleness from his dad. A gentleness Bobbi wished had been attributed to all her offspring.

Josh wrapped a gentle arm around her shoulder and placed a soft kiss on top of her head, bringing a smile to her face.

'Yum. Tuna sandwiches, my favourite.' Bobbi watched the flicker of distaste in his eyes and broke into a smile.

'For you, beef, horseradish, lettuce and tomato.'

Shanna snorted. 'Spoilt brat.'

She elbowed her way past her brother to snatch her schoolbag from the kitchen counter again, taking Bobbi by surprise with a stunning smile. 'Thanks, Mum.' She landed a fast kiss just above Bobbi's ear and ruffled her hair in a quick role reversal. The time would come, but Bobbi wasn't ready for it yet. She was still adjusting to her eldest daughter's see-sawing hormones.

Josh staggered back a step with over-exaggerated surprise as he swept his own bag off the island, one hand on his heart.

About to yell again for her youngest daughter, who'd disappeared upstairs, Bobbi swallowed the breath she'd gathered as Toni flew into the room with Craig hot on her heels. His eyes calm, his face was nevertheless flushed with effort.

Shanna snatched up her little sister and swung her in a quick circle, sending Toni's long plaits swinging wide while the little girl giggled.

Bobbi cast her eldest daughter a grateful look. She might be the diva of the house, but there was a kindness to each of their children she was grateful for.

'Thank you, Shanna. Toni, your hair looks beautiful.' Craig manhandled his daughter upright and tugged her uniform into place.

'Mum. Mum. You haven't forgotten my school trip today, have you?'

With mild panic, Bobbi flicked her husband a quick look. She'd just spent the best part of thirty minutes with Toni, and the child hadn't opened her mouth, except to push food into it.

Craig raised his hand to smooth gentle fingers over the top of his daughter's bright blonde head. 'I'm coming on the school trip with you today.'

Craig's lips kicked up at one side and his eyes crinkled at the edges as they met Bobbi's, conveying, 'and you've forgotten' without opening his mouth.

Toni tipped her head back and scrunched up her face with a

huge, gappy-toothed grin. 'Oh, they love it when you come on the school trips with us, Daddy. You're the best.'

Bobbi tried not to take offence. Despite her job, or maybe because of it, she was too uptight. On the infrequent trips she'd volunteered to help with, she'd felt her entire time had been spent head-counting not only her own group, but everyone else's too, desperate not to let any child go missing. In all fairness to her, that was ever since Mrs Robinson, the Year Two teacher, had mislaid one of her own group when Shanna was that age. It wasn't confidence in herself Bobbi lacked but rather the abilities of the other adults.

The polar opposite of her, all the children loved Craig.

Built like a line-backer, with the temperament of a teddy bear, Craig Channing was the mildest mannered person Bobbi had ever come across to the point of frustration at times, but everybody loved him, including her.

They'd met when they first worked at Tesco together while they were both at college.

University hadn't been an option for either of them. Neither Craig nor Bobbi's parents had been to university back then and didn't believe in it. 'Get yourself a career,' they'd said. 'It'll hold you in good stead. A piece of paper won't get you anywhere, but a skill will.'

Craig had tried out as a builder's assistant. He was going to be a brickie, but he hated it. His love of driving pointed him in the direction of HGV driver. Much of his time was spent driving long distance, over to Europe. That's where the money was. He wasn't short of a note or two.

Bobbi found a job in childcare with the local council. It hadn't been a driving ambition, but she found she liked it. She was good at it. So, she was the one who went to university, eventually. By the time she did, they already had two children and during that time found out she had a third on the way. She attended part-time. One day a week while she worked a full-time job.

Still so young when they first met, it probably should have been the end of their relationship, but unlike a lot of their friends, Bobbi and Craig stuck together. They'd kicked all the wildness out of their systems, partying each time Craig returned home, until they were both ready to settle down properly.

Ready, but completely taken by surprise with the arrival of their eldest son. So, like his father, an easy child, but not quite the timing they'd expected.

When Bobbi realised she was pregnant, only two months into their marriage, it didn't matter.

To say they were besotted was an understatement. Deeply in love with their little boy from the moment he was born.

The following two children, Matthew and Shanna, were planned. In a fashion.

Toni was their little surprise.

When they both thought they were done with having children – three was quite enough for any family, especially as Shanna proved a little more challenging than their other two offspring – along came Toni and blew every preconceived idea of being a parent out of the water. She was force of nature.

Always so much better with the children than Bobbi, Craig's long-distance driving accommodated their lifestyle. Away frequently at the weekends, it meant he was often there during the week, so they didn't need childcare as often as many people did.

Bobbi sometimes wondered how they'd managed to have four children together. They went through long periods of not seeing each other. Then again, the old adage might hold up of 'absence makes the heart grow fonder'. It seemed they never ran out of things to say to each other.

He always had such fabulous ideas, always made the best

suggestions. Probably because he was only there for short spurts and the job of disciplinarian never fell to him.

It was Bobbi who was left to tell their eldest daughter not to wear make-up, to remind their youngest son, Matthew, for the twentieth time that he was likely to get detention if he didn't get his homework in, and to nag their youngest to find her school shoes and that they would be *exactly* where she left them, wherever that might be. Toni was in the habit of stripping the moment she walked through the front door, each item of clothing dropped in a trail through the house to her bedroom.

Craig was convinced she would grow out of it. Bobbi had her doubts. She could only hope for Toni to find a perfect partner when she was older. One who would run around after her and treat her like the perfect princess she was.

Craig picked up the coffee cup Bobbi had filled for him, drained it, opened the dishwasher, inverted the mug and placed it inside the top rack. He slid the door closed again as he spoke over his shoulder. 'I can drop Shanna and Matthew off at school first. They'll be a bit early but I'm sure that's fine.'

'Matt had early football practice. He's gone. I'll get the bus, Dad.' Shanna moved fast, dashing to the front door, and called over her shoulder, 'See you later.'

Confusion slid over Craig's face. He'd not yet come to terms with the fact that his eldest daughter was going through the 'deeply embarrassed by your parents' stage. One on one, she adored her dad, and that would never change, but that slide of discomfort in case he hugged her in front of her friends would last a short while.

Bobbi took the dishcloth out of the sink, gave it a squeeze and swiped it over the countertops, leaving them clean for when they returned. 'I'll drop you. Otherwise, you're going to have to park in the car park. It'll cost a fortune.' She turned to scoop up her work items.

Easy, Craig gave a shrug. He'd not think twice about paying, but that money would cover the cost of another family meal.

Arms full of files, a laptop slung over her shoulder, Bobbi herded them all out the door, eyes constantly scanning, mind buzzing as she checked each one of them over to make sure they had everything.

She let the flow of conversation wash over her as she put her old grey Peugeot 405 Estate into gear, reversed out of the drive and negotiated the early-morning traffic.

They weren't short of money, but the older the kids got, the more expensive became the clothes, the shoes, the hair products. Bobbi wasn't averse to giving them a lesson in life by saying no, but she firmly believed if they could afford it, the kids could have it. None of them would go to private school, like her sister Tess's son. If Bobbi couldn't afford for them all to go, none of them would.

So, they would all get their education from the below-standard local secondary school, and their bright minds would have to carry them through. Things weren't like they were when Bobbi and her three sisters were girls.

Schools these days were run more like prisons. High walls and bloody barbed wire fencing. The decision for what appeared to be heavy-handedness to the innocent and uninformed had come fast on the heels of the Dunblane massacre, where a gunman walked unchallenged into the school and shot dead sixteen pupils and a teacher. He injured a further fifteen within a five-minute frenzied attack. Closer to home, and only a few months later, a machete-wielding paranoid schizophrenic entered St Luke's Infant School in Wolverhampton. Bobbi remembered the incident with clarity, watched with horror as it unfolded on TV at the time back in 1996 and had nothing but admiration for Lisa Potts, the woman who had put her life at risk to save three- and four-year-old children.

She never had an issue with the security requirements to

protect children. It was the clampdown on other issues she objected to. The seeming lack of trust in all parents and their ability to make intelligent decisions for their children.

No longer could Bobbi pen a quick note if one of the children had a doctor's or dentist's appointment. No. The pyjama-wearing squad had seen to that, unable to keep their own kids under control, the truancy rate had rocketed and now all parents had to physically present original documentation to confirm appointments. They had to provide evidence. Not even a photocopy of the damned letter would do or email of a scanned copy. It had to be the original. In case some wily parent had tampered with it. A waste of time for parents, school admin staff and surgery staff.

It was a fact of life now and no amount of objections were about to change the situation for this generation.

Respect had faded.

It hadn't been that way when Bobbi was a child. Her mum and dad would 'dress' for parents' evening. Her dad in his cheap suit, Mum in her finest frock with a slick of lipstick across her lips. These days, you didn't look twice when they turned up in their pyjamas.

She shifted in her seat and tried to think of something else, but it was a personal bugbear.

If every parent did the same as Bobbi and made damned sure their own children attended and stayed at school, they wouldn't have a situation. Parental responsibility. The defining lack was evident in every aspect of Bobbi's life from her own children through to other people's she dealt with on a daily basis. Professionally, she exuded every non-judgemental message she could, but that didn't stop her entirely from being disapproving in her own little way.

She dropped Josh off as they passed by the senior school. With barely a grunt from him, he still managed to ruffle his youngest sister's hair before he unfolded himself from the car and lolloped, long-limbed, through the school gates.

With a kiss from each, Bobbi blew out a soft sigh as the car doors closed behind Craig and Toni when she dropped them at the junior school. It allowed her a full five minutes in the silent drive to work just to think.

She let her mind riffle through her workload, starting with the morning meeting she had as soon as she walked in the door. Barely time to draw breath and, in all probability, she'd be hard pushed to grab a cup of coffee if no one had opened the office up before she arrived. That was the norm. The kettle would be cold and empty.

Her phone buzzed to signal an incoming WhatsApp message.

'Oh, god!'

Who'd forgotten their lunch? She glanced over her shoulder at the back seat. Empty. Thank heaven for small mercies.

If they'd forgotten their PE kit or anything else, then they would have to do without, and take the consequences. Today, she couldn't be late for work. A team leader herself, she had her one-to-one with her manager. It would hardly be an auspicious start if she hauled in twenty minutes late. And it would be twenty minutes by the time she went through the whole rigmarole of getting in through the school security system, answering a million questions before they'd let her hand over a PE kit.

Bobbi drew up outside the red-brick offices with their 1980s flat-style windows and delved in her handbag, fishing out her phone. She snatched her bunch of keys from where they dangled. No keyless fob for her like Tess had. Bobbi's car was fast approaching its seventh birthday.

She scooped up her laptop and files and wrestled her way out, leaning against the open car door for a second as she caught her breath. She was still going to be late.

She pressed her thumb against the recognition pad on her

phone and, juggled everything as she bumped her hip against the car door encouraging it to slam shut. She glanced at her phone screen.

Her handbag fell to the floor, the contents spilling onto the tarmac drive. A small bottle of contact lens fluid rolled down the slope, followed by two gold-tube lipsticks and four Tampax. Tampax she wished she no longer needed but as she was currently staggering her way through perimenopause, she had a combination of hot flushes and heavy periods that would start without warning.

She ignored it all as she stared at the Four Sisters' WhatsApp Group, which included Tess, Bobbi, Alexis and Sarah.

Alexis: We need to talk!

Tess: Urgent???

Alexis: Abso-fucking-lutely.

Tess: When?

Alexis: ASAP!!

Sarah remained silent. Bobbi never answered. Not yet.

4

'Night, Bobbi.'

'Night, Elaine.'

'Night, Sandy.'

Much as she loved her younger sister, Alexis could be a right bloody pain in the arse. A drama queen, so Bobbi thought as she packed away her briefcase and swung out the door of the now empty, sweltering office. She switched off all the lights behind her as she went, pausing briefly to set the alarm and lock up.

As the second eldest of the four girls, Bobbi often found herself the peacekeeper, the pacifier. The closest in age to Tess, the eldest, with her slight air of superiority and four years between them. There was a wide gap between them and Alexis, and even wider between them and Sarah. Alexis always declared herself the middle child. Theoretically, she was, but so was Bobbi.

Bobbie often thought she'd followed in their mum's footsteps by having that surprise menopause baby. You'd have thought she'd have known better.

She hitched her handbag up and sighed. She'd barely had a

moment to think. This wasn't a nine-to-five job, but sometimes, like now when the weather was hot, they treated it like one.

It had been a bloody long, hard slog of a day and she wished the whole team hadn't downed tools and dashed out of the office bang on 5.30 p.m., like it was a greyhound race, leaving Bobbi, the race loser, to lock up.

To be fair to them all, it was a rare day any of them finished on time.

She'd worked in Children's Services longer than most, but she hadn't made manager yet. Still team leader, as Esther drifted her way towards retirement. Esther, her manager, worked shorter hours currently, due to stress. Probably the stress of having to lock up after everyone else.

If she'd not had a slightly disappointing one-to-one where Esther took far too long to tell her far too little, then perhaps Bobbi could have scanned her way through another three or four files. If Esther was stressed by talking codswallop over a cup of coffee, how would she feel if she did some real work?

'Bobbi, you're doing fine.' Esther had smiled as she sipped at her decaffeinated coffee.

Damned by faint praise, it seemed.

'Am I in line for promotion?'

Esther's lips pressed together in a regretful line. 'I'm sorry, Bobbi, but there's nothing available. Not here. Not now.'

Which meant Esther had no intention of retiring imminently.

'I think there's a vacancy coming up in Coventry.' She placed her coffee back down and reached for her laptop. 'Would you like me to enquire for you?'

'No. No, thanks, Esther.' That would be a nightmare of a journey. Almost an hour away, on a good day, but the route she'd have to go, she'd be lucky if it didn't end up a four-hour round trip every day. It wasn't worth it.

She gave her manager a tight smile. 'It's too far. I still need to be here for Toni.'

'Hmmm.'

Bobbi couldn't understand the tight-lipped disapproval from a woman who barely worked and hadn't for the past year. 'How about acting manager?'

The woman sent her a puzzled look. 'Where?'

'Here.'

Almost in slow motion, Esther leaned forward to softly close the lid on her laptop. 'There's no need. Phil, our service delivery manager, as you know, is quite confident that I'm performing my job satisfactorily.'

She wasn't, though. It was Bobbi and the rest of the team who propped her up continually because her failure would be theirs.

Esther cocked her head to one side, suspicion floating through her eyes. 'Have you heard differently? Do we have a problem?' Indicating she thought she may have a problem with Bobbi.

Bobbi brought her mug up to her mouth to hide her discomfort. 'No, I just thought perhaps you could do with some more support. With working shorter hours.'

Esther sniffed. 'I have all the support I need, thank you.'

Yes. She did. At Bobbi's expense. Literally, as Bobbi wasn't receiving extra remuneration for the additional work she was doing.

Esther was the epitome of relaxed perfection. She had the ability to bat off any and all queries. Except, somehow, her GP had signed her off sick with stress for three months and now she was back on an introduction to work, shortened hours. Without for one moment portraying any sign of stress.

The rest of them ran around with wild hair and strained faces.

Some days, when Children's Services were stretched to the limit or they had a child or children to look after until they could get a hold of one of their emergency foster carers, it was more often than not Bobbi who took the lead, stayed behind until the job was done. It wasn't beyond her to have to stay until midnight. Child protection. That was the job.

Protection of the innocent aside, just once, when they were having a quieter day, couldn't someone stay and offer to lock up?

After all, three of the team didn't even have kids. Two of them had kids in their late teens who probably wouldn't thank them for being home too early. None of them had four, like her. Four kids to juggle. After-school clubs, gym, swimming, football.

Craig might be a wonderful dad, but his job made him more absent than present at weekends, which meant Bobbi never had a moment's downtime. At least when Craig was off during the week, he could take himself to bed while everyone else was either at work or school. That was the life. Stress free, listening to audiobooks while driving around the country. Perhaps she should re-train.

She couldn't re-train to not be a mother.

She slid into the car and started the engine running, leaving the door open for a moment to let the whoof of intense heat out. She'd parked where the shade cast long fingers at this time of day, but it was still like a boiler room inside the car. At least the steering wheel wasn't untouchable.

She flipped open the cover on her phone and logged into her bank account using facial recognition. Clever, these things.

A message from Craig scrolled up.

Running really late. Late there, late lunch, late leaving. Major crash closed the road for the last hour. Any chance you can pick us up? We're both knackered. I haven't got the strength to wait in this heat for the bus. Neither has Toni.

Bobbi checked the time.

What time?

We're just pulling up at the school gates. Five mins.

No pressure.
She sighed and tapped her answer.

I'll be with you shortly.

She checked her bank balance. It wasn't overly healthy. Everything cost so much.

Mainly food. The bane of her life.

Josh and Matthew ate everything in sight. If there was something in the fridge in the morning, by the time Bobbi returned home, it would be gone. No amount of nagging could persuade them to leave it alone. They were constantly ravenous. Even raw chicken, which a few months ago had been guaranteed not to be touched, would disappear in a dusting of Bart's Raj Masala, spitting vegetable oil and steamed rice, now Josh had become a caveman and discovered the art of 'fire'. Well, he'd learned how to turn the gas hob on and could use the microwave.

It wouldn't be so bad if they considered that their main meal of the day, but it appeared they'd lost their appetites and found a lion's. No longer boys, they hovered on the cusp of manhood. Despite Matthew being the younger, at fourteen he'd matured so much quicker than Josh. His voice deeper. The dark shadow of a beard on his face by the end of the day. He was taller, broader, more muscular and he ate like there was no tomorrow.

She slipped her phone into her handbag and pulled out of the car park.

She'd have to call in at the local Co-op along the road to the school and pick up something quick to prepare. More expensive than Aldi, but that was in the opposite direction and time was at a premium. She needed to get home.

If Alexis had called a family meeting, then they were likely to be in it for the long haul.

She parked the car and dashed through the store, trailing one of those black wheelie baskets with the telescopic handles behind her. She lobbed in a selection of pastas. Quick, easy. Cheap. Although she wasn't sure it would keep them all going. It would be cheaper to roast a whole chicken, potatoes, and vegetables but she simply didn't have the time.

Bobbi peered in the reduced section at the end of the chilled cabinets. Never anything left by this time of the day. Although... she dipped her hand in and dragged out a family-sized trifle. Seventy-five per cent off. Bargain. Hardly her idea of family size, but a treat. Maybe for a family of three. Although she'd bet her life Shanna wouldn't touch it. There'd be some excuse. She'd get fat, she'd break out, too much dairy. The boys would love it, so would Toni. And dammit, so would she. If there was any left by the time she'd cleared up the dinner dishes.

She added a bag of mixed leaves and a cucumber, glancing at the price of tomatoes. Why were they always so expensive? At this time of year, wouldn't you think the price would come down? The kids hated the big, tasteless ones that cost less. They wanted the vine-ripened mini ones. All a bullshit marketing ploy. Weren't all tomatoes grown on a vine? Just not necessarily ripened on one.

She chose a small box of cherry tomatoes. Not vine-ripened, per se, but if she slipped them from the packet, they'd never know.

Or would they?

Why were kids so perceptive these days? When she was a teenager, she'd had no idea about global warming, fertilisers, imported products. Food was food. It was served up, plated in front of her. She didn't even have the choice to eat, or not to eat. She just ate. No questioning, no moaning, no discussion. Bulimia, anorexia, lactose intolerance, gluten allergies. They didn't exist. Certainly not in her family's world. With five females, their mum couldn't afford for them to develop any kind of syndrome or issue. Hormones did not exist, were not spoken of. Nor was being overweight, under-weight, too tall, too short. They were what they were.

Now, every magazine, TV programme, radio show, friends' discussion was rife with anxieties about food. Not how much it costs, and isn't that a sin to waste it, but how to get rid of it once you'd consumed it by fad diets and peculiar exercise regimes promoted by 'influencers'.

She lobbed a red pepper into the basket.

When Bobbi was in her late teens, early twenties, exercise classes were called aerobics. Now, you needed a degree to under-stand what you were supposed to be doing. Was it Zumba, boxing, step aerobics, spinning, barre, Bikram Yoga, boot camp? The list was never-ending. If she needed advice, she'd have to ask her older sister, Tess.

Bobbi pushed her hair back from her face and stood in front of the open chiller doors for a long moment while the hot flush swept over her. It zapped her brain and left a fine sheen of sticky sweat over her entire body. She closed her eyes and rested her cheek against the sliding door, puffing out a few breaths. This was what happened when she rushed.

She opened her eyes and slid the door closed. Pushing away, Bobbi ambled down the aisle. Her inner thighs rubbed together, sweat coating them. It wasn't just when she rushed. She rushed all the time. The flushes just happened to coincide with her rushing. And when she wasn't rushing. In fact, all the damned time.

She ran her fingers over the back of her sticky neck as she reached the checkouts, ignoring the self-serve ones. She'd rather be served by a human.

She unloaded her wheelie basket and stood upright, catching a soft downward draught from the air conditioning vent above.

Processing her own basket of food was always a trial. That's why she preferred a human. Nothing ever blipped through successfully on self-serve.

Especially when she had alcohol.

Alcohol. Wine.

Dammit.

Bobbi dumped the items back into her wheelie basket, snatched the handle back up and spun around, bumping into the man standing too close directly behind her.

'Sorry, I'm sorry. I forgot something.'

He mumbled under his breath, and she ignored him as she dashed to the chiller cabinets against the back wall. She'd buy rosé, but Tess, her older sister, would probably wrinkle her nose at it. She snatched up an icy bottle of wine and read the back label. White. Sauvignon Blanc from Marlborough. Serve cold. Crisp and zesty with citrus notes. That would be Tess's choice. Whatever the hell citrus notes meant. Her sister would pretend to have a greater knowledge.

Wine was wine as far as Bobbi was concerned. She'd no preference between white, rosé or red. She couldn't care less what was in vogue. She just wanted it to taste nice. She preferred her reds sweetish, her whites dryish. No more than £5 a bottle – on special offer so she felt as though she was getting more for her money. She'd never be classed as a wine snob. She knew what she liked and would prefer one nice glass to a whole bottle of nasty stuff, no matter what the price.

This time, she swept up two bottles at £7 each, reduced from £11. Or so the label declared. Had she ever seen it at full price? She didn't know. She'd not entertain paying that much for wine for herself. Nor would she buy two for herself.

One would never be enough if Tess was coming. She only lived a street away, so she'd walk around. Have a skinful and stagger home. God knows what time Bobbi would guide her out the front door, but she needed to monitor how much she drank herself because she had work in the morning. A 9 a.m. start, officially. Unlike her older sister, who had all the time in the world. She didn't work, didn't need to, although she was classified as the office manager of her husband's financial advice company. A tax dodge, if ever she'd seen one.

Bobbi snorted as she joined what was now a queue, albeit only three people in front of her. One had a full trolley, though.

She tapped her foot and prayed they'd open another till.

Office manager. Tess would be bloody lucky if she knew the key-code to get into the building, never mind work in it. Tess wouldn't be able to tell you the colour of the carpet as she'd not set foot in the place for the past seventeen years since darling hubby had gone it alone. Although, that wasn't quite right. She'd turned up for the opening ceremony and drank the champagne her husband had bought dry. It was a one-off in those days, but now it seemed to have become a regular habit. One that might just need to be discussed.

Darling hubby, who, give him his due, had made a damned fortune. For his long hours and hard work, he'd managed to provide for his family. Wife and son. Tess didn't work and Ashton had somehow managed to worm his way into university without actually lifting a finger to make that happen. One of life's drifters. Bobbi had no doubt the boy would shine like a silver buckle. Just like his daddy.

She stuffed the shopping in her woven carrier bag and waved her phone over the contactless machine, glancing at the time just before her debit card obscured it. She better get a move on, it was almost 5.45 p.m. and they'd descend on her at 8.30 p.m.

Poor Craig and Toni. They should have been back at school by 3.30 p.m. What a long day for juniors.

Bobbi would have insisted they hold their meeting at Tess's except she didn't have a babysitter. Josh and Shanna had their own arrangements tonight. They were absolute stars normally, but it wasn't fair with this late notice to put on them when they'd both arranged to be out.

There was no way she'd trust fourteen-year-old Matthew with Toni. The pair of them would be in cahoots. They'd have the house painted every colour of the rainbow when she got home. Or the guinea pigs would be running riot around the lounge floor. Florrie would be pregnant again. Because Florrie had been Freddie, until he became pregnant, and they realised he was a she. Wasn't it just the way of things?

The place was a mess and she'd no time to clear it up, run a quick vacuum around the living room floor. Although, thank heaven for small mercies, all the breakfast crockery was stacked in the dishwasher by Craig, and she'd wiped down the kitchen surfaces before she'd run out the door this morning. Just as she got that message from Alexis.

The one she'd ignored until she'd had her mid-morning coffee in front of her.

Pretty sure she knew what it would be about, the last thing Bobbi needed was a family meeting so Alexis could air her rising hysteria and communicate it to the rest of them. There was always some bloody drama in her younger sister's life. If she could make it about herself, Alexis surely would. It was always about how whatever news any of them had impacted on her life, her emotions, her opinion.

Bobbi sighed, guilt stabbing at her as she tugged open her car door and slipped inside, punching the air conditioning on as soon as the engine started and winding down the window just to get rid of the stale greenhouse air that had managed to build up in the five minutes she'd been in the shop.

She was being unfair to Alexis. Bobbi was just exhausted herself. She saw all three of her sisters on a regular basis. At least once, sometimes twice, a week. It was nice to see them individually, because when they all got together, they were a pack. All vying for attention and supremacy. None of it done with malice or spite, but just a natural constant shifting. Alexis had always been the most demanding, the most fragile.

She wondered about her other sisters, what would be on their minds?

5

'Look at those rainbow colours.' His voice, pitched in a soft calm tone, squeaked at the end, too high, too excited. I was just as excited, squatting next to him, intent on the captive fish.

'Look.' I shuffled closer, my small fingers pointed to each of the fish. 'One, two, three...' I giggled as one of the fish flipped out of the water, then flopped back in, darting around in tight circles. 'Four, five.'

The boy's fingers twitched against the side of the jam jar.

Panting with the heat of the sun, he leaned back and placed the jar between his blotchy red and white thighs. 'Why day you sit down?' He patted the ground by his side. 'Aye it hot?'

I plopped down next to him; the wide legs of pale blue shorts, two age sizes too big, bagged out, leaving my skinny legs exposed to the glare of the sun.

The boy pulled the jar from between his legs and handed it across. I held it with both hands, studying the flash of fish in the jar.

'I'm Gary. Gazza, they call me. What's your name?'

I told him. He smiled.

'Do you live around here?' Gary shuffled, leaning back to rest on his elbows, one hand rubbing a bloated tummy as though it hurt.

I nodded, still distracted.

'*You'm posh, aye yow? Yow day speak like us.*'

I remained quiet, feeling his criticism.

'*D'yow live in the new houses?*' *Gary pressed.*

With a shake of my head, I replied, '*We live in the pub.*'

'*The pub?*' *Gary turned sideways and studied me with curiosity.*

'*The Bull's Head. We moved in a couple of weeks ago.*' *Preoccupied, I dipped a finger in the water, skimming it across the back of one of the tightly packed fish.*

Gary reached out and wrapped his meaty fist around my hand, pulling it away. '*Yow day want to touch them, you know? Yow can burn them.*'

'*You touched them,*' *I defended.*

Irritation passed over his face. '*I day have a choice. I was quick, though. Kept the burn to a minimum.*'

He took the jar away and wedged it in the sand on the far side of him to keep it from tipping over.

'*I didn't know that.*'

Gary narrowed his eyes at me as if he was annoyed with me. '*Well, you do now.*'

I chewed the edge of my thumb, saying nothing, uncomfortable in the face of his simmering anger.

Gary seemed to relent, his voice softer when it came. '*We'll get yow some more in a bit, but I'm just going lie down for a minute. It's so hot and I went out last night on the piss. I'm too knackered to move.*'

He flopped onto his back, his eyes closing, his broad face slack. '*Yow should lie down too. Look at the sun on the inside of your eyelids.*'

Gary patted the sand beside him. He squinted at me through narrowed eyes. '*Just relax, kid.*'

A little stiff, I lay down. I could hardly reach over him and take my jar and fishing net, could I?

'*Close your eyes. See the orange glow.*'

I lay back, aware of his heavy breathing filling the air. Something didn't feel right. An intangible fear fluttered in my tummy.

The weight of his hot hand rested on my stomach, making my muscles bunch. 'Relax. Let the sun warm you.'

Rigid, I squeezed my eyes tight.

'There. That's better, aye it?' Gary stroked his thumb in butterfly-light circles over my stomach, his fingertip edging up the bottom of my yellow T-shirt until the dry skin of his thumb rubbed against my softer, younger skin.

My mouth went dry. Mum wouldn't like this.

I didn't like this.

There was something not right about the way Gary was breathing. Like he was in pain. My muscles bunched as I got ready to move.

'How old are you?' His voice held an unnatural huskiness.

I squeezed the word from between clenched teeth. 'Nine.'

'That's a nice age. I liked being nine. Most the time. I broke my arm when I was nine.'

I said nothing.

'Nice T-shirt.'

'I got it for my birthday.' I opened my eyes and rolled my head to look at him.

'When was your birthday?' Gary propped himself above me, his cheek resting on one hand with the other flattened on my stomach as he boxed me in against the sand.

'Yesterday. I got the fishing net, too.' I couldn't concentrate with the heat radiating from him.

'That's nice.'

He smoothed his hand, so it brushed the waistband of my cotton shorts with a vague tremble.

'Did you get these too?' There was a warble to his voice, so it broke on the last word.

'Yes.' My voice escaped, barely a whisper.

Gary gathered up the hem of my T-shirt, his knuckles skimming my skin as he edged his fingers under the wide elasticated waistband of my shorts. His eyes closed and he groaned, an unnatural look passing over his face. Pleasure. Pain.

This wasn't right.

I bolted upright, terror racing through my veins as his hand flexed against me before I knocked it free.

I leaped to my feet and rubbed agitated hands against my cotton shorts, sweat forming on my palms.

There was something so wrong, so terrible here.

'I have to go.' My voice was high-pitched, frantic. 'My mum's expecting me. She'll be waiting for me.' I cast a quick look at my fishing net. I'd have to lean over him to get it and, instinctively, I knew that would be a bad move.

Gary rolled to his knees as I hopped from foot to foot. He raised a face mottled with heat, eyes glowing with anger.

I gave an over-exaggerated turn of my head and raised my hand. 'I think I can hear her calling.'

On his hands and knees, he started to lumber to his feet. I took advantage of his slowness and whirled, streaking from the little inlet, into the thin covering of bushes and vegetation.

Terror gnashed its sharp teeth as I raced through the undergrowth, the bushes snagging my new T-shirt and shorts, thorns digging mean scratches into my bare arms and legs as I ran for my life.

6

Bobbi tried her best to be sensitive to Alexis's vulnerabilities, but there were times when she craved her own peace and quiet. Times when she'd spent an entire day fighting for a child to get the protection it deserved. Days like today when red tape hindered often urgent operations and all she could do was press the buttons on the computer and wait for the green light.

She wanted to do more. She certainly had more she needed to do after the girls left tonight.

'Alexis.' She'd kept her voice down low when she called her sister.

'Bobbi.'

Bobbi heard the panic in her sister's voice as its normal tone hitched up an octave. There was no way she could engage with Alexis now. The time wasn't right.

Hormones and heat had sapped every ounce of strength from her and all she wanted to do was go home, pour herself a glass of wine and just sit while the kids did their own thing in the back garden. Her feet throbbed like a bitch. Swollen with the heat.

Really, she didn't even want to cook tonight. Not even pasta.

'I got your message. I can't talk right now. Can you arrange with the others to come over at 8.30 p.m.?'

It hadn't seemed right to send a message on the group chat, but she regretted that decision. She didn't need her sister to say she was disappointed, she felt it in the heartbeat of silence before Alexis mumbled her agreement.

'Okay.'

'See you later.'

'Yeah.'

Guilt had rolled in her stomach at the dead air between them. Alexis was so important to her, but Bobbi had other priorities right now.

That's the way things had to be when you had, not just a family, but an entire brood to tend to. Bobbi couldn't remember a time when she'd not been responsible for someone else. Neither Alexis nor Sarah had kids. Or husbands, for that matter.

Although Alexis had been through her fair share. Of husbands. Two and counting. Currently, she didn't have anyone, as far as Bobbi knew, which explained why she was in demand mode. If she had a man on the scene, they wouldn't hear from her for the next six months or so. Not until that relationship crashed and burned. As every one of them did once they found the real Alexis under all that pretence of happy smiles and perfect life. There hadn't been a man yet who'd been capable of dealing with Alexis's reality.

Bobbi's reality was her family.

Toni and Craig would be starving after their school trip. Sounded like they'd been through hell. It was a long day for them and hot. So hot.

She'd sling together the pasta and throw it in the oven while she grabbed herself a quick shower to wash away the grime and sweat of the day. Shanna and Josh would help set the table and pour drinks.

Guilt prodded her in the ribs.

It wasn't really fair. She couldn't expect Craig to bath Toni and read to her before bedtime when he'd spent an entire exhausting day with a busload of over-excited squealy school kids. Especially as he was back on the road early in the morning. A five o'clock start, he'd said.

He'd want to put his feet up, watch TV for an hour and then off for an early night. When he found out her sisters were coming at Alexis's behest, he'd probably hide in their bedroom to keep out of the way.

Not that he didn't love them all like his own sisters, but he'd prefer to avoid the drama.

Bobbi needed to get Toni off to bed herself. If she knew her youngest, she was going to be hungry, tired and a little bit naggy. If she got wind her aunties were all going to be arriving, she'd drag her feet and make damned sure she could see them all. Then that was going to be a late night, and an even naggier child the following morning.

Bobbi couldn't expect her older children to see to her. They'd got their own arrangements tonight. She'd do her best to let them get on with them. They all pulled their weight, but this was last minute, and they couldn't be expected to drop everything because her plans had changed.

Besides, she'd barely seen her youngest, and after the day she'd had, she wanted to spend some time with Toni. She felt the pull to curl up with her youngest for cuddles.

She never put responsibility on her children, never felt the desire to make them feel accountable. She'd seen far too many cases of parents making their older kids responsible for the younger. The couple who locked their four- and two-year-olds out of the house every Sunday afternoon so they could have sex. The woman who was so scared of her husband, she almost dropped her baby out of an upstairs window while her teenage stepson absconded with her housekeeping money across the back lawn.

Bobbi pulled up outside the school and hit the unlock button as the little one dashed ahead of her dad towards the car. She flung open the rear door and leaped inside. At least someone was cheerful, which actually meant that Bobbi was about to have a most exhausting couple of hours before her sisters arrived. Then there was more work to catch up on later.

She hated to think matters were sliding at work, but they were. It wasn't that she didn't work hard enough, just that the workload got heavier, and the newer members of staff struggled to keep up. All the experience had leached out of the office in the last eighteen months. Changed career direction. Burned out. Retired.

She could only hope Alexis and the others didn't stay much longer than ten o'clock, then she could get a couple of hours in. If she could see straight by that time.

She smiled at Craig when he slumped into the front passenger seat, groaning as he made the car rock. Exhaustion swamped his eyes, but he still afforded her a weak smile.

'What a day!'

She could have said the same, but she patted his knee with admiration and sympathy. It was more than she would do. A whole day at Dudley Zoo with a pack of children running wild.

'How did it go?'

'They were animals.' He glanced over his shoulder at his daughter as Toni plugged in her seatbelt and then snatched up her headphones so she could play on the tablet Bobbi had left on the back seat. Not state of the art, a hand-me-down from Josh. Bobbi blinked at her young daughter. She thought she'd be rabbiting on about the trip, but then she saw the slump of Toni's shoulders. Perhaps she would have a peaceful evening after all.

Craig dropped his voice. 'And I don't mean the ones behind the bars.'

'Toni?' She cast him a surprised look. She expected better from her youngest. A child filled with sunshine and mischief, but never truly naughty.

He shook his head. 'Hysterical for the first hour on the coach, like the rest of them, all high-pitched voices and overly dramatic, and then she settled. She was great around the animals, but to be honest, you'd think some of them had never encountered anything with fur, feathers or scales. No bloody respect. They were all too bloody shouty, so the animals all buggered off to the back of their pens. We ended up hardly seeing anything.'

'Oh. That's not good.'

Bobbi glanced over her shoulder and pulled out into the traffic.

She let a beat of silence hang between them before she told him.

'The girls are coming tonight. Alexis called a meeting.'

She knew he wouldn't outright moan, wouldn't ever criticise her sisters, but all the same, she imagined he'd wanted a peaceful evening.

'What time?'

She kept her voice low, just in case Toni tuned in to her parents' talk instead of the tablet. 'Eight-thirty. She wanted to come earlier, but I said no.'

Craig stared at her with bloodshot eyes. 'You said no. To your sister? Are you having me on?'

Strictly, she hadn't actually said no. 'I stuck to my guns.'

He rocked back in the seat again and grinned. 'That was avoidance if ever I heard it.' He sighed. 'Bloody hell, from one zoo to another. I'll say hi and get off to bed. I've an early start and to be honest, I'm not sure I have the energy to pull myself into bed.' He glanced behind him at Toni and then faced Bobbi again. 'I'm not sure I'd have the energy if you dragged me into bed.' He let his head drop back against the headrest and sent her a sloppy grin that made her heart knock against her ribcage. It still did it for her, after all these years. Made her skin tingle.

'I don't think I'll have an early night.'

'Not if Alexis is coming, she's ever likely to stay until the wee hours.'

Craig was right. At the age of thirty-nine, Alexis was young, free and single and still demanding all their attention. Always had been. She wasn't the youngest, but she considered herself a middle child, which wasn't precisely true either because there were four of them. There were no middle children. Or there were two middle children, strictly speaking, depending on whose perspective you took. Alexis took her own perspective. The one that suited her best at any given time. Bobbi snorted inwardly. It was a moving perspective.

'And Tess will leave when all the wine is gone.'

Tess, the eldest, would settle down with a glass of wine in her hand and she would drink until she was turned out hopefully quietly, so she didn't wake the kids. She'd teeter her way along the street to her huge house in the gated community.

Bobbi wasn't expected to notice how much Tess consumed. It was hard not to.

'I only bought two. Is that mean?' She shrugged. 'She worries me. Now isn't the time, but I'm going to have to speak with her.'

Craig raised his eyebrows. It wasn't a prospect Bobbi looked forward to, but the time was fast approaching where she needed to have a heart to heart with her older sister. Before that, she had other matters to attend to.

'It is a school night, and the others will bring drinks, too. If she'd bring more than one bloody bottle herself, it wouldn't be so bad.' Craig kept his voice a gravelly whisper and shot a glance at Toni, only to find her absorbed in whatever game was loaded on the tablet in front of her. 'She'll bring one and drink three, easily.'

Bobbi wondered if Tess did that on a regular basis or whether it was just when she came to visit, which was at least once a week.

It wouldn't surprise her if it was a developing habit.

Tess had nothing to go back home to. Her husband would still be at the office until god knows when. And now her son, Ashton, was off to university this year, she had very little to keep her occupied. Bored, it meant she frequently pitched up at Bobbi's house, which was only a ten-minute walk away from the better part of the neighbourhood, with little more excuse than there was no one at home.

It wasn't as though she offered assistance of any kind. Tess didn't babysit or even help out in any way. Now her one precious child was off her hands, she didn't seem to know what to do with herself. A lost soul.

Too much time, too much money. Not enough responsibility. A woman who'd never worked but for the three years after secretarial college when she'd been a PA to the managing director of some major wealth management company.

Tess, Bobbi's big sister had stolen Graham from his wife. Twelve years his junior. Now she puzzled why the man continued to have affairs.

In Bobbi's opinion, once a cheater always a bloody cheater, and he always had been a cheater, she suspected.

Why he'd never left Tess for yet another younger woman was beyond Bobbi. He wasn't interested in her sister, just how good she looked on his arm. The trophy wife.

Bobbi loved her big sister to bits, but she hadn't got a clue why she stayed with that man.

7

'God almighty!'

Tess stubbed out her cigarette. The last one she'd be allowed for the next few hours. God forbid she smoke anywhere near Bobbi or her precious bloody children.

With a guilty start, she crushed the cigarette even more, surprised at the thought sliding unbidden into her mind. She loved them all, really. She was just feeling bloody antsy.

She swirled the red wine around her glass and stared at the drip pattern down the sides that labelled it an 'excellent' wine. Her own bitterness turned it to vinegar on her tongue.

Only excellent would do as far as Graham was concerned.

Personally, she couldn't give a damn. She'd just as well drink a bottle of Bobbi's cheap, sweet Australian plonk than the overpriced French Fleurie Graham insisted they have delivered from the local independent wine merchant. At twice the price of the supermarkets. Fleurie! She wasn't even that keen. She liked white wine. Graham insisted on buying red. That's all he ever drank, therefore so should she.

Supporting local business, Graham claimed.

It was all about giving the right impression. Impressions counted in Graham's world. Tess didn't give a flying fig about Graham's world. Apart from his ability to earn enough money to support her so she didn't need to slog herself to death going to work. Like her sisters.

Bobbi, for one, was definitely showing signs of the stress of life. She looked older than Tess, even though she was four years younger. Her dull skin mottled under cheap moisturiser that appeared to be fighting a losing battle against the not so fine lines feathering across her cheeks. Like little ripples across a pond, fanning from the corners of her lips all the way to her ears in ever-increasing brackets.

The dark smudges under her eyes were testimony to too many late nights. Not having fun but trying to catch up with workloads that would never reduce. She was working herself into an early grave.

She seemed to have given up on the fight to stave off old age. No longer wearing make-up or even attempting to have her hair styled and dyed. If she expected to keep that husband of hers, who, let's face it, seemed to have grown into himself rather than grown older, then she should look after herself.

Tess ran fingers through her own hair. She went every six weeks to the hairdresser's, without fail. Graham encouraged it, or possibly insisted. Every three weeks to the nail parlour. Her nails were strong and long but having them gelled kept them that way.

Immaculate. As her husband required. Desired.

The sneaky little shots of Botox had kept the wrinkles at bay over her forehead and around her eyes. She needed a little more than sneaky around her own bracketed mouth. Still, she hadn't admitted it to the girls. Not yet.

Perhaps she'd get a session for Bobbi for Christmas.

Shorter than the rest of them by a couple of inches, Bobbi's body had plumped out in recent years. After three children, her waistline had expanded, but seemed to return more or less to normal, but since little Toni came along, evidently at the 'wrong time of life', there'd been far more give in Bobbi's muscle-tone. Her waistline definitely had not pinged back.

Adorable and loved, Toni was turning out to be a handful, more than the other three put together, leaving Bobbi with no time to herself. Or for Tess.

Who in their right mind had four kids these days? Even Tess's generation, when they were girls, there was a shame in it. A sneaky peek from under a fringe, a sly poke of an elbow, an insinuation that it wasn't right. That somehow her parents were uneducated. Just because they loved children.

Tess didn't so very much.

Oh, she loved her own son. Ashton was the apple of her eye. A perfection she couldn't top. He'd been nothing but a sheer joy.

She took a long swallow of her wine as she acknowledged the lie to herself. But nobody else. Not even Graham. Especially not Graham. He'd nurtured an edgy, privileged attitude in their son which seemed to have expanded as he approached his exams. To the extent that Tess thought he wouldn't pass them. Miraculously, he had. Although she held a secret discomfort that Graham had somehow had a hand in that. She wasn't sure how, or even if it was possible. But there'd been a shiftiness to both of them during those brief exam-sitting weeks.

Now Ashton was heading for university, she was at a loss what to do. No longer was she Mum's taxi service. She was redundant. She'd thought he'd spend the long summer vacation creating memories for her to hold on to, but he passed up that precious time for a trip to Budapest, just after he'd arrived back from a quick jaunt to Spain. She'd found herself floundering as he spoke to her with a certain disdain he appeared to have inherited from his dad. Dropping off clothes from his recent trip that would be better served being thrown in the bin. She wouldn't shame herself by giving them to charity. After all, people knew her around here.

They'd expect standards from the Leaming family.

Graham made sure of that.

Other than keep everything running smoothly, Tess had become superfluous to everyone else's needs. Nothing to do and no real friends of her own. Apart from her sisters, who no longer seemed to have time for her.

The four of them had been so close for so long, but age and circumstances had changed the dynamics. Tess had taken herself off to golf during the week, and found, much to her disgust, that she was useless at it. No coordination. That's where the 'ladies wot lunch' all convened. Which excluded Tess.

That was the thing about money. It didn't open all doors. Reputations did.

The exercise classes Bobbi used to join Tess in were no longer on the schedule. Partly due to time, partly because of money. Just because Bobbi and Sarah couldn't afford a private gym didn't mean Tess had to miss out, or lower her standards by going to the council-run gym Sarah worked in.

Alexis never exercised. She said there was no joy in it. Her job as a paramedic was physical enough without having to power her muscles through hours of blood, sweat and tears. Literally. Every day. Tess marvelled at the fact her younger sister lugged around the equipment she did without collapsing under the weight. Alexis's upper arms were almost as thick as Tess's thighs.

Tess still kept her body trim, her skin soft, her hair in a shoulder-length bob. Not a grey hair visible. There was no reason to go grey. Especially when you were blonde. Appearances.

If she expected to keep her husband, she needed to keep her

figure and her looks because god knows she'd noticed his attention straying lately. Not that he'd necessarily done anything about it.

She tipped her head back and drained her glass. She glanced at the clock and sighed. She would far rather sit out on her patio furniture and finish her bottle of wine on her own while she listened to the sweet sound of evening birdsong filling up her otherwise empty life.

Instead, she reached for an unopened bottle of wine from the wine rack and placed it on the wooden surface of her kitchen island to take with her. She hesitated. She glanced at the clock, reached for the open bottle of wine and glugged some more into her glass.

She drank it down. The whole lot in one go.

If she was about to suffer one of Alexis's histrionics, she needed to gird her loins, as such.

Tess scanned the room. Her keen gaze bounced off every surface before she smoothed her forefinger over the top of the light oak mantlepiece.

Her expression soured. It wasn't good enough. Graham was not going to be happy with their new cleaner. Again.

She breathed out through her long, narrow nose. He had no idea the extent she went to just to find a decent cleaner, never mind one who was excellent beyond words. Which was what he sought. Or, truth be told, what he expected her to seek.

The only one good enough had long since retired.

When they weren't right, which they invariably were not, off she went again in pursuit of her husband's cleaning perfection.

It was utterly exhausting. Sometimes she wondered if it would be less stressful if she cleaned their huge, empty house herself. Little more than a wife, she'd become more of a housekeeper.

Her dyed black eyelashes fluttered as she skimmed a middle finger under her eyes to smooth away lines the Botox hadn't yet been employed on. Once, not so long ago, she noticed they'd be there first thing in the morning but during the day, time and gravity would smooth them out long enough for the evening light to be kind to them. These days, whatever was there in the morning was there when she went to bed, only there were more and they were deeper, together with the bruised look that goes with lack of sleep.

Her sisters would notice. They always did. Concerned noises would escape their lips as they expressed grave misgivings about her lack of sleep/work/sex/play.

It was always the same. The eldest of the four of them, there was a long gap between herself and Sarah, who at thirty-four still had that smooth, alabaster skin of a life untouched by misery. No matter what steps Tess took to care for her skin, deterioration had set in. Just as it had in her marriage.

She shouldn't moan. There was nothing much to moan about. Other than the deepening brackets around her downturned mouth. Resting bitch face, they all joked.

She leaned into the mirror to check the feathers of fine lines radiating from a mouth that once, not long ago, had been full and generous. Now it seemed pinched and mean. She thought she'd been kind to her skin. Looked after it.

She didn't smoke. Well, not heavily, in any case. Just the odd one on a social basis. Or when she was alone in the evening, having a glass of wine on the patio. Or a gin and tonic. And goddammit, she was entitled to something good in her life, wasn't she?

Unlike her sisters, she had nothing. Her life was empty.

Her son had taken off for a tour around the world before he started university in the autumn. It was the quick jaunt to Spain that had given him the taste for it. He'd barely given her a backward glance before he held his hand out for a wad of spending money. Off he'd sloped. She probably wouldn't see him again until his course finished in three years' time. Four if he took the extra year to study in Mexico. If his dad funded it.

His dad. Her husband. He would. 'Let him sow his wild oats while he can' was his philosophy.

She didn't understand the differentiation. Graham had sowed his wild oats all his life.

She took a last look around, before she slipped into the kitchen and placed her empty wine glass by the side of the sink. She'd wash it later, before Graham came home and gave her one of those glances of disapproval.

Perhaps she wouldn't drink if he came home earlier. If he deigned to eat a lovingly prepared evening meal with her. One that she'd spent time and patience preparing. Just in case. Not tonight, though. If he came home earlier than normal, he'd find the house empty with nothing in the oven.

It would serve him right.

With a defiant toss of her head, she scooped up her house keys and popped them in the pocket of her wide white linen trousers. She'd not mention to her sisters her concerns about Graham's possible affair with a younger woman. His secretary, she assumed.

After all, there'd be no sympathy from that quarter. That's how she got him, wasn't it?

She snapped the door closed behind her.

8

'Oh, god. Oh, god.'

Tears filled my eyes as my chest tightened with sheer terror.

I ran as though the very devil himself was after me. Little did I know then that he was.

My feet hit the overgrown towpath alongside the Pensnett Branch Canal the locals called The Cut.

The flat soles of my plimsoles skidded on the slippery surface of loose pebbles.

Straight as a die, the canal passed the front door of The Bull's Head, then onwards to The Wallows. We'd barely been there a few weeks, but the locals revelled in telling us that over the years, there'd been many a person ended up in there. Either dead before or after they'd been rolled or tossed in.

If he caught me, would he toss me in, drown me? Never to be seen again.

Cut during the Industrial Revolution, it was polluted to such a degree that one slip and you wouldn't survive being sucked down into the depths. If you survived drowning, the toxins in the water would poison your lungs.

Which was the reason I'd gone beyond, to the freshwater Fens.

Something I'd never do again.

My breath soughed with panic as I pelted along the narrow path, overhanging branches slapping into me every step of the way.

I heard my name bellowed from behind me. I stumbled as I chanced a look over my shoulder, my skinny legs tangling so I staggered.

'Wait, wait.' Gary's voice cracked as he broke free of the undergrowth and lumbered along the path after me. He wasn't as fast as me, but his legs were longer and they ate up the ground between us. His stomach wallowed from side to side like a balloon filled with water.

'You've forgotten your net, your jar.' His voice held a wheedling note I no longer trusted as water and fish slopped over the edge of the jam jar. 'Day yow want your fish?'

I said the first thing that came into my head. 'My mum, she's calling me. My dad will be looking for me.' I turned my back and ran.

The small bridge that crossed the canal came into view and with fear streaking through my heart, I sprinted towards it. Shoulders back, head up, arms pumping like pistons. I ran for my life.

I pelted over the bridge which angled sharply to take me back the way I'd come, bringing me out on the opposite side to Gary.

I stood across from him, barely able to breathe, small sounds wheezing from my straining lungs.

He paused. His gasps filled the air with great bellows of noise while he rested his hands on chunky knees.

I swallowed. My own legs had turned to jelly while I stared at him, riveted to the spot.

What would he do now?

His face florid, he raised his head.

Gary straightened. Anger glowed like hot coals as he met my own terrified gaze.

His jowls shook as he raised a slow, threatening hand and pointed straight at my face.

'I know where yow live, brat. Yow told me. Yow live at The Bull's Head.' He stabbed his finger at the pub behind me. My home. My refuge.

I straightened to match his stance, bravado kicking in as I realised he couldn't catch me. It was over.

'I'm telling my dad on you.' I meant it. My dad would knock the living crap out of this boy, and if he didn't, my mum was sure to.

His voice raised, panic underlying his conviction. 'I know where yow live. D'yow hear? Don't yow tell anyone. Don't yow tell.'

I hesitated, indecision flashing through me. Why wouldn't I tell?

'If yow tell, I'll come into The Bull and kill yow. I'll kill your mum and dad, too. I'll fucking kill 'em in their beds.'

I widened my eyes, unable to strip my gaze from his.

A sliver of confidence edged its way back into him and Gary raised the net and cracked the thin bamboo cane of my fishing net over his knee. It split in two and he threw it to the ground, fury vibrating over the space between us.

He repeated himself one more time through gritted teeth.

'I'll kill your mum and dad. I'll slit their throats for them while they sleep in their beds. Your whole family. I'll kill the fuckin' lot.'

I stumbled backwards, catching the glint of triumph lighting his eyes as he made a move towards the bridge.

Behind me, faint voices erupted in a wild burst of laughter as a family stepped into view. People I didn't know, but I stumbled towards them, towards safety, regardless.

I must have looked a mess, because the woman, tall, willowy, eyes the colour of the summer sky filled with concern, stepped closer to me, leaving her two children a step behind with her husband.

'Are you okay, bab?'

I glanced across The Cut, but Gary had slinked into the bushes. Was he just a bad memory? Or would he really follow through?

My hair stuck to my scalp, my face flamed. What could I say to this nice lady?

Nothing. Because what if I did, and Gary made good with his threat?

To kill my mum, my dad. My sisters.

While they were asleep. Defenceless.

My gaze strayed to the other side of the canal where an empty jar lay shattered on the ground, fish flopping wildly, and a broken, abandoned fishing net next to them.

I turned away and looked the woman straight in the eye.

'I'm fine. I thought I was lost for a moment, but I know where I am now. I know what I'm doing.'

9

Already covered in a fine sheen of sweat, Sarah, the youngest of the four sisters, tipped her head forward and scrubbed her hair almost dry with the small hand towel she'd brought with her. She shouldn't really, she always ended up looking like a dandelion clock as her fine curly blonde hair stood up in a wild frizz about her head.

'Hey, Sarah.'

She looked up as another woman stepped into the airless changing room and started to strip down to the swimming costume she wore under her clothes.

'Hey, Marie, how's it going?'

'Oh, you know. Same as always, can't moan.'

'Who would listen anyway?'

They both laughed.

'What's the temperature like today in there?' Marie jerked her head towards the opening to the pool.

'Cold.'

'Excellent!'

'It was wonderful. Refreshing.' Sarah sighed out her pleasure.

After her brisk thirty-four-length swim, which equated to a mile, she felt rejuvenated. 'And then you get in here and can't dry off properly and everything sticks. I wish we had air con, especially at the moment. I don't want to moan about the weather, because it's gone all too fast, but god, it's hot.'

'Bab, you ay going to get air con in council-run facilities. You'll have to go up the road to the private one for that.' Marie let out smoky chuckle.

'Chance would be a fine thing.'

'That'd be a waste of good money when you have all this, right here, to use for free.'

Sarah smiled. Marie was right. She couldn't afford the luxury of a private gym membership, not when she worked at the council facilities as a gym and swimming instructor.

Tess was a member at the private gym but seemed not to use it as much as she used to. If she had the opportunity, Sarah would have spent her life in there. The best gym equipment, a fabulous pool she was sure was maintained to a far higher standard.

Perhaps she should have found herself a rich older man. Like Tess had. Stole him from his previous wife. Not an admirable trait, but Tess got him, his house and a beautiful son. Ashton was only sixteen years younger than Sarah. She'd sat for him when he was a baby. A gorgeous little boy, full of energy and laughter. He'd filled the house with his presence.

Sarah was going to miss him. They had a special relationship. There was the same age gap between her older sister and herself, but somehow she felt distanced from Tess. Oh, there was no doubt she loved her, but they'd never been as close, never had quite as much in common. Not quite as close as she was to Bobbi and Alexis nor had as much in common as Sarah and Ashton.

Pity stirred in her as she imagined Tess missed her son. Now she was left alone with her ageing, pretentious prick of a husband. His greasy, thinning hair tied back in a ponytail like he thought he was the coolest dude on the planet. He'd always been that way, but there was something about men of a certain age where their desperation showed in their paunch bellies and pony-tail hair.

He'd always made Sarah uncomfortable. Possibly because he was old enough to be her grandfather. Not quite, maybe, but he was twelve years older than Tess, which made him sixty-two. It didn't stop his roving eye. Even as he got older. Possibly because he was getting older.

He'd never made any suggestive comments, or inappropriate moves, but there was something about Graham Leaming that Sarah couldn't take to. Just a vague suspicion. A discomfort.

Just as well he worked so damned hard, both on and off the golf course, and she didn't get to see him often. Birthdays and Christmas. That was fine by her, she was more than content to see her sisters. She frequently did.

'Are you coming on or off duty?'

Pulled out of her introspection, Sarah met Marie's eyes as she leaned in and combed fingers through the mess of her semi-dry hair, taming it as best she could. She twirled it, teasing fine curls into smooth ringlets as she prepared to go to Bobbi's house.

It wouldn't last.

The heat would soon have the curls unfurling into a crazy frizz. She often wished she had the sleek smoothness of Tess's hair but suspected the sleek and smooth came from the hours her older sister spent at the hairdresser's, because she was pretty sure the wildness had been in Tess's hair when they were younger. They didn't have many photographs from back then, and there was a big age gap between them, but Sarah was convinced she could remember Tess's bright blonde hair bouncing around her shoulders in fat locks.

'Off.' She gave the other woman a weary smile. 'I was in at five this morning.'

'Bum. That means you ay doing step tonight?'

'No. I'm off to see my girls.'

Sarah glanced at her watch. She needed to get a move on, otherwise she'd be late to Bobbi's.

'I haven't seen Bobbi for ages. We keep missing each other, what with work and such. Give her my love, won't you? Tell her I'll ring her and see if we can get together for a girls' night.'

'Yeah, it's her house we're meeting at.'

It was always Bobbi's place they went to. Sarah's was too small. Not that Sarah objected to going to Bobbi's. Guaranteed, there'd be a constant stream of junk food from the kids' cupboard, and alcohol from the adults'. Even though she wouldn't be drinking tonight. She was driving, after all.

'How's the bab?'

Sarah startled until she realised what Marie was asking. 'Toni's fine.' She grinned. 'A complete dynamo. What about Jack?'

Jack was in the same class as Toni. 'Good. He's with his dad this week.' Marie rolled her eyes. 'He's been text bitching about the buz being late from the school trip. I day know what he wants me to do about it. He's the one who insists on having him every other bloody week. I'd prefer to keep him myself. He always comes back knackered and stressed when he's been to his dad's.'

Sarah's smile faded as she turned from the mirrors to dig through her backpack. She didn't really know what to say.

'I haven't seen Tess for ages either, is she still on the school committee?'

Sarah shrugged. 'I believe so.' Although it hadn't been mentioned recently, which was another concern Sarah had.

'Give her my love, won't you?'

'Sure.'

Marie shoved her belongings into a locker, took the key out and pinned it to the strap of her costume. 'Take care, bab. See you soon.'

'Bye.' Her voice faded as the woman slipped from the changing room.

Tess. There was definitely something going on with Tess. Perhaps Sarah needed to have a quiet word with Bobbi, because if she asked, she wasn't sure Tess would open up to her.

Sarah was glad they weren't going to Tess's house; being that much younger, she felt as though she had to be on her best behaviour. The woman was beyond OCD, to tell the truth. Sarah soon learned her lesson to never, ever drink red wine at Tess's house. Make it a white one. The stain doesn't show, and the cold haughtiness doesn't flow. It was much easier.

And the other point was, Tess treated Sarah more like a daughter rather than her younger sister. Her gaze falling on her, a vague flicker of disapproval lighting her eyes. No wonder Ashton had bummed off to the continent.

Sarah felt she couldn't express herself in the same way she could to her other two sisters without a sense of superiority from Tess.

By the time they'd been at Bobbi's for an hour or so, though, and Alexis had worn whatever subject had sent a hornet into her knickers to a fine dust as she loosened up with a glass of wine, Sarah could tell them her news.

An hour in which she would barely have touched her wine.

Tess certainly would. She'd already be three glasses down and not noticing anybody beyond the first half-hour. That was a little unkind. But lately, Tess had developed a habit of getting the first glass of wine down her neck as quickly as possible.

With her trademark non-judgemental way, Bobbi took charge to pour her a small first glass, because it was like a switch inside Tess's head. Once she got that first drink out of the way, gulping it down like a glass of water, she slowed. But if she was pouring the glass herself, it would be filled almost to the brim. And if she didn't slow down quick enough, she'd be legless, words slurring, long fingers flicking as she expressed her dissatisfaction with life. When she was sober, none of those things would be expressed. In fact, Sarah wondered if her big sister even remembered what she said when she was drunk, or if the words coming out fell into a black hole of denial once she was sober.

It was definitely a conversation she needed to have with Bobbi. Tess had always liked a drink, but since Ashton left home, it had escalated. An awkward conversation, because it felt like she was being disloyal, but she wasn't willing to take it direct to Tess. Bobbi was far better prepared to deal with the issue.

Sarah glanced at the time again. She'd let it flash past while she stood in front of the mirror, procrastinating. She dipped her hand back into her rucksack.

Taking out a tube of primer, she squeezed a small amount out and smoothed it quickly and efficiently across her pale, freckled skin with her fingers. She hadn't got time to mess around. They'd be expecting her and if she was late, it would be a black mark. Although Bobbi would never comment, Alexis, the sister closest in age to her, would make a meal of the situation.

'Oh, you're late. The rest of us managed to get here on time, Sarah. Why is it that you have to be the late one?'

Probably because Sarah didn't care enough to rush. If she knew her sister well enough, it would be 'something out of nothing', once again.

She teased another curl, dropping it as she remembered she had primer on her fingers, and then opened a small bottle and applied a light layer of tinted moisturiser to her face. She tried her best to keep her skin fresh and dewy looking, but she couldn't afford the expensive stuff Tess recommended.

Besides, it was just a shitload of money for what? Moisturisers that promised to keep wrinkles and blemishes at bay and look after her skin. Tess used the best. She could hardly boast about it. Despite the Botox she'd absentmindedly mentioned the last time she'd had a drink, she looked older than their mum, who looked damn good for her age. At least, the last time Sarah saw her she had. Shamed by the thought, Sarah lowered her head and stared into her make-up bag before she picked up her blusher and swirled a fat, stubby brush around in it.

As she swept the brush across her cheeks, she studied her reflection in the mirror.

No, it wasn't about what you put on topically. It was about what you put inside your body. Sarah was careful about that. Especially these days. She didn't smoke. She drank very little and ate health foods, in general, apart from when she overindulged at Bobbi's house with the kids.

It was the way to go. She considered becoming vegan. She ate very little meat as it was. Chicken a couple of times a week and the occasional piece of fish, when she could afford the nice stuff from Morrison's counter. Although she had been advised in her condition to think otherwise.

She leaned into the mirror, took the mascara wand from its case and quickly dashed it along her long blonde eyelashes. God, she wished she could afford to have them tinted like Tess did. It might actually work out cheaper if she did. The amount of mascara she put on every day, twice a day. Once before work. And once after a swim.

Perhaps next year she'd ask for gift vouchers for her birthday to put towards it. Annoyed she hadn't thought of it sooner, Sarah plopped her mascara away. It didn't seem fair. She'd already celebrated her birthday earlier in the year. February 14, Valentine's Day, which always seemed unfortunate for her. She never received a double whammy of flowers, but flowers for her birthday were life's constants even from her sisters, and she couldn't moan about that. Who didn't love a giant bouquet of flowers? Even though they were double the price just because it was Valentine's Day. She just sometimes wished for a bit more imagination. Like an eyebrow and lash tint.

Sarah dumped the rest of her make-up back into the small bag and then into her backpack. She stuffed in her towel with the plain black swimming costume rolled inside and crammed the smaller towel she'd used for her hair on top. She swung it over her shoulder and made for the door.

The strong smell of chlorine clung to her despite using a fragrant citrus body wash and shampoo. It wasn't a smell that could be disguised easily when you were in it every day, it simply oozed from her pores. There was no point trying to conceal it with a waft of perfume. It would probably only sour it.

She shouldered open the changing room door, hoping to avoid the casual flasher they occasionally had in the men's changing rooms opposite. There was something about the heat that brought the pervs out to play.

She headed to the reception desk to sign herself out. She raised her hand in a casual goodbye to her colleagues and made her way out of the scruffy building into the car park.

'Have fun.'

She smiled. 'You too.'

She loved her job there. It was inspiring. But she was underpaid and overworked, as were the rest of the team. On occasion, she'd also considered quite how safe the place was with its old room under the swimming pool that forever reeked of chemicals.

She'd been approached recently by a private club that wanted her to work for them for a hell of a lot more money than she was currently earning. The only problem was she was stuck for the time being, circumstances being what they were.

She climbed into her little black Kia Picanto she'd had forever and hoped it would limp along for a few more years. At least until she could afford a better one.

With no air conditioning, just a blower that blew out air hotter than outside, she wound down the window with a hand winder and let the hothouse air trickle out, knowing she'd be wet through before she arrived at her older sister's.

As she drove towards Bobbi's house, she smiled to herself, thinking that once Alexis had vented and they'd all given her hugs, reassuring her that her latest drama really wasn't a crisis, perhaps Sarah would get a chance to tell them her own fabulous news.

She could hardly wait!

10

I crawled from under my bed where I'd slept for the last couple of hours, tightly curled around Kim, our German Shepherd puppy.

'Mum will go mad if she catches Kim in your room.' My sister sneaked in through the door, closing it quickly behind her before she scrambled down next to me and hauled the sleepy puppy onto her lap for cuddles.

'Where is she?'

'Behind the bar.' Her eyes, filled with concern, studied me. 'You okay?'

I nodded, ducking my head so she couldn't read my expression.

'You look like you've been crying. What happened?' She gave me a gentle nudge with her elbow as Kim turned onto her back to punch puppy paws at us.

I glanced up, towards the high window, as storm clouds flitted over the sun to block out the light. 'I ripped my new clothes.' I turned my head to my sister. Should I tell her what happened? Could I?

'I'll kill your mum and dad. I'll slit their throats for them while they sleep in their beds. Your whole family. I'll kill the fuckin' lot.'

I swallowed the confession as my attention was drawn back to the heap of clothes I'd dumped on the floor. Clothes I'd never wear again, even if they weren't filled with tiny nicks in the material where bushes had snagged at them, and spots of blood. They were contaminated. With the touch of him. The feel of his hot hand on them, on my body.

I'd locked myself in the one bathroom we had, stripped and scrubbed my skin raw with Mum's Camay soap and nailbrush, just to get the touch of him off me.

My skin was raw.

I was tainted.

'How did you manage that?'

'I was down by The Cut and nearly fell in. I lost my fishing net.' A sob escaped as I nodded at the T-shirt, shorts and knickers. 'I've ruined them.'

She took a long, drawn-out breath. 'Mum's going to kill you.'

I flinched.

'...I'll kill the fuckin' lot.'

Tears welled in my eyes and I blinked them away. 'Don't tell her. I shouldn't have been there.'

My sister wrapped her arm around me. 'It's okay, don't worry. We'll think of something.'

She rolled forward onto her knees, hooking the shorts with her index finger and then dragged them back, skimming them over Kim's exposed belly as the dog squirmed onto her back. She dangled them and Kim's mouth opened, her sharp teeth grabbing at the material.

My sister grinned at me. 'Mum's going to yell at you for leaving your dirty clothing where Kim can get them. She's told us before, Kim's a baby.'

She gave me a conspiratorial elbow in the ribs. 'She doesn't know any better.'

11

Alexis reached for her car keys with shaking fingers after her twelve-hour shift.

She flashed a smile at her partner. 'Night, Jim.'

'Night.'

'Take it easy with that wife of yours.'

He sent her a lopsided grin. 'We're having a spicy curry, followed by hot sex.'

'Nice to know. Thanks for that.'

He shrugged. 'That's what they recommend when the baby is overdue.'

She looked at her fellow paramedic of the past three years. Eyes veiled with tiredness, his crooked smile widened to show straight white teeth.

'And doing what you do every day, you don't know better?' she asked.

He sent her a look full of mock exasperation. 'Of course I do. But why disillusion the poor missus, when she's intent on pressing these things on me?' The gentle Irish accent that had been smoothed out over the past twenty years of living in the West

Midlands grew stronger as his sense of humour kicked in. She'd noticed the power of it under times of stress, too.

He was stressed now that his wife was ten days overdue with their first baby.

She hesitated, jiggling her keys in her hand. 'Baby will come when it's ready.'

The smile fell from his face and he nodded. 'It's taking its sweet time, and in this heat, she's knackered.' He blew out a breath. 'Fingers crossed it's soon. You got anything going on tonight?'

She forced a smile. 'Seeing my sisters.'

'Lovely. A witches' coven. Have fun.'

Despite herself, she barked out a laugh. 'See you.'

He'd always referred to her meetings with her sisters as a gathering of witches.

Leaving him behind, she made her way to her car as heat bounced from the dry tarmac of the car park.

Thank god she'd been working today, otherwise she wasn't sure how else she would have dealt with things. As a paramedic, there wasn't a single minute of the day in which they could afford to think about themselves. Their minds were continually occupied with the welfare of others.

Now she had to face her sisters without going into meltdown, which was precisely how she felt.

It was strange how she could hold it together while she was at work. Perhaps that's why a lot of people like her gravitated towards the care sector. Because they'd been through trauma so unmentionable that they felt the desire to help others. Because she understood what it was like to deal with everything that surrounded trauma.

How was she going to do this? How could she tell her sisters that the monster was back? What would they think?

They'd look at her in that certain way they had ever since that disgusting man had laid his dirty hands on her when she was a child.

No amount of counselling could account for the way in which her sisters would always regard her because even if she felt the horror of the incident fading, they were always there as a reminder. Pity lurking in the depths of their eyes.

Bobbi, with her mother's instinct that, by all accounts, she'd been born with, rather than grown into. It was just her nature. A brilliant mum to her four children. A brilliant sister. Empathetic.

Alexis knew that when she told them, Bobbi would be the first to fold her into her arms and hug her to her plump bosom, more like a mother than an older sister. The age difference between them making her older sister more maternal than sisterly.

Tess, older still, would stand aloof and separate, as though her fragile body was about to crack if she let any emotion flow through her.

Sarah, younger by five years, would observe her as though she was a stranger, the effect never quite touching her. She'd been too young to know, to understand. Shielded from the very moment it happened so that nothing ever affected her. She'd only found out about it when she was in her late teens and Gary Philpotts had been in prison for a short span. They never seemed to be able to catch him quite at the right moment, never had indisputable evidence to bang him up for good.

Positive he wasn't the brightest candle burning, Alexis never understood how he'd managed to fly under the radar. He'd been caught for misdemeanours, but never the real crime. The darkest one.

Maybe because people like her, like their family, didn't tell. They kept their mouths shut and heads down, minding their own business until their business raised its ugly head and became everyone else's.

But they still all had each other, despite everything. It was Bobbi who counted, though. Who always would.

A part of Alexis would crumble to join the rest of the broken bits in that deep well inside of her that she kept buried so as not to hurt the others. The hurt they felt was for them to deal with. It wasn't their fault. Each one of them seemed to carry the guilt that it had happened to her and not them.

She breathed in to the count of five, out to the count of five, just as she'd been taught. She closed her eyes, brought her hands up to the centre of her chest and placed the backs of her fingers together. Along with her next exhale, she lowered her hands and released the tension again and again, knowing that no amount of relaxation technique would ever rid her of the complete horror and fear that lurked inside her.

She opened her eyes.

She touched the back of her hand to a forehead that had suddenly broken out in sweat as her stomach clenched. She could attribute that to the scorcher of a day that didn't seem to be losing its heat, or she could face facts and acknowledge she was having a panic attack.

Gary Philpotts had walked free. Again.

She shuddered.

Her adult self should no longer fear him. It was children he liked. Children he sought out. He wouldn't come after her again. Although he'd never let her forget.

He'd found her when she was a child. Barely old enough to know her own body.

Would she ever forget how his rough, strong fingers had touched her, abused her? How he'd left her not only physically damaged but mentally and emotionally for the rest of her life. No longer a victim, but a shell of a being who could never trust. Never love. With a mum she no longer saw. And sisters she could never fully rely on, despite their support, because when she'd needed them the most, they hadn't been there.

She'd had nobody there. Not then.

She did now. They'd be waiting for her. To support her. To comfort her.

Alexis blinked the tears away and touched a fingertip to the inner corner of her eye. Dammit, she wasn't going to cry.

12

Mum's voice called my name from the pub below our living quarters.

I scooted down the stairs, almost stumbling over Kim as I reached the bottom. She'd grown in the last few weeks from a small puppy to a gangly teenager, confidence in herself burgeoning.

Unlike me. I'd withdrawn into myself, spending much of my time curled up on my bed, Kim by my side, reading a book.

If Mum noticed, she never said, too busy to see us apart from the occasional, 'I've left your lunch on the side.' Or, 'Don't you want to get some more fresh air? It won't be summer forever.'

I didn't want it to be summer. I didn't want to wear skimpy clothes that showed my skinny arms and legs, and flimsy T-shirts I could see my budding breasts through. I wanted winter to come when I could cover up with no one to question why.

'Oh, what have you got that on for? You must be roasting.' She nodded at my long-sleeved T-shirt as I slipped through the door into the snug room all the old ladies gathered in during the evening. During the day, it seemed deserted, except for the lingering smell of stale cigarettes and spilled beer.

I shook my head. 'I'm fine, Mum.'

'Here, would you take this to Mrs Caldwell? You know where she lives.'

'But Mum...' A whine slipped through my voice, only to be trodden down by Mum.

'I haven't got time myself, the heatwave's brought a crowd in.' She handed me a glass pop bottle with a screw top. 'It's the slops from the bitter, to wash her hair in.' Mum's eyebrow flickered up. Funny how all those old ladies, who swore by the shine it put on their hair, didn't have particularly shiny hair. 'She says she's off her legs, but somehow she'll manage to wash her hair.'

We all suspected why Mrs Caldwell was off her legs, and it wasn't because she used the dregs on her hair.

Kim's low keening came from behind me on the other side of the door leading into the domestic part of the pub building.

'Can I take Kim with me?'

'No.' Mum shook her head. 'It's too hot for a puppy.'

'It's too hot for me,' I whinged, scared to set foot outside without company, but everyone else was out playing. I had no one to keep me company. To keep me safe.

Mum scooped up another dark bottle as she came through the hatch leading to the bar. She lowered the hatch behind her and held the bottle out to me. 'Have a bottle of pop. Ask your dad to flip the lid for you. There's a good girl.'

She disappeared into our living quarters, probably to grab a well-deserved pee, and left me alone, the raucous noise from the bar filling my head.

I raised my arms and leaned on the cool brass hatch, placing the bottles next to my elbow. I waited to grab my dad's attention as I watched him serve the patrons along the extensive length of the main bar.

We weren't allowed behind the bar. Never. Not even when the place was closed and we helped scoop up full ashtrays and beer-soaked mats.

I picked at my thumbnail as I waited.

We weren't often given a bottle of pop, but on occasion we were rewarded with one. Normally on a Sunday lunchtime after we'd helped to clear up. We'd never had pop before we came here. It hadn't been something we were even aware of as children. On a Sunday afternoon, though, we got time to spend with our parents. The only time. Mostly, they were exhausted.

I linked my fingers together and waited impatiently for Dad to look my way. The anticipation of having that bottle of Coca-Cola with its red and white flowing logo in my hands was almost unbearable.

Dad looked over and gave me a small, desperate grin as he served yet another thirsty customer.

I let my attention wander over the long bar.

My gaze clashed with Gary's. Ice-blue eyes pinned me to the spot. I couldn't move. Couldn't speak.

He put his index finger in his mouth and sucked it. Although I had no idea what he actually meant by it, I sensed it was a lewd threat.

He raised his glass and tilted it in the direction of my dad as his other hand came up, his fingers slashing across his throat without his narrowed eyes ever taking their attention from me.

Horror crashed through me. He did know who I was. He did know where I lived. He could kill my mum, my dad, my sisters.

I lunged backward, my elbow catching the glass bottle just as Kim, in all her puppy enthusiasm, raced through the door, my mum tripping over her. 'Oh, for goodness' sake.'

Mum stumbled into the snug, reaching out as she fell face first into a wooden barstool and blood spurted from a split lip.

13

Alexis's bloodshot eyes stared around the room at each of them in turn. Her lips pressed tightly closed as they all listened for any movement from upstairs in case Toni erupted from her bed if she got wind of the fact that her aunties were there.

The overpowering smell of garlic and savoury food filled the house, closed in by the heavy, hot weather despite the wide-open doors onto the narrow patio.

Bobbi curled her fingers around her younger sister's as she pressed a small glass of eighteen-year-old Glenmorangie whisky into her hand. The one Graham had bought Craig last Christmas.

Craig didn't drink.

No more than an occasional beer. It wasn't worth his driving licence and livelihood. Graham didn't appear to have any appreciation of that fact. He liked a glass of single malt himself. So, surely, Craig must. He'd stroke his hand over his ponytailed hair and say, 'It's a man thing.' As he gazed around at the four women as though they didn't have the same level of importance as him.

Tess's husband could be a pretentious prick.

Bobbi guided her younger sister into the one armchair in the room and then sank down onto the footstool beside her, her hand on Alexis's knee. Tess stood stiff and unyielding on the other side of the small lounge, her arm resting against the fireplace. Her glass of wine already half-empty.

This wasn't one of her younger sister's overblown histrionics. This was serious. Bobbi resisted the temptation to take her into her arms just yet. Let her get it out. Tell them.

'What's happened?'

Alexis opened her mouth and Sarah bolted into the room.

All three of the occupants already there raised their forefingers to their lips. 'Shhh...'

Sarah froze for a split second and then sank silently onto the overblown DFS sofa that had seen better days even before Bobbi had finished paying for it. Her gaze shifted from one to the other of them.

'What is it? What's happened? Is Mum okay?'

'Mum's fine.' As far as she knew. It had been a while and she was due a visit.

If anything, it would have been Bobbi calling them for all matters concerning their mum. She was the one most in contact with her.

Tess reached for the glass of wine Bobbi had put ready for her sister on the mantlepiece and handed it to Sarah as she took a sip of her own. 'Alexis was just about to tell us.'

Voice cool, it held a small remonstration for Sarah's typical lateness. That lick of disapproval their older sister just couldn't quite help. It was a reflection of Graham's character. One of the small idiosyncrasies he displayed that had rubbed off on his wife. A touch of the hair, a raising of both eyebrows – not too high – a barely perceptible tightening of the lips.

Bobbi gave Sarah the slightest shake of her head in warning.

She wasn't interested in getting into an argument. There was something wrong.

She gave a light squeeze of Alexis's knee. 'Tell us.'

Alexis swallowed and, in the pause, you could have heard a pin drop.

'Gary Philpotts, he's fucking got away with it again.'

Bobbi blew out a breath and then reached for her own chilled glass of wine from the small wooden side table as the still air thickened. 'Wow!'

Sarah's lips parted. 'What the hell...?'

Tess drained her glass and reached for the bottle to refill it. 'How do you know?'

They all spoke at once, words flooding into the room until Alexis let out a gasping sob, her hand pressed to her chest as the stress she'd held at bay broke through the barriers and tears filled her eyes.

'It's all over the newspapers. The bastard. He's on the prowl again. Nothing's going to stop him. Some poor little girl is going to be raped again. Just like I was, and nobody is going to do a single thing to stop him. No one ever does.'

Bobbi reached out, enveloping her younger sister in her embrace.

14

Tess gathered up her house key and phone, which was all she'd brought apart from the two bottles of wine they'd not quite finished off. Alexis had brought a bottle, but she couldn't recall seeing Sarah with one. Bobbi had possibly provided another two. Would it be rude of her to swipe up the left-over wine and take it home with her? It was possibly only a glass, but she could finish the bottle before she went to bed.

Just to relax her.

If she opened a fresh bottle at home, only for one glass, she'd get that look from Graham in the morning. Like she was some kind of alcoholic, and he was keeping count. She wasn't. But he was. She just liked a glass of wine. She could stop anytime she wanted. If just he wouldn't give her that look full of judgement.

The toe of her knock-off Manolo Blahnik sandal caught on the edge of the hallway carpet on her way to Bobbi's front door. Just because she had money didn't mean to say she had it to throw away. Not everything she bought was the genuine article. Not that anyone knew, apart from her. Only a really discerning eye could tell. She didn't really associate with people like that. Graham spent his days dealing with the rich and famous. But he only worked for them. He preferred to lord it over the ordinary folk outside of work.

As she stumbled, someone wrapped a steadying hand around her elbow before she hit the ground and she let out a giggle.

'Shh. Don't wake the kids,' Bobbi muttered in her ear, her solid arm around Tess's waist.

Tess turned and wrapped her arms around each of her sisters in turn for a wholehearted hug. A little on the strong side.

'I love you. I love you all.'

She gave each a sloppy smile and touched their hair, their faces. She imagined the sympathy oozing from her face. 'I know it's a bad thing, but it doesn't need to touch us, not really. He'll never come near us. Never come near our family.'

She took Alexis into her arms and felt the imperceptible stiffening of her sister's muscular body. As though there was a slight resistance there. A wall she'd erected which stopped her from giving of herself entirely. Drama queen that she was, she might crave attention, but there was a blockage when it came to genuine affection. Which was probably why Alexis could never hold down a relationship.

Tess loved her all the same.

She pulled back and cupped Alexis's face, bringing hers in close. 'I'm sorry he's not got the punishment he deserves, but really, you need to move on. He has nothing to do with us. He can no longer harm you.'

Alexis pulled away, her lips a straight line.

Had she said the wrong thing? Tess always felt as though she was on tenterhooks with Alexis, never quite sure when something she said to her would come back and bite her in the backside. An insult she'd never intended to deliver. An accidental slight. Something that would be nurtured for months before it came out.

About to open her mouth again and apologise, she was instead taken firmly into Bobbi's embrace.

Bobbi's hugs were always the best.

Tess might be the eldest, but Bobbi was the most maternal of them all. Without their mum there, Bobbi was the mother figure. The kingpin. She held them all together. If it wasn't for her, Tess was pretty sure Alexis and Sarah wouldn't see her as often. They rarely came to her house.

Tess might have the more expensive property in the exclusive gated community which kept the rougher element from the door, but Bobbi's four-bedroom, two-bathroom house was somehow more inviting in its messy homeliness.

Graham wouldn't have a thing out of place. Not that he was responsible for the tidying up. He simply wouldn't tolerate a thing out of place...

Their house was more show home than home.

15

Sarah tucked her arm through her older sister's and set off along the street at a gentle stroll to accommodate Tess's intoxicated weave.

One sip of the whisky had been enough for Sarah. She shouldn't really have even consumed that, but the shock had left her reeling.

Poor Alexis. She couldn't imagine how she felt.

Tess stumbled again and Sarah righted her. Tess was the tall, willowy one. She made a pretence of exercising, but there was nothing to her. A featherweight. Unlike Sarah. Shorter by a couple of inches, athletic. Her upper arms thick through weightlifting, her body toned, her legs – unlike Tess's skinny, straight up, straight down legs – bulged with muscles.

She wasn't going to be able to keep up that regime for much longer. Not the weightlifting. Too much stress on the body. She'd continue to swim and run, keep up her fitness regime. There was no need not to.

'Nearly there.' Words slurred from Tess's mouth as the heavy night air seemed to take her from tipsy to drunk.

Sarah tapped in the security code to the community gates,

which was a farce, because everybody knew it. The gates screamed rich people live here. Come and steal from them. Their crime rate was no less than the rest of the surrounding areas, but the insurance claims were considerably higher.

Sarah regretted not driving them both there as it meant she had to walk back to Bobbi's to collect her car; she hadn't wanted Tess throwing up inside it. That would only set Sarah off on a round of retching.

Sarah took the key from her older sister and inserted it in the lock, pushing the door wide. She glanced at the empty driveway. Graham might have parked his car in the triple car garage, but it was unlikely. He normally dumped it on the drive for the neighbours to admire.

'Isn't Graham home?'

Tess sent her a strained look as she stood in the doorway. 'Probably working late. He seems to do a lot of that lately.'

They stood in silence for a moment and then Sarah pulled the key from the door when it became obvious that Tess wasn't going to. She handed it to her. 'Goodnight. See you soon.' She leaned in and gave Tess a gentle hug, as though her older sister might break. She loved the smell of Tess, more so when she hadn't been drinking, but all the same, she could smell the scent she dabbed on behind her ears. Jo Malone, she'd said she wore, Myrrh and Tonka. Cost a fortune. Something Sarah couldn't imagine ever affording.

She pulled away and sent Tess a smile, hoping it didn't reflect the pity in her gaze. She wouldn't want Tess's sterile life. An empty house, a husband who held no affection for her. She far preferred her own life. And it was about to get better.

'Do you want to come in for a drink?' Tess leaned against the doorframe.

Sarah shook her head. 'No. Thanks anyway, but I have to go to bed. It's late enough and I'm on the early shift tomorrow. I have to be up at 5 a.m. No wiggle room. We have the 6 a.m. swimmers on the doorstep hammering on the glass if we don't open bang on time.'

'Oh. Okay.' There was sadness there, layered with a desperate loneliness.

Regret churned inside Sarah, but she needed to go. Her swollen feet throbbed like a bitch in this heat.

She reached out and stroked the hand Tess curled around the door. 'Close the door. Go to bed.'

'Okay.'

The door closed and Sarah was left alone on the doorstep. Regret shimmered through her and she raised her hand to knock. Perhaps she should have stayed. Just for a while.

The scent of jasmine her sister's gardener had planted hung heavy on the air.

A silence descended in the strange twilight of the summer night.

Sarah let her hand drop and turned a slow circle.

A prickle of unease sent a chill over her skin. A skitter of insects, a cool breeze that wasn't there.

Knowing that vile man was out there, possibly in search of another child whose life he would ruin, gave her a deep sense of unease.

She rubbed her arms.

Tempted to knock on the door and tell Tess she'd changed her mind and wanted to come in, Sarah waited. Her breath held so she could hear any movement above the beat of her own heart.

Monsters were out there. Not all of them got the justice they deserved.

Some of them still lurked in the shadows.

16

I crossed skinny arms over my chest and hugged myself, rocking back and forth to gain some comfort.

What a bastard.

I'd heard that word. It was a bad word.

Dad had used it once when he thought we were out of earshot, but I was sitting second step from the top of the hallway stairs.

That was always the best way to find things out.

That's how I found out Gary Philpotts had offered to do some gardening for us.

It wasn't so much a garden as a field of overgrown dandelions and cow parsley enclosed by an eight-foot wall. On top of the wall, there was a thick layer of mortar in which broken glass had been stuck, jagged points upwards. This was the deterrent of the day, when alarms weren't commonplace, and pubs were broken into regularly for the night's takings which were invariably kept on the premises.

Dad had neither the time nor the interest to do anything with the garden, but it appeared he'd found someone who had.

My heart quaked every time Mum sent me out with a bottle of pop or a packet of crisps for him. How could I tell her?

What could I tell her?

I left the rear door to the pub wide and raced out to plonk whatever I'd been sent with on the low stone wall so overgrown with ivy, the red bricks were barely visible.

Twice I'd escaped him, racing back inside before he raised his head and caught sight of me.

The third time, he was waiting.

I placed the bottle on the brick wall and whirled around, ready to race back to the pub.

Gary was there, leaning up against the pub wall, next to the wide-open door, a crooked grin on his face. Something I'd come to recognise as evil.

'Good to see you. I'm so pleased you've decided to look after me properly. It's no less than I deserve.'

He let out a humourless laugh.

Fear froze me to the spot, my knees too weak to move.

He pushed himself upright and took a step towards me.

'Perhaps we can take up where we left off...'

My muscles quivered. There was nowhere to run. Nowhere to hide. If I tried to lunge past him, he'd be able to grab me with one of his meaty fists. His hands would be on me again and this time, I knew there would be no second chance for me. Somehow, in the weeks since I'd last seen him, he'd grown in confidence.

Could that have been because he got away with it the first time?

The sound of my dad's deep voice echoed from inside the pub as he called my name.

'Here. Dad, I'm here.'

Whether it was the panicked squeak in my reply that brought him to the back door I never knew, but he narrowed his eyes as he looked from one to the other of us.

Gary seemed to shrink, once again a spotty-faced teenager, with flushed skin and sulking eyes.

My dad said my name once again, and I slipped under his raised arm into the pub as he leaned in against the doorframe.

I dashed through the cool hallways up to my bedroom, panting as though I'd run the 100-yard race.

Nothing was ever said, but I was never asked to take refreshments to Gary again. After a few weeks, he was gone. The damage was done, though. The garden was no longer a haven.

Not only that, but I'd lost another opportunity to say something. To tell my dad.

But I didn't.

I was as guilty as sin.

17

Alexis scrubbed rough hands over her face. Perhaps she shouldn't have had so much to drink. She was back on duty in the morning. She certainly shouldn't have had the whisky to start with. She wasn't used to spirits. And then to add wine into the mix was lethal.

It had seemed like a good idea at the time. She thought it would settle her nerves.

With the pitch and roll in the back of the taxi, she was no longer sure. She stared out of the window, trying to rid herself of the image of Gary Philpotts. The one she remembered from long ago, coming back to haunt her as though it was yesterday. Her memory vivid.

It didn't help to close her eyes. His face filled her vision as he rose above her.

She snapped them open.

Hot bile rose in her throat.

She'd not gone into her detailed memories to her sisters. She didn't need to inflict that on them.

She should have stayed at Bobbi's, but her older sister's house was already over-crowded without her muscling in. As Tess left, Alexis had changed her mind about staying. The little flicker of relief on Bobbi's face had proved she'd made the right decision. Bobbi would never object, her motherly instinct so strong it encompassed all of them. But it hadn't been fair, and she didn't need to.

She could have left with Tess and Sarah.

Tess's place was a show house, not a home. She'd never feel comfortable there. Tess had had a skinful already, and she'd probably want more once she got home if she had company.

Which meant Alexis would have had to engage with Graham. One of the subjects she agreed on with Sarah was her opinion of Graham.

There was something about him Alexis had never been comfortable with. Not that there were many men she was comfortable with. Her two ex-husbands were testament to that. Both of them mistakes. One at the age of eighteen, which had lasted all of six months, and another again at the age of twenty-six. An act of bravado. An attempt to prove a point which unfortunately had backfired.

She looked up and caught the glance of the taxi driver in the rear-view mirror and watched as the driver's eyes crinkled to indicate she was smiling at Alexis. It was one of the reasons she always booked a female taxi driver. She didn't want to be alone in a confined space with a man.

'Are you okay back there?'

Alexis nodded at the woman.

'You look a little green around the gills. You want the window down a bit?'

Alexis nodded. 'Please. It's been... an unusual night. I don't normally drink.'

Balmy air wafted in through the window as it slid halfway down.

'I hope that's better for you.' The words were kindly spoken.

It seemed Alexis had struck lucky. She'd hoped Craig would

offer to take her home, but he'd already been asleep by then and she knew he had an early start. She trusted him. One of the few she did. She knew she was safe with him. Bobbi's lovely husband. More like a brother to Alexis. He'd been around more than half her life and never once had she ever caught him giving her a sideways glance.

There had been the possibility of cadging a lift with Sarah. That meant she would have had to wait for her to come back from walking Tess home. That wouldn't have been fair on Bobbi.

Alexis let her mind sift through the evening. Bobbi looked more tired than normal tonight. Stress lines had played around her mouth, deeper than usual, and the bruised look under her eyes showed she wasn't getting enough sleep.

Bobbi worked far too hard. She was there for everyone. It was starting to tell. Maybe the load was too heavy.

Perhaps Alexis needed to back off and give her older sister some room. Maybe the menopause had got a grip on her. It hadn't passed Alexis by that Bobbi had a continual sweat on and her neck and chest turned puce every three minutes. Alexis wasn't looking forward to that stage of her life. She'd escaped having children. Thank god.

She loved her nephews and nieces but there was no way she wanted to cope with the responsibility of another human.

She gave a shudder.

The guilt parents carried. For every damned little thing. For doing the right thing. For doing the wrong thing. For making a wrong decision for the right reasons.

There'd been the time Bobbi and Craig had taken the kids on a trip to the Lake District, staying in a little cottage for the week that belonged to one of Craig's colleagues. When they'd returned, Toni's floppy toy rabbit was missing. The upset, the tears, the guilt. The time spent trying to track the thing down. A cuddly toy! Bobbi had been frantic. Toni insistent she have it back. She'd had it since birth.

There'd been recriminations, Bobbi blaming herself for not checking when in all fairness the child was old enough to have known whether she had it or not. And there was Alexis's problem. She'd not melted with sympathy. She'd stared at Toni while Bobbi beat herself up over a bloody toy. Get her another one. Tell her to get over it.

In the end, the cuddly rabbit had been discovered bundled in with the cottage bedclothes that had been well washed and dried. The cottage owner had posted it back the very next day.

Somehow, that rabbit had never been the same since.

Maybe this was the reason Alexis made a good paramedic. Because there was a part of her she held back. Something missing in her psyche. She might fall apart in front of her own family, but when it came to strangers, to victims, casualties, she didn't have an issue. She could step back out of herself. Assess, monitor, deal. She could separate her own personal issues from incidents, accidents, victims, offenders. Compartmentalise.

Because she'd been a victim. Survived. The hot rush of panic overwhelmed her from time to time but never, she'd discovered, when her mind was occupied with somebody else's needs.

She breathed in, her head still swimming but her stomach had stopped rebelling.

Alexis had come to terms with the decision her mum had made all those years ago on her behalf. Looking back, it had been the wrong decision, but her mum had wanted to protect her, to shield her. Instead, Alexis had lived in fear of Gary Philpotts, knowing he was still out there, somewhere.

If it hadn't been for the support of her mum, her sisters and occasional counselling when it all became too much, she wasn't sure where she would be.

'You all right, chick? We're here.'

The taxi pulled up outside the small block of flats and Alexis scrambled out. It never seemed to be an elegant thing to do, getting out of a taxi when you'd had a drink. At least she wasn't wearing a short skirt. Short skirts were not her thing. Not any more but she'd had her fair share of tumbling headfirst from a taxi, bare arse in the air while she went through a self-destructive period. She didn't do that these days. Had learned hard lessons. Settled down. Become someone with responsibilities, if a cat could be considered a responsibility.

'Thanks.' She raised her hand at the driver before she closed the door as soft as she could, otherwise some wise-arse would start to shout out of their open windows about the noise. Every resident in the block of flats would rouse and there'd be a full-scale shouting match. It happened every Friday night, particularly in the summer when windows were open, and noises echoed around the U-shaped brick flats.

The area wasn't the gated community her sister lived in. Alexis couldn't afford to live anywhere else.

Alexis punched in the security code for the outside door and made her way up the stairwell to the third floor, her shoes tap-tapping on the stairs as she broke into a trot.

Breathless as she reached her floor, she bent over at the waist, taking in gulps of air. If only she could get in the lift, life might be easier, but there was no way she ever put herself in an enclosed space, just in case she couldn't get out.

She straightened, her hand already clasping her bunch of keys at the ready. Longest one poking through her two middle fingers on the off-chance she needed to defend herself.

She raised her hand, ready to insert the key in the lock, and the door flew open.

Her breath jammed in her throat, a rasping gurgle escaping her. She leaped back, her hands balling into fists.

'Hi.'

A figure separated itself from the shadows.

Teeth glowed vibrant white in a smooth black face split with a wide grin.

'Pippa. I nearly shit myself.' Alexis slapped her hand on her heart, adrenaline fighting with relief to make her chest heave.

Pippa grinned harder and stepped forward, her arms open in invitation for Alexis to walk into them. 'I got your message earlier. I was too busy to reply. I thought you might need me.'

18

It was the terrible weeping that drew me closer to the bathroom. A small room in the new council house we'd moved into two years previously when Mum and Dad decided pub life really wasn't for them. It had been a brief dream in their arsenal of dreams. One that had thankfully only lasted three years.

Dad's rapid deterioration of health had dictated that dream come to an end. That and the intolerance of the brewery who owned the pub. There was no such thing as time off for being ill. You had to find a replacement, pay them yourself out of your meagre salary.

And Dad was seriously sick. He'd been gone almost three months. Cancer had ravaged his pancreas and taken him from us far too early. We weren't ready for it. Nobody ever is.

The Bull's Head was only a distant memory. One I'd been more than thankful to put behind me.

I edged the door open and peeped inside the bathroom.

Mum was perched on the toilet seat, my other sisters there too.

Alexis sat in a crimson bath, my mother softly stroking her wet hair.

I froze in the doorway. 'What happened?'

Mum turned tear-filled eyes to me. 'Alexis has been raped.' Her voice held a flat, emotionless tone.

My hand went to my mouth and I stepped inside to join the rest of them, leaving the door wide open. My gaze darted around, barely able to take it all in.

Alexis with her face pressed into her tucked-up knees, a pitiful wailing noise seeping from her lips. The crimson in that bath was her blood.

I sank to my knees on the bathroom carpet. 'What have the police said?'

Mum shook her head, frowning. 'I haven't told them.'

Confusion fogged my mind. 'You haven't told them?'

Mum pressed her lips together and shook her head. 'No.'

'I don't think she should be in the bath. They'll want to examine her.'

'No.'

I turned. 'I'll call them.'

'Noooo! Nooo! Don't call the police.'

Horrified at Alexis's sudden move from quiet weeping to hysteria, I pressed my hands to my chest as Mum tried to comfort her.

She turned her face up to mine. 'No. No police. She doesn't need to be put through this. They'll only drag her through it all over again. She'll be better off people not knowing.'

'You can't hide it. You have to tell.'

Mum's eyes turned bleak. 'Some things are better not said.'

'But what if he does it again?'

Her mouth tightened and she shook her head. 'It's for the best. We need to keep silent.'

My heart thundered and I couldn't catch my breath. Surely, surely it was better to tell the police.

'Who was it?' My voice grated out through a dry throat.

'You're not to tell.' Mum's eyes glowed with a fierce protectiveness.

'Mum!'

Mum came to her feet and reached for a towel, holding it wide so she could wrap Alexis in it as my sister stood and stepped out of the bath into her arms.

Alexis pushed her thumb into her mouth and sucked it as Mum sank back down onto the toilet seat. Pulling her onto her lap, she gave a brisk rub across the top of the towel covering Alexis's shoulders.

Her voice was quiet as she spoke. 'She thought she knew him. He was waiting outside the school gates. She'd seen him before. When we lived in the pub.'

My blood ran cold. A sick premonition pressing down on me.

'Who was it? What's his name?'

I waited a heartbeat, terror curdling my stomach.

I knew what Mum was going to say and it was my fault. All my fault for not telling when I should have done. Now, it was worse. Now my sister had been raped by the same man who had assaulted me.

I should have said something then.

We should say something now.

Mum's eyes hardened as she stared at me.

'Gary Philpotts.'

19

Bobbi pulled a cool cotton nightdress over her head without switching a light on and slipped into bed beside Craig, trying not to disturb him.

She might have to get a bigger bed. She'd really love to cuddle into him but didn't want to touch him, to feel the heat popping from him like a furnace, despite only having a sheet over the top of him. If she mentioned it, he'd only tell her he was 'hot stuff'.

He really didn't understand.

Her feet were comfortably cool after wandering around in bare feet on the tiled kitchen floor while she washed up the glasses she and her sisters had used.

She'd managed to flick through one file before her eyelids refused to stay open. At least she had her first case of the morning ready. She'd read it before, it was more of a refresh, but she could rest easy knowing she'd go into the meeting prepared.

She reckoned on three minutes before the hot flush hit and she'd be soaked through, nightie clinging to her wet body. She'd need to get up at least once in the night, but if only she could get some sleep first.

She desperately needed it.

She closed her eyes, but horrible images filled her vision, so she popped them open again and stared into the misty grey of the room. Not fully dark at this time of the year, their curtains with their thin lining didn't quite keep out the light from the full moon. The shadows slipped long and low over the bedroom floor and crept up the wall opposite. Sharp fingers pointing at her, so she squirmed and closed her eyes again.

Her younger sister always managed to stir up a deep unease Bobbi found hard to rid herself of. The dark side of Alexis's personality clung onto the depressing and transmitted to them all.

She'd become their mood barometer. Whatever she felt, the rest of them did too.

She'd arrive at Easter in a bunny outfit and bounce around with the kids, inducing hysterical laughter with her enthusiasm and excess of chocolate eggs. On Christmas Day, her hair might be a mess, her face gaunt and she'd bear a handful of thoughtless presents and change the mood instantly to morose.

Craig, with his even temper and fondness for all three of her sisters, had once asked which Alexis they were expecting to turn up at the summer party.

Surprisingly, Alexis had done well today. She'd held up. She often did when she was under pressure.

It was in the coming weeks that she was likely to hit a low. When the initial shock wore off and everyone else had moved on. Alexis's mind would dwell on the matter, stirring it from time to time, poking at the embers until they sparked, flickering to life so they burst into flame.

It would be out of the blue. Unexpected. They'd all be taken by surprise. But not really. They should know by now, but it caught them every time. Bipolar disorder. When the sleeping monster stirs.

Bobbi's muscles relaxed, but her mind struggled to give itself over to sleep.

She had so much to do. It was like spinning plates, all of them going off at different tangents, rotating at various speeds. Could she keep them all balanced? Because right now, she thought she was drowning. A slow sucking down into a deep ocean and nothing there to pull her back up. No life buoy.

The demands of work increased daily. Fewer people to carry out a job under so much pressure the department was buckling at the knees. And so was she.

It wasn't as though she couldn't find another job. She didn't want to. This is what she'd always wanted. To help children. To protect them from the monsters and the predators.

Craig had told her she could retire. Retire. What the hell would she do with herself? She loved those spinning plates, that whirling dervish, even if it hammered her into the ground from time to time. It was just a phase. It would pass. Just as it had before.

She couldn't think of anything worse than being a stay-at-home mum. There were some people who were happy to, like Tess. But it wasn't for Bobbi.

She needed her job.

She needed to be needed.

But she needed something more too.

The scratch of ants crawling over her flesh started at the back of her knees, and she sighed. Here it came. When women spoke in whispers about hot flushes, none of them told you about the hormonal rush that bloomed out over your skin and sent your mind into a roaring torrent of white noise. She'd watched her own mum, in the days when periods and menopause weren't mentioned, not even in undertones.

She'd been almost twelve when her mum had given birth to Sarah. Old enough to know everything there was about sex, pregnancy and giving birth. Yet her mum had never discussed it. Never given Bobbi 'the talk'. The best she'd done was say, 'Has Tess given you the little book?' When Bobbi had nodded, mute, her mum gave a tight smile. 'Good. If you have any questions, just let me know.'

Questions she'd had in abundance, but she'd never gone to her mum.

She'd made sure all her own children understood and could talk to her. Even if they squirmed in embarrassment. She'd not left it to Craig to educate her boys in the subject of sex, responsibility, and respect. She'd been the one to do that, and not to edge the door closed again afterward, but to leave it wide for questions, discussion.

She had questions of her own, now.

Her colleagues at work were all much younger than her. Predominantly female, none of them were aware yet of what was to come. Raging hormones had never raised their ugly heads when Bobbi was pregnant. If anything, she'd relaxed into mild and mellow.

She needed to speak with her GP.

It was a matter of getting the time to even make an appointment.

Ring at 8 a.m., they said. Didn't they realise that unless you were retired, the likelihood was you were run off your feet at 8 a.m., rounding up kids for school, or even in work as Bobbi frequently was at that time? What a stupid system. The sooner they had an online booking service where you could see the availability of all doctors in your practice for the next six weeks, and book a time to suit, the better. Until then, Bobbi struggled. Three minutes past 8 a.m. and the slots were all taken.

Tess went to some private practice in London and used a fancy gel of some kind. Bobbi didn't have the time to visit a Harley Street doctor, nor did she have the inclination to spend a couple of thousand pounds each visit.

She closed her eyes and this time her mind didn't turn to her sister's pain, this time it went through its usual nightly routine. She'd try to be organised and ring the doctor's surgery at 8 a.m. Toni had her spelling test. Check she knew them over breakfast. Matthew had a dentist's appointment first thing, Josh would sort himself out. Shanna was stressing over... was it her hair, or her skin?

The flash of heat shot from the core of her, and Bobbi threw back the covers, looking to see how wide the window was. As wide as it could get. She could go and hang her head out of it, but she'd disturb Craig.

She rolled onto her side and waited for the rush to subside, for her mind to turn off, but it refused.

20

That was me that day down by The Cut. That child.

It was me who was tormented time and again by Gary Philpotts. My whole childhood, he was there.

It's an ungodly 4.37 a.m. and the soaring temperature of yesterday has barely dipped. I'm wide awake with the memory of the incident so fixed in my mind. Who would have thought memories could linger and be quite so vivid? They never have been before. It's almost like someone pressed the 'on' switch in my head and replay started. Boom! Full technicolour. A bit like when you go along to those speciality 5D cinemas. Only add in an emotion so intense it rips out your guts and leaves them dangling down, a mass of tangled ropes on the floor at my feet.

I keep my eyes closed as I listen to the stillness of the house in the early hours. Despite every window being open, and only a cotton sheet to cover me, sweat still slicks my body.

I'm trying to resist turning over yet again. It achieves nothing, except maybe a cool puff of air for a nanosecond as the sheet wafts away from my body.

It has to be the hottest July on record. It feels like it to me, at least.

Temperatures soar. Tempers fray.

Mine hasn't. There's no need.

It doesn't matter what I see in the newspapers. No matter what I hear.

I won't allow it to affect me.

Despite all my good intentions, my muscles twitch and persuade me that I do want to turn over. I roll and find myself on my feet by the side of the bed with no real understanding of how I came to be there.

While I'm up, I might as well go to the toilet.

I pad on silent feet, drawing in a soft breath as I open the bathroom door and step onto the cool tiles. I could lie face down on them. Just for a short while.

Instead, I pick up my toothbrush and give my teeth a quick brush, skimming it over my dry, swollen tongue as though I had a skinful last night. But I didn't. Maybe it would help if I had.

I run the cold tap and fill a short, stubby glass with water. I pop a couple of paracetamol I don't really need out of their blister pack and throw them to the back of my throat. Just for something to do. It seems like a good idea. Maybe I'm running a temperature. I gulp the whole glass down in one go, leaving myself gasping for air, and place it back on the small white shelf on the cabinet beside me.

I rinse a flannel through, gently dab it over my face first and then place it on the back of my neck until the heat dissipates. I could leave it there when I get back into bed, but then the pillow will get wet.

I wring it out and put it on the side of the sink then risk a look in the mirror which I'd been trying to avoid.

I knew it.

Bloodshot eyes stare back, more green than hazel. I blink away the haziness, recognising the lowered lids as another sign of sleep deprivation. And yet I'm wide awake.

I could stay up, but that means by early evening I'll be dragging my arse around the floor after me.

If I go back to sleep at this time, I'm going to wake up feeling like shit.

It's not much of a decision to make, so I creep back into the shadowed bedroom and pull on clothes I'd left in a neat pile that I'd not had chance to put away after the washing was done.

I thought I'd managed to push thoughts of Gary Philpotts away, but I can't balance the injustice of it all in my head.

21

Gary cracked open eyelids crusted with sleep. He rolled his lips inwards, smacking them together in an effort to drum up saliva and slick the thick, dry tongue stuck to the roof of his mouth so he could swallow.

The bare bulb in the ceiling light swam in a hazy mist before his blurred vision. He rolled his head against the hard, cushioned arm of the furniture he lay on to check his surroundings.

His left leg lolled off the side of the settee. The hem of his shorts hitched painfully into his crotch to squeeze at his balls. He flopped his hand over the swell of his white stomach and farted as he struggled to tug down his T-shirt which had hitched up around the top of his chest.

With a guttural moan, Gary rolled off the settee and landed on all fours. His hands and knees felt the weight of his body. Already bruised, he suspected from whatever the hell he'd got up to the previous night when he'd glugged down several cans of lager and stuffed his face with pizza and Doritos to celebrate his success.

It wasn't exactly a 'not guilty' verdict so much as 'insufficient evidence'. Someone ballsed up somewhere. The police, the CPS, the admin trail in between. Who gave a shit? He was off. Free.

A hollow celebration, as it turned out.

Letting out soft grunts, he placed his hands on the arm of the settee to push himself to his feet. He swiped the back of his wrist over thick, cracked lips as he swayed. For a moment, a dull confusion swamped his mind as his head reeled.

He yanked his T-shirt down again over his middle as he scoured the floor. His gaze hit on the four empty bottles of toffee vodka. That made far more sense of his banging hangover.

His stomach pitched and rolled at the thought of drinking another drop of the sweet, rich nectar.

A vague recollection swam through his mind of him staggering around the corner to the off-licence the previous evening, or possibly the one before that, to spend the last of his benefits on the bottles. Old man Singh's nutmeg eyes had met his and then strayed away, devoid of judgement.

He knew, though. Just as all his mum's neighbours knew. Mud stuck. They studied him with suspicion now.

It was time for him to move again. He had no choice. It wasn't his house.

They'd put him on the registered sex offenders list, now. Everyone would know.

He may have got away with the offence, but it was all over the *Express* and *Star*.

He'd managed to avoid any conviction involving that until now. He'd been dodging and weaving that one for the best part of thirty years. A little bit of drug dealing was the only thing he'd been caught red-handed for.

That had been his own stupid fault. Selling to kids who were obviously young. He'd had a game plan. One that hadn't worked out. He'd learned his lesson. Two years away for dealing drugs.

When he came back, he proclaimed to have gone clean. His mum passed the word around.

It wouldn't make any difference. Now this particular news was public. With no one to protect him, he'd have a brick thrown through his front window any time soon.

He raised his head and gazed at the front window. He was surprised there wasn't a brick through it already.

Flat footed, Gary made his way to the small downstairs toilet. He raised his arm and leaned against the wall to stop the room from spinning. His eyes glazed over as the stream of bright yellow pee splashed the sides of the toilet pan, missing to splatter over the edges onto what used to be a pale-green bathmat, now crusted and urine stained.

His mum would have beaten the living crap out of him if she saw the state he'd let it get into. He didn't care. He wouldn't be here for much longer. It would be someone else's problem.

He wiggled his penis back and forth to get the last drips off the end before he tucked it into his stained underpants. He hauled his old shorts back up.

Instead of washing his hands, he rubbed them on his grubby T-shirt before he turned and stumbled back into the living room to slump down on the settee. He rolled onto his side to give his aching stomach support. A dull throb came from a liver he'd misused well.

Gas bubbles popped and fizzled in his gut. He needed something to eat, but the thought of food made his stomach lurch. He needed a glass of water.

He reached up and ran stubby fingers through thin stringy hair. Once pale ginger, instead of turning grey it had morphed into an insipid colourless fuzz lying in greasy straggles over his almost bald pate. He drew his hands down his face and the smooth-shaven cheeks his solicitor had insisted on for his court appearance now rasped with thick grey stubble.

Perhaps it had been even more than two days since he'd fallen off the wagon.

Gary squinted at the remote control on the coffee table poking out from under the pile of unopened post.

He couldn't be arsed to reach for it. The greyed-out TV screen could remain blank for all he cared. He let his gaze stray back to the letters.

There might be a court summons amongst the messy pile. A bailiff's letter at the very least. He couldn't believe they hadn't tossed him out of his mum's council house already. The small two-bedroom semi-detached she'd lived in for the past twelve years. A place he'd always bunked down in whenever he got into trouble, ran out of rent money himself, or generally wanted to hide from the world.

He was beyond caring. His mum had gone. Dead. All that bloody grease and fat she'd eaten over the years, not to mention the amount of gin she'd consumed, had finally caught up with her.

'It's all your bloody fault,' she'd have said, if she could talk. 'The stress you've put me under with your dirty little antics. Filthy pervert. You should be ashamed of yourself.'

And he was. Totally ashamed.

No amount of shame could stop him, though. It was an obsession. A dark power that overwhelmed him and drove him on, no matter how many times he promised himself he'd stop. He couldn't. It was in his nature. Always had been.

'Pathetic weakling.' His mum spoke to him from the corner of his mind, where she squatted like a bloated toad.

He clapped his hands over his ears, but it couldn't shut out the words inside his head.

'A son of mine, accused of being a kiddy fiddler. You scum. How dare you come back here and expect me to take you in! You filthy little shit.'

But she had taken him in. Clocked him around the face with fingers gnarled with arthritis. Pulled at his hair until he yowled, tears streaming down his face.

He'd stayed because he had no choice. Nowhere else would have him.

She'd taken him in each time because he was her only child. He knew she'd never turn her back on him, despite what she said every time he left.

'Day yow come back again. I worr 'ave it, yow know. I worr...'

He'd have to find somewhere now, though. She'd been gone for almost three months. He'd still been claiming her benefits. The council would want the two-bedroom house back once they found out, if they didn't already know.

The funeral went ahead while his court case was being held.

Now he had nothing. No home, no mum, no money. He wasn't sure which of those held the most importance.

He scrubbed thick swollen eyelids as hopeless tears came again. Who'd have believed he'd be lost without her? At one time, he couldn't wait to get away. To have his independence.

Independence had been his downfall. Maybe she would have kept a better grip on him and his lack of self-control.

Then again, he'd never had much control. He'd lost it completely this last time.

The memories curled in his mind. Ones he'd drowned out with vodka came back to haunt him. He wanted someone to stop him, someone to make all those deep, dark desires go away. No matter how much he hated himself, he still couldn't stop.

The doorbell pealed. A sharp stabbing noise which reverberated in his head. The sickening roll of his stomach threatened to spill the contents of vodka over the dirty, stained carpet at his feet. It would be pure lager and vodka and a messy churn of cheap pizza as he had no memory of the last time he'd eaten properly.

During the last few weeks, he'd barely eaten at all. Not since his mum's death, his court case, her funeral. There'd been so much. Too much to deal with. He'd lived on the contents of the small fridge and sparsely populated cupboard. Cold baked beans, crisps, tinned meatballs.

He had no idea why he was still so flabby. He could grab the thick layer of skin on his stomach and hold it in his fists. Like his mum used to, just before she gave a vicious twist.

'Fat git. Why don't you do something about this?'

Underneath it, the fat had shrunk to leave an empty bag of hollowed-out skin that flopped in a disgusting apron to cover his penis. He couldn't remember the last time he'd seen it. At least he could still feel it.

The doorbell pealed again, and he lowered his feet and pushed himself upright. His body swayed. He waited until he felt stable on his feet before he slouched barefoot to the front door. Too hot to hurry.

It wouldn't be the bailiffs, not yet. Surely they'd give him more notice to vacate under the circumstances.

He cast a quick glance at the unopened letters.

Perhaps they had.

He yanked the door wide and slumped against the doorframe.

Vague recognition wallowed in his head as his gaze clashed with one swimming with dark fury.

_____

22

Heat scorched the back of Gary's neck as he hunched over to watch the small fish. His skin stretched tight like an over-inflated tyre around his belly as he rolled forward, constricting his breath, so it came in short, laboured puffs.

The slick oiliness of last night's three cans of cider slid through his stomach as his bowel contracted. He'd not had anything to eat since the greasy sausage and chips supper his mum had brought him from the chippy at about five o'clock the previous day. The gloopy mess of mushy peas his mum insisted he have to balance his diet spread thick across the top of the chips to spoil the taste and send them soggy.

Ravenous, he'd stuffed them in his mouth in silence anyway before she lost her temper and threw them in the bin like she frequently did if he made comment. Or even gave her a look. Or didn't look, or failed to say thank you. It wouldn't matter if she had one of her moods on her. He was bound not to get his dinner. He should be grateful when he did.

It was free, wasn't it?

She slaved away in the steam and the grease of the Holy Plaice without acknowledgement or thanks, with ungrateful customers and miserable colleagues.

All for what?

'To keep you in food? Greedy little sod that yow am.'

Not that she provided him with anything else to eat. If it was in the fridge, it belonged to her.

'Day touch tharr, or I'll flay the skin off you.'

Except for the milk. He was allowed some of that as long as he didn't guzzle it, and certainly he wasn't allowed to drink straight from the bottle. He'd learned that the hard way.

If there was food in the practically bare cupboard, he had to ask permission. Last time he'd sneaked a cheap, paper-thin biscuit thinking she'd not notice, she'd virtually yanked his hair from its roots. He'd learned his lesson then, too. Never steal from his mum.

One meal a day was enough. It sustained him, didn't it?

'Yow wouldn't be fat if yow weren't having enough to eat.'

He wasn't stupid enough to believe that. During school time, the unhealthy school dinners and stodgy puddings sustained him, but in the school holidays, there was nothing but grease and fat.

Maybe once he moved out, into his own place, he'd eat what he wanted, lose weight, wear clothes that didn't come from the local charity shop. Convinced she bought them too tight just to ridicule him, he kept silent on that front too.

Last time he'd made comment, she'd got a pair of scissors to the joggers she'd bought for fifty pence and shredded them in front of his eyes.

'Ungrateful git.'

Not that he'd have worn the insipid pale mustard bottoms. It had saved him a job of 'accidentally' ripping them.

He could only be grateful he was required to wear school uniform during term time, so he wasn't distinguished from the other kids in the sixth form. Except for his greasy hair and body odour because she only let him have a shower once a week and timed him, switching off the boiler after five minutes if he wasn't done, so the water ran icy cold.

'What is it yow don't understand? We're on a meter, you pleb. I cor afford to heat water for yow.'

He'd taken to sluicing a little water over his head and rubbing in the pea-sized amount of cheap shampoo he was allowed so it was already frothed up before getting into the shower.

Already fine, his hair had started to thin at his temples and push his forehead back, so the thick swathe of yellow pustules surrounded by angry red acne lay exposed across his forehead for everyone to see.

The boys teased him unmercifully. He was only allowed to join their group to be the butt of their jokes, their bullying.

The girls were sympathetic as they always were with the downtrodden, offering advice on which incredibly expensive products were available to him.

He ducked his head and told them to fuck off. It didn't take long before they got the message.

It wasn't what he could apply to his skin that made a difference, even if he could afford the cure-alls, but what went in his body to poison it on a regular basis.

The three cans of cider the boys had reluctantly let him have the previous night might be good for him. At least it was fruit based, if that made a difference.

Gary rolled to his hands and knees and puffed out a relieved breath as the pressure of his stomach squashing his lungs eased. He might have to slope off home again, just to go to the loo, but his mum would be there until eleven, and he might earn another slap around the face for the way he spoke to her the night before when alcohol lent him confidence normally lacking. He'd not stumbled in until almost midnight and she'd thrown a hissy fit.

'You're only seventeen, yow shouldn't be drinking.'

All the other boys were. Why did he have to be different? He was seventeen! He wasn't used to it. The alcohol had gone straight to his head.

She grabbed him by the ear until he howled. 'Yow shouldn't be out so late. The police'll have yow, and I'll not have trouble on my doorstep.'

She wound his hair around two fingers and yanked. 'You'm just like your dad. Drunken arse that he was.'

The dad he'd not seen since he was two. A man he had no memory of.

The soft lap of water on the shore provided him with a sympathetic reflection of a pale, round face undulating with the bright golden sunlight streaking across to wash away his ravaged skin and leave it unblemished and fresh, just as it should be.

He squinted for a moment longer until another fish flashed through his reflection, sending ripples racing across the surface to wipe his image away.

He raised his head, his eyes still narrowed as a scuffle sounded in the bushes to his right. The powerful sunrays blinded him for a long moment while they sent black blooms across his vision.

He held his breath, blinking away the darkness. He scrubbed the back of his wrist against his top lip to remove the beads of sweat that threatened to drip into his mouth from the straggly line of bumfluff that had started to appear recently, much to his mum's bitter amusement.

'You'll be a man soon. The day you turn eighteen, yow'm out of here. I won't put up with your slobbishness one day longer than I need to.'

He squinted, his heart leaping with unnatural desire as a child stepped into his eyeline. The brilliant white hair reflected the sun in a halo across its head and Gary's breath was stolen in a rush of forbidden lust.

It was wrong. So wrong and his mum would thrash him if she could read his thoughts, but she wasn't there and she couldn't possibly know what he was thinking. Could she? Did she know what had lurked in his mind for so long? Was that why she hated him so much?

He hadn't broken his arm like she'd told the authorities. His mum had broken it for him with the floppy end of the vacuum cleaner thrashed down on him. But he didn't tell anyone that. He didn't say she'd moved them for the umpteenth time after questions had been asked at the hospital. Too many broken fingers, a broken rib once. No one noticed when she broke his other wrist when he was eleven. She didn't take him to the hospital that time. Just strapped it up herself and said it would heal soon enough.

When it turned purple, she panicked and ripped the bandage off, so blood flooded back into his hand, burning until the tips of his fingers tingled back to life.

She'd not broken anything since, although she'd not been soft on him. A broom handle to the ribs, which may have been broken, he'd never been sure. Although it had been weeks until he could catch his breath again. A leather belt to his backside, where bruises didn't show, a man's slipper to his belly. Though god only knew where she'd got that.

By the time he was fifteen and bigger than her, she'd resorted to deprivation of food, sharp slaps to his flaccid cheeks and a cruel tongue to whip at him and undermine his self-confidence.

Gary forced the dark thoughts from his mind and let it turn to even darker ones.

He kept his moves painfully slow, so the kid didn't notice him through the thin covering of bushes and take flight.

As he straightened, his stomach gave another sickly lurch. He could hold on. Just for a little while. He could hold on.

23

I knew where he lived. Gary Philpotts.

I'd made it my business to know.

He disappeared every so often, possibly trying to break out from under his mother's watchful eye. Not for long, though. He always returned to the little semi-detached council house she'd lived in for years.

Probably to lie low for a while.

As the saying goes, like a bad penny.

I parked my car two streets along. One of the better neighbourhoods, with slightly newer cars so mine didn't attract attention.

Shoulders hunched to my ears, hands tucked in my trouser pockets, I struck out. Keeping my head low, I cut through a couple of passageways, deserted in the early-morning light. Already sticky, it was going to be another long, hot day.

I reached the end of the alley almost opposite Gary's mum's house and waited, looking both ways for movement. Tempted to lean against the red-brick wall, I checked it first. My nose wrinkled. God only knows what was smeared up it, but I didn't want to come into contact with it.

The place was a slum.

It wasn't unfamiliar territory. I'd returned a number of times over the years. Just to watch. To check. Some kind of false reassurance that I knew where he was. What he was doing. I'm surprised he'd never been caught before now.

Apart from that short stint in prison, when he was drug pushing. A new venture for him it turned out he wasn't very good at. Unfortunately, there hadn't been much cocaine on him and nothing at his mum's. His sentence had been minimal.

I squinted, scanning the bank of dirty windows in the shabby houses opposite.

Nothing moved.

It was too early for school kids. They had another week before they broke up for the summer holidays.

There was no such thing as 'dog-walkers' in this part of town. They opened their front doors, let the dogs out to shit on the pavements and let them back in again when or if they returned.

If you informed them it was illegal, you'd be told to piss off and mind your own business. If they knew where you lived, you'd have that dog shit posted through your letterbox. Minus the envelope.

As if on cue, a perky Jack Russell-cross trotted past, stopping when it sensed me near. Unperturbed, he sidled over and started to cock his leg up the corner of the wall next to me.

I hissed at him. Quiet, under my breath. He hesitated, leg half-cocked. Not so quiet, I looked him in the eye. 'Bugger off.'

Evidently accustomed to that terminology, he lowered his leg and pranced away, nose in the air, the cheeky git.

My chest expanded with a long breath I hadn't realised I'd been holding.

I was going to do this.

Whatever 'this' was, the time had come for a confrontation.

No longer the scared child hiding under my bed, I knew I had to warn him off. Keep everyone safe from him.

I stepped from the cool darkness of the alley into brilliant early-morning sunshine and crossed the road.

A rusty gate hung twisted on one hinge against a broken wall of red bricks, half of which lay in a haphazard pile in the garden. I imagined a car had hit it. It wouldn't have been insured and the council would take an age getting around to fixing it, if it had even been reported. It was hardly as though any counsellors lived down this neck of the woods.

I paid little attention, while taking in a quick glance at the rest of the shabby frontage of the house. It could barely be called a garden. A few tufts of hardy grass poked through between rubble and wilting dandelions. No better or worse than the neighbours either side.

Considering he'd classed himself as a gardener at one time, I was surprised he'd not done more to spruce up his mum's front lawn.

It was littered with crap.

Abandoned fence panels that had been left to rot, a roll of wire fencing I was surprised hadn't been nicked. A broken garden fork. A litter of split plastic plant pots as though they'd been dumped there after he'd finished a job.

An attempt had been made at some time to attract birds. A variety of feeders lay on the ground, empty. The metal pockmarked and corroded.

What may once have been a pretty, ornate birdbath, steel leaves twisted into a heart-shape over the shallow bath with a sweet little bird on top, was propped beside the front door. Perhaps they'd given up trying to push the thick three-foot-long spike into the hardened earth.

I eyed it for a moment, a sudden thought making me catch my breath. Why would you leave such a lethal weapon lying around? With all that had gone on, I was surprised no one had thought to lob it through his window.

I turned my attention back to the grubby front door.

Now what did I do?

The doorbell dangled limp from the wall. Did it even work?

I took a breath in. Indecision held me fast.

What was I doing there?

I had the choice. Ring. Or walk away.

I pressed my finger to the bell, unsure whether anything had happened. I tried once more when there was no immediate answer.

Grime covered the frosted panel of the front door, so I pulled my long-sleeved T-shirt down before I hammered on it with the side of my fist.

Inside was silent for a long moment and then I heard the quiet shuffle of movement.

A blurred image approached, and I stepped back to give myself breathing space. What would I say? What would I do?

The door swung open, and Gary Philpotts leaned heavily against the frame.

'Whadya want?'

The words that I'd struggled to formulate in my head still wouldn't come. I stood there silent as Gary peered at me through rheumy eyes, a dull, grey pallor to his skin. With not even the decency to recognise me.

The spark of annoyance in the pit of my stomach ignited, bursting into a raging flame.

My lips drew back in a sneer. 'What does your mum think of you, Gary? She must be dying of shame.'

The pitiful colour he had in his face leached away further to leave him a chalky shade of white.

'She's dead.' His voice hovered just above a whisper.

'Dead?'

My stomach cramped. If she was dead, the tentative thread holding back his perversion was cut. She'd kept him on a tight leash for so long, but every so often, that leash slackened. Whenever that happened, I know he got up to no good. Disappeared off grid. The men he associated with crawled out of the brickwork until old Martha reeled him back in again.

He'd served time, although not enough and not for the right crime.

According to the papers, he'd be on the sex offenders list now. But that wasn't enough.

The trouble with being on the sex offenders register was that he'd never work again, because paedophiles rarely got a chance. Which meant he'd have even more time on his hands. Without Martha, who would keep him on a tight leash? Who was going to control him?

It wasn't my place to, but how many more children would suffer at his hands because I hadn't spoken out?

I swallowed.

Gary folded his arms across his chest as he narrowed insolence-filled eyes at me. 'Do I know you?'

What the hell was I doing there? There was nothing I could say that could influence this man. This monster.

I took a step back, just as an ugly smile spread over his face. 'Are you going now? Because it's almost time for the kiddies to go to school. And I like to watch.' His sly gaze slid behind me. I turned to look at the bus-stop, where kids would gather in less than a couple of hours.

'The seniors are a little old for me, but when the juniors come past...' A pointed, cracked tongue darted out and swiped across his thick lips.

My stomach lurched. 'You sick bastard. I don't know how you managed to get away with it all these years. Someone should have made you pay.'

His eyes narrowed, brow furrowing before his face cleared, a smile playing across his lips again.

'I know you. Oh, my god, how did I not recognise you?' Laughter bubbled from cruel lips. 'You're old now, and your hair's different, but those eyes. They're still the same.' He leaned against the doorframe and my stomach pitched.

Shit, he knew me.

'I had you once.'

He was mistaken there. It wasn't me, but my sister. But I wasn't about to correct him.

'Have you come back for more?' He slipped one hand down his groin to stroke his penis through thin, grimy shorts in a sick taunt. 'They say you can't keep a good man down.'

I ground my teeth in helpless anger.

What the hell had I done? What had I expected to achieve coming here?

All I'd done was expose myself to him. Dive into a whole new nightmare.

His hand dropped from his shorts at the same time as the smile dropped from his face. Eyes hard as ice-chips bored into me.

'Fuck off, bitch. You're not the right age for me.'

I don't know at what point I lost my mind, but once I did, there was no getting it back until I was done.

It had never happened to me before.

Well, yes, I'd had my dark moments that we don't talk about. A slip. A mistake. Nothing like the solid black velvet curtain that dropped over my vision that morning. Not that I'm telling of, anyway. Not right now. That's for another day.

Rage tore through me, a torrent I couldn't stop.

He stepped back, his hand on the door, ready to shut it.

Red fury washed over my vision. I reached out and grabbed the nearest thing to hand.

I didn't know what the hell kind of weapon a birdbath made, but I snatched the weighty thing from where it leaned against the wall and smashed the thick end of it into his smug face.

His laughter exploded from his mouth in a bloody gush as he stumbled backwards.

He held one hand up in front of his face to stop me as I powered towards him, elbowing the door wide so hard it rebounded and slammed shut behind me, trapping me inside his house with him.

I didn't care. He didn't frighten me. Not any more. Too much of my life had been lived in fear of Gary Philpotts.

He no longer held the power. I did!

His foot caught in the curl of the ragged hallway rug and he slammed into the floor, sprawling at my feet.

Without a second thought, I twirled the birdbath around in my hand and, holding the heavy end with both hands, plunged the thick spike through him.

It snagged on his flesh, for a heartbeat, like a needle when you push it through leather, before it split his skin like a ripe melon. With my full weight bearing down on it, the weapon slid through his body with little resistance. With no bones in the way to stop the advance, the spike pierced through Gary's soft tissue.

When the metal hit the floor under him, fire licked through every muscle and sinew in my arms, jolting my shoulders so the wild scream I'd not even been aware of cut dead in my throat.

In the silence, our eyes met. We stared at each other.

A strange understanding passed between us.

I'd done the world a favour.

Gary opened his lips and a trickle of blood oozed out. Perhaps he'd bitten his tongue when the birdbath smashed into his face. But the pink frothiness that followed indicated something far more sinister.

The sharp spike had torn through his lung.

24

I straightened, taking my weight from where I leaned against the metal birdbath. The top gave a gentle wobble in my hands, but the shank held fast.

Shock held me frozen as I watched Gary's pale blue eyes fill with tears. The years hadn't been kind to him. He was no longer the enormous, robust young man of my memory, but more a withered shadow of my nightmares. The weight he'd heaved around had fallen from his bones in recent months to leave his skin slack and sallow.

He let out a choked cough, as though he wanted to say something.

The same pink bubbles coming from his mouth leaked from his nose and spluttered out, little droplets filling the air.

I stepped back, horror swimming through my veins. I didn't need his blood on me and so far, there'd been enough distance to avoid that.

I raised my hands to my face but couldn't bring myself to cover my eyes as I stared at the man I'd stabbed. More than that, I'd skewered.

My knees turned to water and I crumpled to the floor at his side.

What had I done? What the hell had I done? What had I become? As much of a monster as him?

I turned my head and stared at the closed door.

How long had we been there? Locked in our final conflict.

I listened to the silence. No sound of movement to indicate the day had begun in the neighbourhood. Despite the bright summer light, it was still early.

My yell had surely been loud enough to wake the dead.

I turned back to Gary. He opened his mouth wider, trying to speak, but only a wet gurgle came from him. His eyes fixed on my face as though looking for an answer.

There was no point. I didn't have one myself.

I turned my attention to my accidental weapon. My fingerprints were all over it. The whole of the birdbath would be covered in them.

I touched it and the little bath on top wobbled. I leaned my head in as close as I dared to Gary.

Confusion slipped over his face, his milky, unfocused eyes squeezed shut. A tear rolled down his cheek.

I pushed aside the regret that edged its way through. A small smile curved my lips as I peered down at the garden ornament. The bath was screwed onto the metal stake.

I couldn't allow myself to feel anything. Nothing. Nothing at all. Not regret, not sympathy. My heart needed to be dead inside because I had to sort out this mess that I'd got myself into.

Gary's head flopped to one side so he no longer faced me.

Shock still held me in its grasp, but strength borne of necessity returned to my limbs. I leaned back on my heels, my head to one side to better study him. Blood seeped from the puncture wound and soaked through his grubby T-shirt. It trickled in a thin line to form an ever-increasing crimson puddle by his side.

I should call an ambulance. I should call the police. Turn myself in.

I considered it.

What would that achieve? He was going to die.

They would never believe it wasn't deliberate, I hadn't meant to do it.

I hadn't.

When I'd set out, it had never even occurred to me that I was about to commit murder.

I ran my gaze over his inert body. He wasn't dead yet.

If I yanked the prong out of him, he'd bleed out quicker. It could all be over in a matter of moments. That would be the kindest thing to do.

But I don't feel kind. The blind fury still snaked its way through me, not quite sliding away.

With cold deliberation, I ran my options through my head.

'I could make this easy for you, Gary.' I said it out loud to give myself conviction. 'Make it quicker by pulling this thing out of you.'

He let out a soft, pleading whimper.

'Is that what you want me to do?'

He gurgled a wordless plea.

My blood ran icy cold. I placed my fingers on the birdbath. It gave another wobble.

If I pulled out that stake, blood was going to go everywhere. So far, I paused to look down at myself, I hadn't got any on me. Yet.

My fingerprints were on the weapon. All over it.

I could wipe down the straight shaft easy enough, but the bath itself was full of wrinkles and divots.

I deliberately rocked the top and peered at the connection. The top was screwed onto the shaft.

I made quick work of unscrewing the top of the birdbath and placed it beside me as I took a tissue from my pocket and gave the metal shaft a vigorous rub. How much did it take to remove fingerprints?

As the pool of blood spread, almost touching my knees, I came to my feet, steadying myself without touching floor, wall or Gary Philpotts.

With a quick glance, I dashed through the open toilet door, used the tissue to flush the loo and threw it down, watching it swirl away through the stained and splattered bowl.

Panic nudged aside the shock and I dashed back to Gary's body.

How long had I been there? Were people starting to stir?

I crouched down and picked up the birdbath, tucking it under my arm. The metal felt cool through the thin cotton of my T-shirt that soaked up the slick sweat coating my skin.

I gave a hasty glance around.

I'd touched nothing, other than hammering on the door with the side of my fist. They couldn't get fingerprints from that. Could they? Instinct that I'd believed was to protect my hand from the dirt had served me well when I'd pulled the long sleeve of my T-shirt over it.

With one last look, I sniffed, taking in the stale scent of rust and BO, with the overlaying powerful smell of fresh blood.

I refused to let myself dwell on it. I needed to get out of there. To save myself.

I turned on my heel and took four short strides along the hallway. I yanked my sleeve down over my hand again and turned the lock.

Without looking back, I hooked my foot around the bottom of the door and let it slam, leaving the stench and the horror behind me.

25

It wasn't that I felt no remorse for what I'd done. I'm not some kind of psycho. I knew it was wrong. But it felt so right. Not good, per se. Just right.

Given the choice, would I do it again? Hell, yes! But I wouldn't necessarily have done it the way I did.

That slide of sharp point through flesh, fat and sinew makes me shudder every time I close my eyes. It's not like carving a leg of lamb, or a rib of beef. The 'pop' as the point pierced his skin and then the give as my weight lent power to the weapon.

And what a weapon. Who would have thought an innocent garden feature could cause such damage?

I can't help laughing to myself. Death by birdbath.

It wasn't as though I drowned him. Nor did I wield the weapon in front of him, threatening him with it. For god's sake, I'm not a trained killer.

It wasn't murder. It was an accident. An horrific, sick accident.

It happened so fast. He didn't put up a fight. I took him by surprise. Truth be told, I took myself by surprise too.

Who would have thought I'd react the way I did?

Perhaps it's not my choice of weapon under normal circumstances. But those circumstances weren't normal.

It didn't feel good to kill him.

It did feel good to rid the world of him.

Maybe I could have been a little kinder and finished him off straight away. Cut his life short somehow to save him the agony of dangling between life and death. What was I supposed to do? I couldn't risk hanging around or ferreting through kitchen drawers to find a knife sharp enough to slit his throat. That would be a deliberate act. And it hadn't been premeditated.

I wrinkle my nose in disgust. I wasn't capable of slitting someone's throat.

I wonder how long it took him to die.

Part of me still wants to call an ambulance. Call the police.

I step everything through in my head.

It isn't about saving him now. It's too late for that.

What about me? What's the right thing for me to do? Do I want to confess and spend the rest of my life behind bars? I don't think so.

Is it better to confess than to be found out? I have no idea. I suspect the courts may be more lenient if I explain.

But I don't want to explain.

Why take that risk?

This has been my secret since I was nine. What would be the point of burdening everyone I love with that knowledge now? The one I thought I was protecting them from.

The secret that had caused more harm in the long run. If only I hadn't kept it to myself in the first place.

No. There's no point confessing. The damage would be irreparable.

I'm pretty sure there's nothing to point to me. After all, I've never been in trouble with the police. My fingerprints won't be on file. Nobody, to my knowledge, saw me and I'm not sure it's the kind of area where people have little CCTV cameras all over the place. Mainly because most of them wouldn't want the police on their doorstep.

Also, I turned my phone off before I left it in my car. After all, I didn't need anyone knowing my location. Questions might have been raised.

Every nerve ending that had been set on edge from the moment the court case turned belly up relaxed.

This changes things for me.

I feel differently about myself. About what my role in life is.

I have a much clearer idea of what I now need to do.

26

My hands are shaking so badly, I have to wrap them around the Costa cup just to stop the tremor in them, as though it's a freezing cold day, but it's certainly not freezing. In fact, sweat runs down the length of my back as my teeth clench against the shock.

I've dumped four of those fat little sachets of sugar into the cappuccino because that's what you're supposed to do, isn't it? Plenty of sugar if you're suffering from shock. Or is that blood loss? I have no idea. My brain has turned to slush at the mere thought of blood.

I close my eyes and swallow. Not sure I can even drink the overly sweet coffee. But my closed eyelids just play out the scene again, so I blink them open.

I'm trying to keep my shit together here. I can't afford to lose my nerve. But the memory of what I've done won't back off and leave me alone for a while. I hardly slept a wink the previous night and exhaustion has left me even more vulnerable.

I study my fingers, curled around the cup. Not only are the nails bitten to the quick, but little slivers of skin have hardened around them and stick out from bloodied spots in miniature spikes to catch on every item of clothing and torture me some more.

I haven't bitten my nails so badly since I was at junior school. Then, I used to do it in class. I massacred them until my fingers looked like fat little stubs. I always found it strange that the shorter your nails, the wider your fingers looked.

This wasn't about my nails, though. That was just a response to my reaction.

Whatever triggered such violence in me now stirred other dark, long-ago memories that I thought were dead and buried. That worries me too because I know it's not my imagination. I'm not making it up. I just hadn't needed to remember.

Until now.

The churn in my stomach from distant recollections feels like the wriggle of worms making their way to the surface of a deep pile of steaming, rotten manure. Why would something from so long ago explode in my head like a 3D movie playing out?

I try to push it away, but I'm suddenly consumed by it.

I was eleven years old, the final year of junior school. I don't think it was called Year Six back then. Those insignificant details I can't really remember. What I do remember, though, was the headmaster.

Mr Collington.

A giant of a man, or so he appeared to us. We'd thought he was old back then, but he was possibly only in his mid-thirties. That would put him in his seventies now. If he's still alive.

I'd never looked him up or given a second thought to my youthful traumas. Incidents I'd long ago buried for my own self-preservation.

Things happen when you're young. It shapes your future, in a myriad of ways in which we don't necessarily understand or recognise the connection. As the saying goes, we are all products of our environment.

I recognise it now. Now things had been stirred up.

I'd never had any desire or thought to check on what had become of Mr Collington, my headmaster, until recent events dredged up my past, nicking old wounds that had long ago healed and peeling back the scab to reveal all those festering feelings I never even realised I'd harboured all these years.

Something dark stirred inside me. A deep abhorrence of the man.

Mr Collington, broad and imposing, regularly hitched trousers up from where the legs bagged around his ankles, only for them to slide back down again. The belt just about tight enough to stop them slipping off his hips slung under his stomach, Simon Cowell-fashion. But long before Simon Cowell made it fashionable.

The kids sniggered at the small, dark spotted patches on the pale grey material covering his groin. The boys saying he hadn't shaken his willy properly and the splashes showed through his trousers. The girls shushing them with nervous giggles.

His trousers appeared to be clean each Monday, after the weekend. Did he really only own one pair of grey trousers?

I found in me a steadfast caution of the man, for no apparent reason, other than having been through one unfortunate incident. I think back then, even in my innocence, I recognised a like character to the one I'd already come across some years previously. It had taught me a healthy kind of wariness.

When we reached the final year of junior school, we were sent, two at a time, to his office for 'reading' practice.

He sat behind an enormous shiny, mahogany desk, the bulk of him spilling over his chair, squeezing out between wide wooden arms. A book rested on the desk beside his right hand and each of us read an entire page in breathless, jerky sentences with words that blurred before our eyes in our anxiety to please, to get it right, while he rested his forearms on his desk.

His heavy breathing always filled my ears.

Uncomfortable in his presence, I stood by his side, every muscle tensed. In preparation for what, I didn't know back then.

* * *

I know now.

Instinct prepared me for flight. An instinct I listen to every day of my life now. Learned to listen to too late back then. But maybe they were the lessons I needed to learn in order to be the person I am today. Mistakes happen. We learn by them. Grow. Move on.

I'm not sure if I'm actually moving back as these things rear up to haunt me.

* * *

On occasion, Mr Collington would stop me by holding up a hand, nothing more. He'd reach out and slide the book closer to him and point at a word. With the book angled away from me I'd have to shuffle closer, my thigh resting against the back of his hand so I could lean in and read the word.

Now, as it did then, my breath stuttered and held. Every part of me recoiling inside, but unable to distance myself physically.

In case he guessed.

In case he knew.

Towards the end of the school year, as the long days became thick with the July heat, Miss Forster, our form teacher, told us we were to have special lessons with Mr Collington to prepare us for life as we matured.

These lessons were not under any circumstances to be discussed with the younger children in the school. Their time of enlightenment would come. We were special. It was just for us and no one else. Which implied, in turn, that it wasn't for us to discuss outside of school, either. A sort of mystique.

With an air of excited importance, we filed into class after lunch. Our eyes, normally heavy with sleep by this time on a Friday afternoon, were gleaming with enthusiasm. We were to have special lessons. And Mr Collington was to deliver them.

Whether this was because Miss Forster had been deemed too young, or too inexperienced to take this subject, it never occurred to us at the time. In retrospect, it was actually because Mr Collington, our headmaster, was a pervert and he'd manipulated matters so that he could teach us all we needed to know. All he wanted us to know.

Did it give him some sadistic kind of pleasure to watch us squirm, our innocent lives tainted by the manner in which he delivered sex education?

Back then, all those years ago, things were different. Girls didn't start their periods at the age of nine as they often do now. I remember the first and only girl in our class at junior school to start her periods at that age. Carol. Big boobs, greasy hair and a savagely spotty face. Everyone knew. They called her a freak. She spent most of her time desperate to remain unnoticed at the back of the classroom, shoulders hunched, arms crossed over her well-developed chest and a strange smell permeating from her.

Her reading ability was far below the rest of ours.

She spent extra time, one to one with Mr Collington.

I wonder what became of her.

Times were different. Better nutrition has led to higher body mass, hence earlier periods in girls. That's the simplified version, but I'm no scientist.

My experience of sex ed scarred me for life. All because of one horrific event.

The sun beat down through a whole bank of windows onto those of us who sat along the right-hand side of the classroom. We didn't have shades or blinds to protect us.

The heat scorched through my scalp. My eyes watered against the brightness.

My sister, when she was here, persuaded the teacher she had such appalling hay fever that they allowed her to wear sunglasses and sit on the shaded side of the classroom in the summer months. But that's my sister for you. She was always more forward than me. I would never have asked.

When Sir came into the room, we all leaped to our feet, shoulders back, chins up. Proper little tin soldiers, all of us. So pleased to be noticed by Mr Collington. At that time. Not so much later, when we all knew.

He closed the door, and we took our seats as he made his way to the head of the classroom where he stood in front of the blackboard, so his wide body almost obscured it from view.

Not a single one of us had anything but a fearful respect for the man. He was a man who wielded the cane quite liberally.

You could have heard a pin drop in the silence he managed to create. Except for laboured breathing through plump, wet lips.

A quiver of fearful excitement circled the room as he invited us to our feet. Anticipation for what exciting things we were about to participate in had nerves pinging.

There's only a vague recollection of how he started the game, but it was fun. Such fun. I'm not sure with all the health and safety regulations and risk assessments any teacher would dare do it these days, but then it was fair game.

Mr Collington talked about families. The make-up of them. The cell that we form. The relationship between our parents and ourselves. He whisked through it, gaining our interest.

Then he asked everyone who was an only child to take a seat.

With half-hearted groans, a dozen or so children sank back down with the sure knowledge their game was over and no prize, should there *be one, would be coming their way. If I'd known then, I would have kept my mouth closed and taken my seat along with them. Along with Carol, who slouched down, crumpled almost in half as though she hoped not to be noticed.*

My excitement escalated as everyone who had more than one child in the family was told to stay standing at floor level.

Those with three were invited to stand on their hard wooden chairs.

With a dropping sensation, I realised that this game was going in a bad direction. Back then, if you were naughty, you stood on your desk, hands on head for the whole classroom to stare at you in your humiliation.

As only two of us stepped up onto our desks when asked who had more than three children in their family, we stared at each other over the expanse of the classroom, nervous smiles dropping from our lips as the discomfort set in.

These days, no such questioning would be allowed. No adult would wield such power in their classroom. Or so we'd like to believe. But predators find their way. I've learned to be on the look-out for them. I reckon I would recognise one the moment they walked into a room full of people.

Phillip Whitman stood tall and lanky on his desk, in the shade at least, while the sun beat down on my head and a light-headedness made me sway as I stepped up. I steadied myself.

For an age, we waited on those desks, silence descending like a scratchy blanket before Mr Collington spoke. He pointed at Sandra Newton, one of the 'only' children. 'What does your father do for a living?'

She swallowed before she offered him a tentative smile. 'He's an accountant, sir.'

Mr Collington nodded approvingly. 'Very nice.'

He pointed to another 'only' child. 'And yours?'

'A doctor, sir.'

'Good. Good.' He squinted at a third child. 'And you? What does your father do?'

Alfie shrugged. 'I dunno, sir. He's a manager, sir, at Brierley Crystal.' He blushed to the roots of his red hair. 'He doesn't talk about it, sir. Says it's confidential.'

Mr Collington smiled. 'A manager. That's good.'

I swallowed as his gaze passed over me and moved on. A bead of sweat trickled down the back of my legs.

There was a pause before he addressed Phillip. 'What does your father do for a living?'

Phillip's lips quavered upwards in a desperate attempt to please. 'He manages a pub, sir.' There was a certain pride in his tone.

A self-satisfied look passed over Mr Collington's features as he turned to me. 'And yours, girl. What does your dad do?'

At that time, it hadn't occurred to me that Mr Collington was exactly aware of this information and had contrived the whole scenario. That the position of headmaster with no one to answer to lent itself perfectly to his sadistic nature.

I squinted at him through a beam of sunlight that danced with dust motes. 'He owns a pub.' I wasn't so sure. My dad was an engineer by trade. The pub was a diversion from his normal work. We hated it. Us kids. We no longer saw our parents, except on a Sunday afternoon for a few hours and when we arrived home from school. Mum still made sure there was a hot meal on the table for us bang on 6 p.m. before she dashed into the bar to serve by 7 p.m., leaving us to wash, dry and put away the dishes. No such thing as a dishwasher in our house back then.

She was no longer there to supervise our homework. You either did it, or you didn't. It was right, or it was wrong. We took the consequences either way. Maybe it was a good life lesson for us. After all, all of us are strong, independent women. Character building it would be classed as back then, I'm sure.

At my confession, Mr Collington's face brightened as if I'd just given him a Ferrero Rocher. Not that we knew much about them with their high-priced sophistication. Perhaps a Walnut Whip. That was my dad's favourite.

Mr Collington rubbed his hands together, making a dry, rasping noise and then dropped them to his side as he gave a slow nod, his attention drifting around the classroom, a silent invitation for the watching pupils to join him in his sport.

When his gaze fell back on Phillip his eyes turned shrewd. 'You. What's your name, boy?'

'Phillip, sir.'

'And you?'

I told him. I said it loud and clear and never tagged 'sir' onto the end either. My dad taught me that to be called 'sir', a person needed to earn that respect. My respect for Mr Collington had rapidly slipped down the toilet pan during the last few minutes and was about to be flushed.

A sharp pain stabbed under my breastbone and my breathing became stilted with the sure knowledge something bad was about to happen.

As heat bloomed in my cheeks, I raised my hand to wipe the sweat from the back of my neck, all the time watching Mr Collington as his plump lips twitched upwards in a lopsided smile.

'Pub managers.' His nostrils widened as the air whistled through them. 'See, children. Can you see, there's a connection here between large families and lack of education?'

The room held its breath as every child froze. Shock rippled around bouncing off the walls.

The insult, almost a physical slap, had me reeling. My dad wasn't uneducated. He was intelligent. Brilliant, even. He knew about things I could never imagine learning. He could do maths in his head. Three pints of lager and a packet of crisps... not quite. But four pints of beer at 77p each, a twenty-pack of Lambert and Butler King Size cigarettes at £1.15, two packets of scratchings at 10p each and he had it all totted up in his head. He didn't have to ring it up on the till to know. I've watched him.

And when a £20 note was handed over, he counted out the change back-wards. Not forwards like kids are taught now.

My dad could fix a motor engine with his eyes closed. He wasn't uned-ucated. He was clever. I'd go so far as to say, brilliant.

Like a well-honed comedian, Mr Collington used that beat of silence to observe us all, to deliver the next cutting remark without a change of expression.

'Those uneducated men. Working class, with no idea how to treat a woman. Men whose way of life is to drink.'

Silence pushed down on the oppressive heat as each one of the chil-dren came to the same realisation as me. This subject was roaming off down a dim and distant path of foulness. The stench of it hung like a cloud over us.

My face blazed with embarrassment, but I couldn't lower my head to avoid everyone's glances. I was above them. Their faces upturned to see me. So, I looked at each one of them instead. The muscles bunched in my jaw as I ground my teeth together and balled my hands into fists at my side, ready to pounce if a single one of them should snigger.

Not one of them met my gaze as they dropped their heads, clearly relieved it wasn't them he'd targeted.

A flicker of a frown creased my brow as his hands slipped from his side to rub the tops of his thighs, either side of his groin. My discomfort grew. I might not have been old enough to understand what was going on, but I was wise enough to realise it wasn't right.

'You see, what happens is these men, your fathers.' He waved a hand to encompass Phillip and me. 'They have a few too many drinks and their baser instincts take over. They go home. Or in these cases, they just need to go upstairs. Even more convenient. And they put upon your mothers.' He pointed his finger at one and then the other of us. 'They press them into having sex when they don't want to. And then, along comes a little mistake. Another baby to swell your mummy's belly.'

Horror filled me until I thought my head might explode. My dad didn't do that. He wasn't like that. He loved my mum. He loved all of us.

My head throbbed under the heat from the sun. Black clouds washed over my vision, and I swayed, precarious on a desk with a slight list. It felt more like a see-saw to me as it rocked from side to side and I adjusted my feet, spreading them wider to give more balance, conscious that they were now at the outer edges of the desk.

Did he mean I was a mistake? That my sisters were mistakes?

'That's not true.' I glanced at Phillip. Pale skinned, anyway, his golden freckles stood out stark as the colour leached from his face to leave it grey.

I returned my attention to Mr Collington, grinding my teeth. The whites of his eyes showed as he left the centre of the room and stepped closer, tipping his head back to glare up at me. 'What did you say?'

I shifted my weight again as my bladder gave a hard twinge. 'I said that's not true. My mum and dad love me. They wanted me.'

One derogatory eyebrow raised. 'I seriously doubt they wanted you. As I said, you were probably an accident. That's what happens when there's so many.'

As the comment sliced me open, my mouth dropped wide to the accompaniment of uncomfortable sniggers from the other children. How dare he? How could he stand there, his hands touching his trousers in an obscene caress and accuse my dad of something so vile?

I tried to wet my lips with my tongue, but it stuck. 'I wasn't a mistake. They wanted me.' My voice was less convincing this time, quieter, lacking in confidence.

Like a cobra, Mr Collington reared his head back, readying himself to strike. Even in my innocence, I could tell.

I recoiled.

'Are you sure?' A sly nastiness crept through, what I now recognise as sarcasm. 'Did they really? I think you should ask them. Why don't we make that your homework?' He circled around to encompass the entire class, get them in on the joke. Include them in my degradation. 'You can let us all know in next week's lesson.'

Only now, as an adult, do I realise he knew. Knew no child would ever willingly go to their parents to ask such a question. His disgraceful behaviour was safe inside that room. None of us would take it to our parents.

I touched the back of my hand to my wet forehead and swayed again, the hot sting of humiliation filling my eyes with tears. 'They love me.' My words came out a hoarse whisper.

'I'm sure. At least Daddy probably does. Does Daddy sometimes slip into your bed at night, when your mum is already asleep, and tell you how much he loves you? Is that how you know?'

Horror filled me at his words. I had no real understanding of what he meant, but it was filth. A disgusting slur on my family. My dad.

Despite my initial anger and bravado, there was not a thing in this world I could do to deny what he said.

He was our headmaster. The man in charge. The man everyone looked up to. Even the parents.

I could do nothing as he stepped back and picked up the long ruler from his desk and tapped it on his hand. A subtle, but blatant threat.

Defeated, my head swam.

The scald of my own urine washed over my thighs, trickling down my legs to pool a bright yellow stain in my white ankle socks. The soft splash hitting the desk grew louder in the silence of the room.

Humiliation scalded my cheeks as I stared at my feet, knowing my shoes would forever smell of my own wee.

I raised my head, anger searing my chest, ready to fuel the words branded on my brain. I didn't care who he was, who looked up to him. My dad was right. You never called anyone 'sir' unless they deserved it.

I opened my tight lips. 'You filthy git. You vile man,' I wanted to scream at him from my higher stance, but the words never formed as a wave of dizziness hit me and I fell, down, down into a yawning black pit.

27

If only I'd said something all those years ago, to my mum, to my dad. To any one of my sisters. But, for the second, and by no means the last time in my life, I hugged this dirty little secret close to my chest and kept my mouth closed.

Shame and embarrassment held me in check. Shame that Mr Collington had held my dad accountable for something he declared wicked and vile, of which at that tender age I had no proof otherwise and no one to ask. I'd been too ashamed to mention it just in case he was right about me being an accident. Unwanted. Because he should know, shouldn't he? He was there to teach, wasn't he? A man of position and standing who I'd been told I must respect.

I had no doubt the second accusation the Head made was completely untrue. My daddy loved me and there was, without any doubt in my mind, nothing lurid or obscene about his love for me.

A trickle of doubt filled my heart. What if he was right about the first thing, though? What if I was unwanted?

If I voiced the question, did I want to know the truth?

The thought has always lingered in the back of my mind. I try to push it away, but let's face it, it's there, embedded in my subconscious. A part of me.

What if I told my dad? He'd thump Mr Collington. I knew he would. And then what would happen to me? I wouldn't be allowed to go to school, and I liked my teacher. I liked Miss Forster. She made me feel safe. If only I didn't need to see Mr Collington again, everything would be all right and besides, it wouldn't be long until I went to secondary school. I'd passed my grammar school entrance exam. Surely Mum and Dad would let me go there. Dudley Girls' High School.

But if Dad hit Mr Collington, none of my dreams would happen.

Along with that, there was the indignity that in peeing myself, all I'd achieved was to make Dad look even worse in that man's eyes. As if I'd helped him to prove his point to the whole class.

When my dad turned up at the hospital to pick me up, I held my silence. He came because Mum didn't drive, and someone had to stay behind to keep the pub open. At that time, she was struggling, but they couldn't just throw everyone out and close it because one of their daughters was in the hospital.

I heard what the nurse said to Mum on the phone. It wasn't life threatening. A few little stitches. Possibly concussion. No, of course it was okay if just my dad came to pick me up.

Lunchtime business would have been lost otherwise.

Maybe if it had been Mum, I would have said something. Or maybe if my nose and mouth hadn't throbbed from the wallop against the desk as I went down.

Even more humiliating, if I hadn't wet myself.

All I wanted to do was go home, pull a blanket over my head and sleep for a million years so the pain both inside and out would go. Twelve neat little stiches straight down from the base of my nose, right down the centre until it touched my lip. He called that little groove from nose to mouth my philtrum. The doctor said I was young enough for it to heal without a scar.

He was wrong.

I reach now and stroke the tip of my finger along the slight white ridge, faded over time so no one else would notice unless they looked very closely. Unless they knew what they were looking for.

According to Mr Collington, he hadn't quite reached me in time. I never asked if he'd been questioned as to why I'd been standing on my desk. Why I'd wet myself.

Those were the days when you were made to stand on your desk, hands on head to teach you a lesson. A hard one. For any reason from not knowing your four times table to picking your nose in class. It sounds Victorian, but actually it's not so very long ago. Nor was the use of the cane, which was regularly wielded in my school and only ceased to be used in 1987.

Kids these days think their treatment is tough.

I squint at my computer screen, my eyes aching, but I'm on a mission and nothing is going to stop me conducting a bit of research outside of my own normal remit.

Funny how it's not so difficult to track people down now. I think I've become pretty adept at stalking. Facebook is a doddle. You don't even have to have an account on there for some kind person to post a photograph of you for the whole world to see.

All I had to do was join the Past Pupils of St Luke's Primary School and scroll through. Admittedly, it took a bit of patience. It was one hell of a long time since I left there.

I figured he'd not been that old when I was there. Through the eyes of a child, he probably did seem it, but looking back, I'm not so sure.

As I study the page, I find myself stroking my finger across that scar, a light tingle persisting. A small reminder of this man's sadistic nature.

I let out a yawn and pick up my cup of tea, which has turned tepid while I've reminisced.

Reminisce probably isn't the right word. That sounds like I was enjoying happier days. I was not. My days were never happier than they are now.

Back then, when I was a child, it was hell. Each Friday for the following three Fridays until we broke up for the summer, when Mr Collington was scheduled to take us for sex ed, I miraculously fell sick at lunchtime. Mainly because I stuck my fingers down my throat and threw up.

Miss Forster declared that my reading was up to par and I no longer needed to see Mr Collington. I wonder now whether that had been at his behest or hers.

My life had taken a turn for the better once I went to Dudley Girls' High School.

I peer closer at the screen, eyes dry from too much scrolling.

Knowing my luck, he'd have been promoted and moved to a larger school, or a secondary school.

Then again, had he preferred, with his predilection for young children, to stay under the radar, remaining in a low-key job? Big fish in a small pond scenario.

I keep looking.

Eventually, there is one of those 'remember the date?' posts.

Photographs of bygone days.

I spot someone I knew.

So many people had jumped on board. Yes, yes, yes. Mr Collington's retirement year. It takes a while longer scrolling, to find the sly comments hinting at the dirty old man he'd turned out to be.

Perhaps he should have been sacked, not lauded with a long-service award.

I study the posts. He'd worked beyond his retirement age, which was unusual in teaching. Quite often, as retirement approaches, they're already burnt out from a life full of stress, admin and relentless children.

Had there been a reason he'd stayed?

Had it suited him?

No wife, apparently. No one. Not even a Facebook page of his own for me to follow, but I no longer need to.

Because someone has just told me where he is now.

'Poor bugger,' they said.

28

'When are you going to tell your sisters?'

Alexis rolled out of bed and slipped her sateen wrap around her, pulling the belt tight around a waistline that had thickened recently. Contentment, some would call it.

'It's none of their business.'

'I think it is.' Pippa sat up and the sheet slipped from her, pooling around her waist and leaving small, pert breasts naked so Alexis thought twice about going to get coffee. 'Alexis, we've been together almost four months now. Don't you think it's only fair to let them know? Besides, I'd like to meet them.'

Alexis shrugged. 'I'm not sure they're ready for that.'

'Them, or you?' Pippa pulled back the covers and slipped from the bed, her slim, lithe body moving with grace as she crossed the room to the en suite.

'Them. Definitely them. It's going to be a shock to them.'

'That I'm black, or that I'm female?'

Alexis snorted. 'They're not going to give a damn about your colour, in fact you might find Sarah checking out your perfect skin. And honestly, I'm not even sure if they'll care that you're female.'

Alexis leaned against the doorframe leading to the short hallway. 'They are going to be surprised, though. I mean, I'm this many years old and never, ever shown interest in the same sex.' It wasn't strictly the truth. She'd noticed. Had the odd inkling that she found women attractive. Even had a crush on one of the female teachers at school. But didn't every schoolgirl? Wasn't that normal?

She'd thought so.

But then, she'd spent all her life trying to prove something to everyone. That she was fine, undamaged. Perhaps the truth was more that she'd overlooked her own sexuality in favour of making her family believe she'd been unaffected by what had happened to her as a child.

Pippa's lips twitched. 'I turned you.'

'No, I don't think so. I've always fancied Jill Gascoigne.'

At the blank look from a woman seven years her junior, Alexis frowned. 'You know! Surely you've seen the re-runs.' She sighed. 'Okay, how about Marcella?'

Pippa's face broke into a smile. 'Ah, Marcella. Definitely worthy.' She narrowed her eyes and grinned. 'And as for Villanelle.' They both sighed. 'But I still turned you.'

Pippa leaned in for a kiss before she swung around and allowed the door to close with soft finality behind her.

Alexis wandered into her compact kitchen and stared from her window onto the street below, watching as people dashed by in their rush to get to work. Barely past dawn, she'd better get a move on or she'd be late for work. Pippa was on at 2 p.m. One of those strange half-shifts she sometimes worked but hated. It never fell in properly with what she wanted to do and meant that five half-days didn't make up the time for three full days. She always seemed to be on the back foot with her shifts. Normally it wouldn't matter, but now she had someone else to consider.

A doctor at Russell's Hall Hospital, Pippa had met Alexis

numerous times on duty before she'd asked her out for a drink. A drink which led to them falling into bed together.

Alexis filled the kettle and switched it on, listening to the noisy shush and bubble as it heated up. She'd make a cup of tea and then grab a quick shower and pull on her uniform.

She wasn't ashamed of falling for a woman. When she thought about it, about her two failed marriages and destroyed relationships far beyond those two, it made sense. Nor had she thought of herself as a lesbian. Was she? A lesbian? She'd never thought of herself as one, never considered it a possibility. She'd always chosen men, never particularly looked at other women other than to admire their figures or envy their skin.

Pippa was different. She just happened to be a woman. Alexis's soulmate.

Alexis just had to find a way to tell her sisters.

There was no shame in it.

She'd seen the hurt flicker through Pippa's eyes. It wasn't fair on her.

Alexis was right. Her family weren't prejudiced. Certainly, skin tone didn't matter to any of them, to Alexis's knowledge. Although she could almost guarantee Graham would have something to say on the matter, if only behind her back. Most probably about how their reputation would be tarnished by having a black lesbian in the family. Then again, he was a dickwad.

So, why was she hesitant about introducing Pippa to her sisters?

She took the lid off a bright red canister, fished out two teabags and dumped them into the mugs she'd left out the night before.

It wasn't because Pippa was black. It wasn't because she was female.

It was because Alexis's sisters would give her that same look they gave her every time she introduced a new boyfriend to them.

Like they knew her, and they knew she was going to make a complete balls-up, just like she did with every relationship.

She poured boiling water onto the teabags, put the kettle down and stared back out the window again.

Perhaps she should take Pippa to Tess's fiftieth birthday party. Would that be a good time and place to introduce her? Or was that unfair on Pippa, throwing her in at the deep end? The whole family, kids included. After all, she didn't want to scare her away.

This time, she wanted it to work.

This time was different.

This time, it was going to last.

29

Bobbi scanned the computer screen, looking for something, anything that would tie this evil scum of a woman into the crime. She knew she was involved. Proof beyond reasonable doubt was her goal. But it just wasn't there.

She scrubbed her hands over her cheeks and peered over her laptop, catching Vanessa's eye. 'I'm really struggling here.'

Vanessa, one of the more experienced in Bobbi's team, put her coffee down and sat up straight to talk over her own laptop. 'You need a sounding board?'

'Do you mind?'

Vanessa stood and made her way around to stand over Bobbi's shoulder, coffee in hand as she looked at the computer screen.

'Which case are you working on?'

'Anslow. The two children. Little girl and boy. Marcie and Alfie.'

'We removed them from their parents about a month ago, yeah?'

Vanessa was a bright woman. Mid-thirties, one daughter aged nine. Had her finger on every case. Mainly due to a photographic memory. Once seen, never forgotten was her joking philosophy, but

Bobbi wished she had a bit of that superpower to her name. She struggled to remember what they were having for dinner recently.

'Yep. Mum and stepdad. Evil. Stripped the kids down and made them stand in the corner hour after hour, staring at nothing. Not allowed to move, not allowed to speak. They were slowly starving them to death. The only meals they had, apparently, were when they were at school. Which is why it came to Marcie's teacher's attention.'

Bobbi shook her head, her chest aching for the children. She didn't normally take things to heart so hard, but this case had really got to her, dug deep into her feelings, under her thinner-than-she'd-realised skin, so when she couldn't sleep at night, the case was what she thought about.

'Marcie's teacher flagged up a problem. She'd noticed the little girl ramming food into her mouth. Taking other children's leftovers. The teacher spoke with her, and then took a look at the younger brother. He was gaunt. Barely eating at all. He'd gone beyond the point of trying to fend for himself. Bruised under the eyes. Not from a beating. They were too clever to beat the children outright. That wouldn't have gone unnoticed for so long. They were abusing them physically, mentally, emotionally.'

Tears pricked at the back of her eyelids. God, she never cried at work. What was wrong with her? She bore down on the emotion, shoved back the tears. They were no good for anyone, not her, the children or the prosecuting counsel.

Bobbi leaned back in her chair and looked over her shoulder at Vanessa as her friend and colleague flipped her long chocolate-brown plait over her shoulder and pulled a chair over to sit down.

'It's getting to you.'

Bobbi nodded. 'I don't think I've ever come across a case of such cruelty.' She tapped the screen. 'He has got to be the most evil person I've ever come across. We've got him. I know we have, but I can't nail her down with anything. Can't find the proof.'

'Have you interviewed him?'

Bobbi shook her head. 'Not yet. I've got him this afternoon.'

'Shit. Do you want someone to go with you?'

Bobbi waved it off, although she was tempted. 'No. I'll be okay. I know I can do it, hold it together for the kids, but you know when you just want to slam your fist into someone's face?'

She caught Vanessa's startled look. 'Uhh.'

'I wouldn't really.' She took her glasses off and laid them by the side of the laptop, giving her eyes a rub. 'But you know when you just want to do something...' Some damage, she'd been about to say, but the slight look of disapproval from the other woman warned her not to vocalise how she felt. They were social workers. Child protection was their job, not beating up on the parents. She'd never had any inclination in the past, but this pair had needled her.

Before she'd become a social worker, she'd worked at a junior school for a couple of terms to get some experience. She'd been young and idealistic. Part of that idealism was wiped from her as the headmistress took her to one side and lectured her on the merits of keeping her opinions to herself.

'You don't see anything in this school, you don't hear anything. Do you understand?'

She was nineteen. She wasn't sure she did. 'No. I don't think I do.'

'Things happen here. You have to realise that not every area is nice. This school serves "the streets", one of the roughest areas in the West Midlands. You upset one of these families by listening to what a child has told you over the sandpit and you're going to find yourself in deep trouble. You won't have a car left, you may not have anything to live for.'

She'd not stayed the full length of time. She didn't believe in turning a blind eye. That wasn't her role in life.

Vanessa tapped the photograph on the screen. 'What about the mum?'

'She's not the brightest star in the sky. She seems amazingly willing to allow him to take the lead, to control her children as though they're his own and he has a say. What woman allows her children to be abused?' She'd not meant for it come out as judgemental, that's not what their team was about. She wouldn't normally vocalise her feelings, but this one had definitely rankled.

She knew better than to let it. She saw it time and again. It never ceased to amaze her, though. Women who turned themselves over to abusive men and allowed them free access to their children.

It happens. Which was why there was a Children's Services, why she had a job. To be there for those children who were ignored, neglected, abused.

'I interviewed her yesterday. It wasn't a happy time, but we have her. She admitted to everything. Blamed him. Said she thought that's the way things should be.' She swivelled her chair around to face Vanessa. 'Do you know he wouldn't even let them watch TV? If he allowed them in the same room, they had to turn their backs.'

Vanessa raised her eyebrows but said nothing.

'How can a mum sit on the side lines without lifting a finger to help? Without objecting to the treatment of her own flesh and blood?'

'Beats the hell out of me,' Vanessa replied. 'Are they settled with the foster carers?'

'Yeah. Tanya is on it.' Another member of their team. Tall, slim, early twenties and determined to make the world a better place. With fire Bobbi felt she lacked these days. She'd had it once, but it seemed to be slipping from her grasp lately.

Jaded was the term she'd use.

Bobbi tapped the plain brown file to the right of her laptop. 'We're working on it together. He'll be convicted. I think there's indisputable evidence.'

'Where is he?'

'Ley Hill. Remand.' The computer screen timed out and went blank.

'Are you sure you don't need someone to come with you?'

Bobbi thought about it for a moment and then shook her head. 'I can manage. It's just getting to me. I interviewed him a couple of weeks ago.' She reached for her own coffee, but it was already cold, so she pushed it back onto the desk and picked up a bottle of water, which was tepid. Probably the same temperature as the coffee. She unscrewed the lid and gulped some down. 'He's intelligent, you know. Manipulative.' She didn't need to try hard to visualise the slithering ripple of evil shadowing his eyes when he'd stared right at her, refusing to break eye contact.

She couldn't help the shudder.

'You've got it in hand.' Vanessa leaned forward and rubbed Bobbi's arm. 'You've done this before.'

Not quite like this. How could she explain? She'd dealt with bad people before, wicked people. Never had she been drawn in so deep.

'You know what gets to me?' She leaned back, depressing her thumb into the plastic bottle until it made a cracking noise.

'What?'

'His sister.'

'Sister?'

'Yeah.' She wiggled her mouse and the screen leaped to life again. She clicked onto another tab.

'Charlotte Gainsford. Charlie for short. We have nothing on her.'

Vanessa leaned in close over Bobbi's shoulder. 'Do we need anything on her?'

Bobbi's mouth tightened. 'Yeah, we do. I reckon she's as bad as him.'

'Why?'

'We can place her there. At that house. A lot. But damned if I can make anything stick. She seemed to spend an inordinate amount of time there. But there's nothing she's admitting to and neither of the other two will roll over. Not even the mum.' She tapped her fingers on her desk. 'You know when you know...?'

'I do.'

'Well, I know. There's something about the two of them together that seems to have made the whole situation even worse. Vile. I don't know what kind of upbringing the two of them had, they certainly weren't in the system themselves. I can't put my finger on it, but that kind of evil doesn't normally run through families naturally without some kind of catalyst.'

'Nature versus nurture.' Vanessa leaned forward and scrolled down to read the scant information on the woman. 'Maybe no nurture involved in their upbringing. Two psychopathic people together.'

Bobbi tapped her fingertips on her lips and shook her head. 'No. They're not. There's no delusion, no madness. They both know with a certainty what they are doing.'

'Pure evil.'

Bobbi nodded her agreement. 'Charlotte Gainsford definitely has a hand in this, but no amount of questioning even hints at her involvement. But she was there. And I damned well know that she participated in the abuse of these kids.'

She stabbed a finger at the screen. 'I know it!'

30

Sarah stroked a hand over the smooth skin of her gently distended belly and smiled. If anyone looked, they could be mistaken thinking she just had bad wind.

Some wind.

She pulled on her swimsuit and turned sideways. Almost flat again with the Lycra material sucking her in. At four months, the baby barely showed, but she knew he was there. She talked to him at night while she cupped her hand under her stomach.

She should have told her sisters by now, didn't have a clue what was holding her back. First it was just getting past the surprise. After all, despite the fact she'd planned the pregnancy, it had all happened so quickly. She'd been in shock for a few weeks. She'd not told her sisters before, because she didn't want their opinions to sway her either way. The decision had to be hers.

Hers was firmly settled now. She couldn't be happier. This was her chance at motherhood, maybe the only one she'd get. At her age, she was going to take it.

Sarah slipped through the inner door into the swimming pool and lowered herself down the steps. No diving in. Not for a while.

She sucked in her breath at the chill of the water in contrast to the heat that had already kicked up outside.

Perhaps she'd tell them at Tess's party.

None of her sisters were backward in coming forward. They spoke their minds and she could just imagine the contradictory opinions from each one of them. Old-fashioned, Tess would be more concerned that she'd become pregnant out of wedlock and want to know when the wedding would be. That would be a fun conversation.

Bobbi would be delighted and full of overwhelming advice and enthusiasm. God forbid that she'd probably saved Toni's baby clothes and want to pass them on. Sarah would be obliged to take them. Well, only the unisex ones, not the girl's clothes.

Alexis... well, as always, Alexis would steal her thunder by doing something to undermine Sarah's news. She'd have another drama, something to detract from Sarah's joy. She always did.

Sarah reached out, cutting through the water in a sleek, practised front crawl that came as naturally to her as walking or breathing. Face in, arms stretching, legs kicking. When she reached the end wall, she rolled, kicked off and stroked out again.

It felt good. The smooth wash of water over her. Exercise that she would keep up all the way through. It was in all the research – if you exercised normally, then you could carry on that exercise. The issue was, she would no longer be able to get into the water with the school children she taught at the local school.

They had their own pool, funded by some famous athlete who'd attended there and wanted to pay back into the community. Or get a tax break.

That pool was smaller than the 25 m one the council ran, but it was nice. The water a touch warmer for the younger children.

She would normally get in the water with them, but from now

on, she'd have to stay on the side and get one of the helpers to slip in.

She considered for a moment asking Tess to help out. After all, she helped with the reading at the same school. She already had her DBS checks in place.

Sarah snorted to herself as she completed another forward roll. Imagine her sister getting her perfect make-up and hair wet. She'd never put her face in the water. She'd probably traumatise the kids.

Maybe not.

Sixty-four lengths, just over a mile, and Sarah stopped, squinting to look at the clock on the far wall. She needed to get ready to go to the school and then maybe later this afternoon, she'd pull an 'Alexis' and summon all the sisters together.

She could do it individually, starting with Bobbi, but really she wanted it out there for them all to know.

Sure now. Confident in herself.

She'd needed time and space to figure out her life.

She had.

Now she had to figure out how to tell her sisters.

There could be no more secrets.

31

Tess pressed her fingers into her eye sockets and groaned. Thank god Graham had already slinked off to work.

She'd listened for the front door to close before she slipped out of bed. Happy to avoid him.

Her head spun as she reached for a pod to put in her Nespresso machine. She'd have a double shot of caffeine. If she could shoot it straight into her veins, she would.

She'd had far too much to drink last night. She didn't even know what time her husband had come home. She really needed to cut back. She'd not heard a sound and he wasn't normally light on his feet.

She wasn't an alcoholic, but she did drink too much from time to time.

Alcoholics drank all day long, didn't they? Hid their bottles of vodka and gin in cupboards throughout the house just so they could access it any time they wanted it.

Graham's old secretary had apparently kept a bottle of gin in her bottom drawer. Had she found the job so stressful, or was it

Graham himself who had driven her to drink? Perhaps he'd pursued her, too, but she'd not been interested.

Tess snorted. That was rubbish. She'd been ancient. Perhaps the alcohol had pickled her, but she definitely hadn't been Graham's type.

Tess was strict on her drinking habit. Never a glass before 6 p.m. Unless it was the weekend, of course. She might have one with her lunch then. Maybe 1 p.m. With the nice weather, it was so easy to have an icy cold glass of Pinot Grigio while she read a good book in the garden.

She didn't need to make excuses. The others didn't need to judge. After all, what else was she to do with herself these days?

Besides, her fiftieth birthday was fast approaching, and while everyone else wanted to celebrate that landmark, she really didn't want to acknowledge it. She didn't want to get any older.

She volunteered at the local school two mornings a week. Helped with some of the children who had special needs and required extra reading practice. It wasn't so very hard. Frustrating. Unrewarding. But not hard.

Most of the children were scared to death of her. She had no idea why.

She wasn't cut out like Bobbi, she knew that. No Earth mother was she. If she had been, she would have had as many children as Bobbi had. One had been enough for her. God knows how she'd survived that. Ashton had been a nightmare when he was a baby. Cried all damned night, and all damned day too.

No one in their right minds should have a baby. Never mind more than one.

She glanced at the clock. Almost midday. She must have fallen back to sleep once Graham had gone. She'd not even realised she'd slept the morning away.

The faint shake of her fingers stopped her as she raised them to her forehead. She had an hour to get ready and make it to the school in time for reading at 1.30 p.m.

She dabbed her fingers over dry lips. Was she up to it? Could she scrape through listening to stilted, strained words today? She had alternatives.

She could call in sick.

Then again, how would that seem? What would they think of her?

She'd never called in sick.

She just had to suck it up and get on with it. Her own stupid fault for drinking far too much.

Shock was not necessarily an excuse for how much she'd consumed but really, would anyone blame her for reacting the way she had?

Had she said anything out of order? She could barely remember getting home. Sarah had walked her. Then she'd let Sarah go back alone.

What a terrible sister she was.

32

'Curry and hot sex didn't work?'

Jim slid her a sideways glance as he manoeuvred the ambulance out of the bay and punched the buttons for the blues and twos in response to Control's emergency call before they'd even closed their lockers on their personal items. 'Worked for me. Not so much for the baby. Still hanging on in there.'

Despite his joke, the strain was starting to show.

Alexis leaned in to touch his arm. 'It'll come when it's ready.'

'No. It won't. It'll come when they say.' He shook his head. 'She's booked in day after tomorrow for a C-section if she hasn't produced by then.'

'That's a good thing. At least they're keeping on top of it, not letting things slide.'

Jim shook his head. 'Nope. She's terrified. She says she doesn't want an operation.'

Their radio crackled to life and Alexis reached for it. 'ETA three minutes,' she responded before they could ask.

'The police have just arrived. They'll have the door in by the time you get there.'

Alexis raised her eyebrows at Jim. 'Just another day in the life of...'

He smiled and overtook the row of cars rapidly pulling over to the side of the road to let them through.

As he pulled up in front of the address, Alexis unhooked her seatbelt, already reaching for their equipment.

A young, uniformed officer stood outside the door, thin face pale, eyes wide as Alexis and Jim dashed through a small garden littered with rusting bird feeders and a couple of old rubber tyres.

'I don't think we need you, except for confirmation of death. I've sent for CID.'

An older officer stood just inside the hallway and gave them a sad smile of greeting. 'I day think there's anything can be done here. Someone's had him. Just watch where yow stand. It's a crime scene now.'

Alexis nodded. 'Do you have anything we need to know?'

'Nothing much I can give you. The house isn't registered to him. It's in the name of a woman.' He chinned inside. 'At the state of the place, it could be anyone. Some homeless person. We day even know his name at this stage.'

He moved to one side to let her through.

She took one step, narrowing her eyes as she came out of the light into the dim hallway.

Her knees buckled and the officer caught her around the waist before she hit the floor.

Air puffed from her lips as she stared at the corpse.

'Gary. His name's Gary Philpotts.'

33

Bobbi wiped down the glass panel on the inside of the oven and pushed the door closed. Craig would be another couple of hours before he got home. It had been a long haul, with a four-hour delay at the docks. There was no point leaving his dinner on low. It would be dried up before he got to it.

She covered it up and popped it in the microwave, ready to blast once he arrived.

With every surface clean, she picked up her glass of wine, a sense of satisfaction filling her.

It would be nice to have him home, even for a short while. She needed to de-stress and he was always good for that. She didn't want to talk to him about work or her worries about Tess's drinking, or Alexis's state of mind, or even the fact that she thought Sarah might be pregnant. She just wanted him there. To talk about their own children. None of which she had any particular worries about. At the moment.

It would be nice to curl up with him in bed. Until the raging hot flush attacked, but she lived in hope that it would be staved off, just for a while

She'd ring again in the morning for an appointment with her GP. She couldn't live like this.

She paused just to listen to the silence from above. No booming TV, no squabbling. Just the quiet background music in the kitchen of Jo Whiley on Radio 2. The boys were both out, but Shanna was having a rare night in and was currently reading to Toni.

Bobbi closed her eyes and sighed. Please let nothing break this peaceful moment.

She opened her eyes as Alexis, still in uniform, flew in through the open patio doors, eyes wild, blotchy face streaked with tears.

Without question, Bobbi set down her wine and opened her arms as Alexis flung herself into them.

'Oh, Bobbi, Bobbi. Are the girls here yet? It's awful. Just fucking awful.'

Bobbi cast a guilty glance at the iPhone she'd not looked at in the past half-hour or so as Tess and Sarah bustled in behind their sister.

'What's happened?' Concerned voices raised in unison.

Bobbi flashed a quick look in the direction of Toni's bedroom. She wanted to tell them to shush, but the urgency was too intense.

Alexis pulled away. 'He's dead. The bastard has been murdered.'

'What?'

'Who?'

'Gary fucking Philpotts, that's who.' She wheeled away, scrubbing her fingers through her tightly ponytailed hair so it pulled loose to straggle around her face. 'I was there. This morning. Gary Philpotts is fucking dead, and I was there.'

34

'There?' Bobbi blinked furiously, her voice filled with horror while her head drained of all blood. 'What were you doing there? Do you mean you saw it happen?'

Tears spilled down her cheeks as Alexis shook her head impatiently as though Bobbi was an idiot. 'No. Of course I didn't. Why would I be there when it happened? Who do you think I am? The murderer?'

Rather than react to Alexis's typical overreaction to a simple question, Bobbi rubbed her sister's shoulder and hung onto her patience. 'Then...?'

Alexis shrugged so Bobbi's hand flopped back down as her sister paced to the patio doors and then spun to face them, fingers twisting through her tatty mid-length chestnut hair. 'We were sent on a job this morning. A neighbour called it in. Said they'd gone around to get their chisel or some shit back from him. He'd had it for weeks, the guy said.'

Bobbi nodded and scooped her glass of wine from the bench to take a sip and wet her dry throat.

Tess sidled up beside her and opened the fridge to take the

already open bottle of wine out. Sarah reached for two more wine glasses and set them on the bench for Tess to fill. She reached for Craig's whisky and splashed some in a tumbler.

In an automatic move, Bobbi held hers out for more wine as Alexis railed.

'He'd looked through the letterbox and thought he saw Gary's shadow at the end of the hallway. The guy couldn't see properly because he said it was quite dark compared to the sunlight outside, but he said Gary ignored him. He said he was pissed off, so he left it overnight and went around again early this morning before he went to work. Stupid git.'

Alexis took a swig of the whisky Sarah handed her and then opened her mouth, gasping for breath as the sting hit the back of her throat. Tears formed in her eyes again, but she scrubbed them away with an impatient dash of her hand.

She cleared her throat. 'When he saw Gary this time, he knew something was wrong.'

Bobbi frowned and cast a look of confusion at her sisters. 'What do you mean?'

'Gary was flat out on the fucking floor. He called the police and us.'

Sick with horror, Bobbi clapped a hand across her mouth. Poor Alexis. She didn't deserve to see that.

'We arrived just after the police. They had to break the front door down for us to get to him.' She paused as she took in their expressions. Confusion, horror, interest. 'He was impaled.'

'Impaled?' Tess lost her coolness to a morbid curiosity and pushed away from the sink to step closer. 'In what way impaled?'

'Like, a huge four-foot stake driven through his body. He didn't die immediately, he could have taken hours to bleed out.' Her voice ground on a hoarse whisper.

Bobbi slapped her glass down and moved to take the whisky

from Alexis. Helping herself to a huge swallow, she screwed her eyes up as the scald hit the back of her throat. 'Shit.' She was going to regret this in the morning. What was the saying? *Don't mix the grape and the grain.*

'They don't know how long he was lying there.'

'God! That's sick.'

'Serves the bastard right.'

'Sarah!' Bobbi turned wide eyes on her youngest sister. 'You can't say that! No one deserves to die like that.'

'Why not? It's true, isn't it? He was a bloody paedophile. He...' She pointed at Alexis and stopped herself just in time. 'Well, he did. He deserves everything he got.'

'Oh, surely, Sarah, you wouldn't wish that kind of death on your worst enemy? That's awful.' Bobbi tried to pacify her sister as Alexis turned a sickly grey.

Sarah stepped forward and snatched up the bottle of whisky. She took the glass from Bobbi's hand and glugged two inches into the bottom before she helped herself to a deep swallow. 'I need something stronger than a bloody sip of wine.'

Bobbi stared at her, a question on the tip of her tongue, then she let the moment go.

Tess gave a delicate sniff as she lowered herself onto a kitchen stool, pulled Alexis in close and put her hand on her sister's back. Voice cool, she surveyed them all, that inkling of big sister superiority edging through her tone. 'Just for the record, Bobbi, he was our worst enemy. All of us. I have no sympathy for him. Good riddance to bad rubbish.'

Bobbi gaped. 'But Alexis found him. I wouldn't wish that on her.' She rubbed her hand over Alexis's knee.

Silence hovered on the air before Alexis broke it. 'I puked.' Shame filtered through her shaking voice.

Tess took an almost inconspicuous move back on the stool as

Bobbi screwed her face up, the idea of Alexis throwing up bringing a ball of acid to her own throat. 'I'm not surprised.'

'I take it he was dead?' Sarah handed the whisky glass back to Alexis, her hand underneath to persuade her sister to take a sip.

Alexis snorted, part laughter, part hysteria. 'Well, yes. Very much so.' She took a drink and slumped against the kitchen counter, so Tess's hand fell away. 'You should have seen the size of the spike. It was bloody enormous.' She rested the glass on the countertop and brought both hands up to her lips. Her red-rimmed eyes turned huge as she shook her head. 'It was like a bloody javelin. Thick galvanised steel, the police said. We don't even know where it came from. The police officer said he'd never seen anything like it. Just a great long stake, about four foot long.' She held her hands body-width to indicate the length. 'Like something you see at a hog roast.'

Sarah gagged. 'Well, I'm never going to eat roast pork again.'

'You don't eat it now.'

'Occasionally, but never again.' She gave another over-exaggerated gag, fluttering her hand in front of her face.

'Sarah!' Bobbi sighed.

Tess leaned forward, her elbows on her knees, glass of wine cupped between both hands. 'I wonder who did it? What do you reckon?' She looked around at them. 'The dad of a victim? Someone who saw the newspaper article?'

'Who reads them these days? Probably on Facebook.'

'I heard something on the local radio the other day,' Tess confessed.

Bobbi ducked her head. 'I wonder. Perhaps it did trigger anger in someone. Vengeance.'

'I don't know.' Alexis shrugged. 'Whoever it was must have been hellishly strong.'

Sarah's face lifted. 'You don't think it was from a whaling gun? You know, the ones you see on the movies.'

Alexis folded her arms. 'I think you're putting far too much thought into this. I'm sure the police will sort it.'

'He probably owed the local drug pusher a shedload of money,' Sarah replied.

'Did he still do drugs?' Flabbergasted, Bobbi stared up at her youngest sister. It wasn't something she'd heard on the grapevine, and she kept her ear to the ground where he was concerned. In her job, she couldn't be oblivious to the potential of a paedophile or a drug pusher. There might not be any convictions or valid evidence in some cases. But she knew. They all knew he'd been convicted previously. They'd not heard anything since.

'How would I know?' Sarah turned away, raising the glass to her lips for a sip.

'I'm surprised, with his size, anyone managed to run him through,' Tess joined in.

Confused, Bobbi raised her hand to her forehead. 'How do you all know so much? How do you know he was overweight?'

'Because he always was. I can still see him now. Slimy bastard.'

Alexis tipped her head back and took in some more whisky. 'He wasn't. He was half the size I remember. Or is that because I've grown up? He always seemed so big, so threatening. But he looked small and fragile in death.'

Bobbi tried not to glance at the clock but couldn't help herself. It was just past 9 p.m. now.

'Mum?'

They all jumped at the sound of Shanna's voice.

'Shanna.' Bobbi put down her glass and stepped forward.

'Is everything okay? Has something happened?' Shanna, dressed in PJ shorts and T-shirt, studied each one of their guilty faces in turn.

'I'm sorry. Did we disturb you?' Tess stepped forward. 'We were just having a drink.'

A doubtful look passed over her eldest daughter's face and Bobbi knew for certain they'd been caught out. But had Shanna heard anything she shouldn't?

'Aunt Alexis had a bad day at work,' she confessed.

Shanna turned sympathetic eyes on her aunt. 'Are you all right?'

Alexis nodded her head, her lips stitched together, but her eyes still frantic.

Shanna opened her arms, and Bobbi swallowed back the emotion as Alexis stepped in for a hug. 'Aunt Alexis, you can sleep in my bed tonight, if that helps. I'll snuggle in with Toni.'

Choked, Bobbi turned away and poured the remainder of her wine down the sink.

35

I leaned into the driver's mirror and tucked a stray strand of my own hair under the neat wig. The style changed the shape of my face, making it rounder, the colour turning my skin a different shade and deepening my eye colour.

I slipped a thick, dark-rimmed pair of glasses on and pushed them up to the bridge of my nose with my middle finger. Not used to wearing glasses, the weight of them was alien. I blinked through the plus one magnifying glass at the googly eyes staring back at me.

Was this wise? I might trip over my own feet.

Turning my head one way and then the other, I inspected my appearance. If I didn't know it was me, I'd never recognise myself. My lips twisted in a crooked grin. I'd have to control that. A tight, simpering smile would be more appropriate. Keep it controlled. Nothing so distinctive as a big, crooked smile.

I slid the cover over the mirror and pushed the visor up, before slipping out of the car. I looked both ways and then stepped away as the locks engaged. I had three streets to walk to the home. I hadn't wanted to park my car anywhere near, just in case it was spotted.

The downside was that it provided a wider window for people to see me, to get caught on someone's Ring doorbell, or CCTV camera.

Then again, there was a risk to everything.

Pretty sure there was a cut-through somewhere along the street, I set off, resisting the temptation to touch the wig.

It was amazing how realistic it was for the cost.

Who would have thought I'd ever dare to disguise myself?

But things were changing, life had just got better. I had purpose.

As I stepped into the cool dimness of the home, I squinted to get my bearings.

'Hello, can I help you?'

My heart jumped as a little woman, make-up free face, hair streaked with grey, wearing what appeared to be hospital scrubs in sick green stepped from behind a doorway. The window must look out onto the entranceway to the home. Who needed cameras when you had a hawk eye like this woman?

My hand still on my chest, I puffed out a quiet laugh. 'Oh, goodness, you gave me a fright.'

Soft wrinkles bracketed the woman's mouth, and like ripples on a pond, widened across her cheeks. 'I'm sorry, I didn't think I was that scary.'

I smiled at her, deliberately keeping my lips from stretching too wide. Maybe I'm being super vigilant, but it occurs to me that showing my teeth could be identifiable. Not that my teeth are anything unique, no crooked ones or chips. Nor are they overly whitened, or for that matter yellowed. I'm quite ordinary in that respect.

'I'm sure you're not,' I replied.

I stopped just short of getting chatty. Don't engage in too much conversation. This is where people fail. Over-sharing. Keep your mouth shut. Tell no one.

Take a leaf out of my mum's book. Never threaten anyone in

public, never put anything in writing, and if you do something bad, never tell anyone. Not your best friend, because friends fall out. Not your sister, because sisters can't bear the guilt. Suck it up and keep it to yourself. Bury the body on your own.

Now, you might think my mum is a real badass, but actually she's a sweetheart. Wouldn't hurt a fly. But if she did, we'd never know about it. Most of us.

I think, maybe, for the first time in my life, I actually understand her philosophy.

'I'm sorry?' I blinked the woman back into focus.

'Yow'm posh, aye yow?'

Nonplussed for a second, I wondered at the accent I used. Too upper class, too identifiable in the midst of the Black Country. Be careful. I need to be vanilla. Nothing to pick up on. 'Thanks,' I replied.

'Who have you come to visit?'

'Mr Collington.'

There was slightest lift of her eyebrows as she tilted her head and I had one brief moment of panic when I wondered if she could see through my disguise, if it wasn't as good as I'd thought.

She sniffed and looked down, reaching over the half-moon reception desk to pick up a pen. 'Would you like to sign in?'

She held out the pen and I could only hope she didn't spot the slight tremor in my fingers as I took it from her. I'd never visited a home before. How was I supposed to know you had to sign in? That wasn't so bad, I could fudge a signature, but you also needed to print your name in capitals too.

I wrote the name I'd practised in case someone asked me who I was. I'd made up a whole life of lies, but it was best to be truthful where possible, then you didn't fall into the wide chasm of trying to remember what you'd said to whom.

'Are you a relative?' The warmth seemed to have seeped out of her while I was forging someone else's name.

'No.' I gave a little shrug. 'An ex-pupil. I heard he'd come here, I thought I'd pay my respects. Thought he might be lonely.'

Her brow dipped, but her words were a contradiction to the deep furrows there. 'Respect isn't often a word I hear associated with Mr Collington.'

Surprised, I stopped myself in time from taking a step forward and asking her to spill the beans. But really. I needed to know. Instead, I held my silence, which seemed to be an invitation for her to spill the beans in any case.

She ripped along the perforated lines and tore off the top copy of the sheet I'd signed, folded it in half and slipped it into a plastic badge holder. 'He told us he didn't have family, and I've never known him to have visitors. Not in three years.' She turned her back. 'This way.'

As I dashed to catch up with her, she strode along a wide hallway with dingy mustard tinted walls and a threadbare carpet.

People often tell you that care homes have the stench of urine, with old people sitting in their own mess for hours on end. That isn't the case, and it's an old belief. It's certainly not what I noticed. A strong smell of bleach battled against a much more sinister underlying smell. That of dying flesh permeating through not only the soft furnishings, carpets and clothes, but the very walls themselves clung onto dead skin cells.

There isn't a solution invented. No matter how clean-scrubbed they are, there's something that tells you they're just waiting to die. The human body was never intended to last as long.

We strode along another windowless corridor, breathless in the July heat. Doors to the bedrooms closed, so no air circulated.

'Most of our residents are downstairs in the games room.' It made me wonder what games they played. Twister? Hopscotch? The question must have registered on my face. 'Chess, Monopoly, Cluedo, jigsaws.'

I kept quiet and allowed her to do the talking.

'Mr Collington doesn't tend to join in. He likes to keep to himself most of the time.' She hesitated and I felt sure she'd left something unsaid.

'Except...?' I prompted this time.

I'm not sure I wouldn't have got more from her if we hadn't pulled up outside a closed door at the furthest end of the hall with only the lift opposite. The silence there was oppressive.

She knocked on the door before pushing it wide.

'Reg? Hello, Reg. I've brought someone to see you.'

There wasn't the gentle condescension I've heard in tones from people when dealing with the older generation, more a barked efficiency of a headteacher's secretary.

I don't know what I'd expected in all truth, but the vast slug of a man was barely recognisable as my old headteacher. A large man before, or so my memory served me, he'd expanded ten-fold, his soft body wallowing in a huge, sickly green vinyl wingback chair. The ones homes have so they can hygienically wipe them down when residents have accidents.

A clear tube snaked up from an oxygen tank by his side. Strapped tight across his broad face. Two smaller tubes were inserted into his nostrils and the soft in and out wheeze of oxygen flowing through to fill his lungs hung in the room like a weak version of Darth Vader but with that underlying sinister cloak.

His jowls curtained onto his chest, obscuring any view of his neck. Folds of skin pressed down, puffing out around his eyes to give them the appearance of those of a black spotted pig, sharp intelligence snapping out of them.

I'm so shocked with the directness of his stare, I hesitate in the doorway. A vague stutter making my footsteps falter. Not many would notice, but he did. I could tell from the calculation in his squinty eyes.

'Reg, I've brought someone to see you. One of your ex-pupils.' She halted just inside the doorway and indicated a chair for me to sit on.

I took hold of the wooden high-backed chair and went to move it forward.

'I wouldn't get too close if I were you. Reg can be a little...' she gave a tight smile, her eyes boring into mine, willing me to understand her subtlety, '...tactile.'

I took my hand from the chair and wondered if I should have touched it at all. The police could take fingerprints, couldn't they? If anything should happen to the headmaster, they'd dust the room down.

I almost shook myself. Nothing was going to happen. I wasn't going to do anything to him. It was hardly going to be a massacre. I was in control. I only wanted to check on him. Make sure he was monitored. Were my childhood memories false?

I didn't want to lie awake night after night as I had done all the time Philpotts had been in court. Sleepless nights had almost ruined my life. That constant churn of thoughts and memories to needle at me, insistent that from three o'clock in the morning I toss from side to side, acid scalding at my stomach.

Dealing with Philpotts had given me the first good night's sleep since I'd seen the article in the newspaper about his arrest. I felt no remorse. Just a deep satisfaction that the deed was done, and he could no longer give me disturbed nights.

Since then, I'd barely got back to normal when memories of Mr Collington invaded my peace and quiet.

The woman turned to him. 'Reg.'

'Mr Collington, to you. I've told you before. Show some damned respect, woman.' His voice snapped out, sharp and uncompromising, and he shot her a look filled with loathing. 'Bitch.' The word was coughed out on a breathy hiss so I wasn't sure I'd heard it.

'And I've told you not to speak to me like that, Mr Collington. I'll have none of your nonsense. If you'd like to live elsewhere, we can always arrange it with the council.' She sniffed and lowered her voice and I swear she said, 'And keep your hands to yourself,' before she sidled out the door.

I lowered myself into the seat opposite, not quite sure what it was I wanted to say to the man, but it seemed I had no reason to worry as he filled the gap himself.

His voice, warm and phlegmy, came out. 'Who are you? I don't recognise you.'

In a self-conscious move, I raised my hand to my mouth and touched a finger to the fine white scar there. 'It was a long time ago.'

'What year?' he snapped back.

My lips parted, but no sound came out. If I told him the year and he recognised me, would I be putting myself at risk of exposure?

I told him anyway.

Satisfied, he smiled, a sick, superior one. 'What's your name?'

I told him that too. After all, what harm could it do? No one else was around to witness the exchange. It wasn't Sandra Mills, the name I'd signed in at the front door with. That wasn't even a name from anyone I knew at school or beyond. Just a simple made-up name.

It wasn't as though I was about to do him any harm.

Was I?

His mouth twisted under the tubing, the laboured sounds of his breath hitched for a moment before resuming the ebb and flow rhythm. The loose skin almost covered his eyes as he screwed up his face.

He coughed through the mucus. 'I remember you. I know exactly who you are.'

36

I flopped against the slatted wooden chair back, breath wedged in a hard knot in my chest.

He wheezed out a soft laugh. 'I don't remember all of my pupils, but I had my favourites.' He raised a hand and dabbed at his shiny lips with a white tissue and then let it fall back into his lap. Thickened yellowed fingernails curled around his fingertips and had my lips pursing with revulsion.

'You weren't one of them.' He tilted his head to one side, his spare flesh gathering in a roll under the right side of his chin. 'But I remember you. You were one of the bad girls. From that big family.'

The stuffiness in the room washed over me and heat rushed up my neck and into my face. I needed air, almost as badly as 'Sir' needed his oxygen. I glanced at the window behind him, locked shut by a long aluminium rail. Perhaps I could reach past him and push it open.

'Were you the one who pissed yourself?'

Laughter gurgled out of him as my eyes flew wide. Surprise and shame.

His eyes gleamed with amused satisfaction. 'I knew you had to be. You look like a pant's pisser.'

In retrospect, I bet dozens of kids had wet themselves during the time he'd spent as a teacher, then a headteacher. He'd said it because the possibility was high. A stab in the dark, and he got the rise he wanted from me, because right here and now, the memory of the humiliation stung like a sharp slap.

I wiped the back of my hand across my chin, where sweat had trickled down from under the wig. My scalp prickled with discomfort, and I wanted to rip the wig off and expose my real self, but I resisted the temptation as I peered at him from under lowered brows.

I'm not stupid, nor am I still a child to be intimidated by him. The whole set up of the straight-backed chair, me sitting on it facing him, was designed to make me feel inferior. He obviously took this tactic with everyone who came in. Carer, visitor. It didn't matter. Well, it wasn't going to work with me.

I pushed to my feet and took three steps forward to tower above him, conscious of the sticky carpet sucking at my shoes to make me wonder if it was urine-soaked or whether that was the memory of my own misadventure invoking the smell.

'Did it give you pleasure, using all the power you were given in good faith to make children wet themselves in fear?'

The sound of the rusty scrape of phlegm in the back of his throat made my stomach lurch.

'I didn't deliberately make you piss yourself. It was merely a side effect of a weak-livered child who had no ability to stand up for themselves.'

'Stand up for themselves?' My voice escalated until I almost shouted the final word. I glanced towards the open door and then back at him. This time, I controlled myself. 'You picked on children who were defenceless, not even eleven years old, and completely at your mercy, all for your own self-satisfaction.'

His eyes glowed and my stomach clenched again as I grasped the source of his amusement, remembering the slow slide of his hand down to his groin as he stood in front of an entire class of juniors. Had he known none of us would speak out? Had any of us? Would anyone have dared?

How could this possibly have happened? Were none of the teachers aware of his lasciviousness? Was it possible for such a deviant to fly under the radar for all those years, never detected? We're talking about the 1980s. Worse had come to light from that era. Things that should never have been allowed in a civilised society. Professionals turning a blind eye with concern for their own position, job, title.

'I was very satisfied.' His voice was a low rumble of humour. His own humour, not mine. I didn't find him funny at all.

I know I promised myself I would behave, but really... he took more than the biscuit, he took the entire packet. Would anyone notice if he just slipped away? He had no family. His carer had told me that, as if in confidence. A snippet of information I might find to my advantage. No one to care.

It appeared she didn't have any particular affection for him either, so would anything be questioned if a man who suffered from respiratory issues stopped breathing?

I glanced at the pillow on his bed as I stood there, possibilities skimming through my mind.

I wasn't entirely sure, in fact, let's be honest here, I had no idea what procedures were in place in a care home, when someone quite obviously suffered from health issues and was old. So terribly old. Surely they didn't carry out post-mortems? What a waste of taxpayers' money. Would they be able to tell if the resident had just naturally stopped breathing, or had been gently assisted? If I squeezed his nostrils together, I bet there would be pressure marks. Pressed a hand over his mouth... Apart from anything else, he was a big man. Was I in any way capable of overpowering him?

There must be another way.

I stepped closer to the bed, barely conscious of the move.

I picked the pillow up and plumped it, all the time watching his eyes, the awareness in them.

'You wouldn't dare.' The hiss came from between clenched teeth.

I smiled.

Is this how good it felt to have the power in my hands?

'Would you like a cup of tea, dear?'

Startled, I spun around, my panicked gaze clashing with that of a short, stout woman who bustled in with a hot drink in one hand for Mr Collington and a small plastic pot in the other.

'Can I get you one?' she prompted, as I'd failed to answer the first time, aware that I'd almost peed myself in front of the head-master for the second time in my life.

'No, thank you.' The words gushed out in a breathless exhale. 'I just had one before I came. It's okay, I'm not thirsty. Thank you all the same.'

Get a grip, woman, I thought to myself as words poured from my mouth. I stopped myself before I said any more.

I glanced down at the pillow I held in my hands, guilt sucking the moisture from my tongue. What had I been about to do?

A switch had been flicked in my head, compelling me to take action. And now it had been prised back again. Mr Collington was safe from me. He had nothing more to fear. If fear is an emotion he'd felt.

I raised my head and the lady's smile spread across her face as she placed the two items on his wooden side table. 'Oh, that's very kind of you, dear, trying to make him more comfortable.' She nodded at the pillow I held in a limp hand. 'Let me give you a hand. He's a big boy, aren't you, Mr Collington?'

He grumbled under his wheezy breath. 'I don't think the idea was to make me comfortable, but to suffocate me. I think she's trying to kill me, woman.'

High-pitched laughter broke from the woman's lips. 'Oh, he is a card is our Mr Collington, aren't you, dear?'

'Fuck off.' His breath wheezed.

I wasn't even sure if I heard him correctly, he seemed to have mastered the ability to disguise his words enough for deniability if he was challenged.

She didn't challenge him, she ignored him as she leaned forward. She took hold of his enormous shoulders with short, square hands and leaned back, puffing out a breath. 'Be quick, now.'

I stuffed the pillow behind him and as she let him go, he slumped back. The air hissed out of the pillow as he almost flattened it with his sheer size. His jowls wobbled like an underset jelly with the mere effort of movement.

The woman moved back, a smile of satisfaction on her face as she looked at me. 'Are you sure you don't want a drink?'

My mouth was parched and sweat trickled down my spine. 'No, thank you. I won't be long.'

She turned a simpering smile on Mr Collington as she picked up the small pot and waited for him to hold out his hand. When he hesitated, she reached out and grasped him by the wrist, inverting the pot so one tiny white pill and two larger caplets sat on his palm. She handed him the glass of water that sat on the wooden table, a permanent fixture I would imagine, and then waited for him to put them in his mouth

From his hesitation, I wondered for a moment if he was about to lob the half-full glass of water at her. Without taking his gaze from me, he threw the tablets to the back of his throat and swallowed them with a mouthful of water.

'There we go now,' she spoke to him as if he was a young child. 'That didn't hurt, did it?'

When she turned to me, her eyes sparkled as though she'd just discovered the secret to everlasting life. 'Just as well you're not staying. He'll not be awake for long with his medication.'

'Sleeping tablets?' It seemed odd to give him something to make him sleep in the middle of the day.

'No.' She shook her head. 'He has to have antihistamine for all his allergies, and then we give him co-codamol. It helps with the pain, but he sleeps like the dead for an hour or so after we give it to him, don't you, Mr Collington? Although it'll take a few minutes to take effect. Long enough for your visit.' She patted the limp hand he laid on the armrest and he mumbled some obscenity under his rasping breath.

Oblivious to his reaction, she reached down to pick up a hand control attached to his chair. 'If you press this button,' she indicated, 'you can tilt the chair back to make him more comfortable once he's had his tea. Mind this, though.' She touched the clear, plastic tubing with her fingertips. 'You wouldn't want to cut off his oxygen supply.'

She chuckled as she turned her back to him and scooped up a pile of magazines from the end of his bed.

'I'm right here, you know. And perfectly capable of doing it myself. If you hand me the fucking control, woman.' His voice filled with vitriol.

With no sign of acknowledgement, she strode towards the door.

He narrowed his eyes at the back of her head. 'Deaf bitch.'

That's when the penny dropped. No wonder she thought he was pleasant. A retired headmaster, what was there not to like? Especially if you couldn't hear his snide, low-voiced insults. She wasn't totally deaf, but I realised she'd watched my lips as I spoke so she could pick up anything her ears missed by lip-reading.

Little did she know what a devious personality he was. Did she only come in to give him his tea and tablets each day? She certainly didn't have the same wariness the first woman had of him.

Maybe I was mistaken, and he was harmless. Just a grumpy old man who'd spent a lifetime looking after children in all their tempers, tantrums and challenges.

Now the rush in my head had subsided, I decided I would give him the benefit of the doubt. That was, until I looked at him.

His piggy eyes stared in rheumy consideration and sent another wave of sticky heat over me.

I indicated the window. 'Do you mind if I open it?' See, I could still be polite, even in the direst of circumstances.

He shook his head and spluttered. 'No. Don't. The pollen from the garden kills me.' His breath rattled in.

I paused, allowing a small smile to curve my lips as the darkness inside me decided to peep just above the parapet and tease. 'Does it, now?'

I leaned across the arm of his chair and grasped the metal handle on the window, yanking it upright so the window burst open all of six inches before the safety catch jolted it to a halt. I don't understand that. Why have a safety catch? Isn't it to stop them throwing themselves out of the top storey of a building? He was on the ground floor. I reconsidered. Maybe it also stopped anyone climbing in.

As I tried to push myself upright, Mr Collington's hard hand grasped the cheek of my arse, his sharp fingernails digging straight through the material of my shorts into my skin beneath. His fat fingers squirmed as they worked their way up, almost penetrating me. A practised move, I'm convinced.

With a shocked squeak, I shot ramrod straight, but his hand

gripped one cheek in a vice-like grip and squeezed so tight it took my breath away. A distant look in his eyes, he stared at me. 'Did you say your name was Carol? I liked Carol, she was my favourite. For years, she was my favourite.'

I flung myself backwards to break his grip and tripped over the small bin I'd stepped over to get to the window. I slapped straight down onto the tacky, threadbare carpet, whimpering as pain shot from my coccyx all the way up my spine.

All the time, the foul man puffed out rasping laughter as I stared up at him from the floor. His broken, yellowed teeth turned my stomach.

'Of course you're not Carol. She had tits, at least.'

Flames of embarrassment scorched my cheeks, just like all those years ago. And like back then, I was helpless to do anything to defend myself against this monster.

Or was I?

I'm no longer an eleven-year-old child on the cusp of adulthood. I am the adult. I am in charge.

Fury banked in the pit of my stomach as I glared up at him. 'You pervert. You absolute freak. I was right. You did abuse us. You abused children.'

His laughter was confirmation enough. Just how far he'd gone with children I wasn't quite sure I even wanted to know. Maybe that was between him and his god, but I'm not sure I could live with the knowledge. Not after so many years. Knowing I knew all that time and could have taken some kind of action to stop him. Prevent him from doing to someone else what he'd done to me. What he'd done to poor Carol. How had he made her suffer?

I pushed to my feet, my hands clenching against the grit and stickiness from the carpet. Disgust curdled and I turned my back on his insanely grinning face.

I hooked my foot around the partially closed door into his small en suite and opened it. Slipping inside, I turned on the tap, squirted liquid soap into my palms, scrubbing them together as I waited for the water to heat up. All the time having to listen to the laboured sound of Mr Collington sucking in oxygen and puffing it out with his vile laugh. I suspected he was forcing it a little as he knew I had to return from the bathroom and face him again.

I held my hands under the almost scalding water to sluice the suds off, my mind rejecting each suggestion I put to it. As I pushed the lever to one side, I let my gaze cruise around the bathroom.

Neat and tidy. Very few personal items. Toothbrush, toothpaste. Deodorant I suspected they only applied once a week, if that, but no aftershave. A stack of incontinence pads, which had me wrinkling my nose for no particular reason other than thinking of Mr Collington's penchant for stroking his own belly and privates.

Next to them was a box of latex gloves. Medium.

I paused, my mouth opened in a silent 'oh'.

A novel idea literally pinged into my head.

37

I caught my reflection in the mirror and grinned. A big, wide, slightly lopsided smile that showed my straight, white teeth my parents had the foresight and interest to get straightened when I was in my early teens. I hated it then. Train tracks. No one had their teeth straightened when I was a kid. Mine had been particularly crooked, though.

Now it seems to be the norm. Now they make it pretty. It hadn't been back then. I'd been teased about it. The only one in my class to have braces.

I leaned into the mirror. It had been worth every painful moment.

I pulled back as I heard Mr Collington snuffle. I think he's probably run out of breath. That might be a good thing. It could make matters a good deal quicker and easier.

I snatched two paper towels from the dispenser and dried my hands. I scrunched them up as tight as possible and shoved the damp towels into the pocket in my shorts. With thumb and forefinger, I carefully extracted two powder-free gloves from the cardboard box. Pausing, I listened for movement outside the bathroom before I stretched the gloves over my fingers. The scent of latex tickled my senses. I'm surprised they used latex for someone with allergies.

I tugged a third paper towel from the dispenser, squirted on hand wash, dribbled on some water and then washed down the tap and the handwash pump. I didn't think I'd touched anything else in the room. Not even the door handle as I'd used my foot to pull the door open. I wadded up that towel too and pushed it into my pocket to join the other two, aware that it was damp, but I wasn't going to leave them behind. I reminded myself not to forget to wipe down the back of the chair I'd put my hands on earlier.

With a quiet sigh, I stepped back into Mr Collington's bedroom and gave him a quick appraisal. His face had gone slack, the contours softening, blurring. His eyelids were at half-mast as though he'd drifted off to sleep.

I turned my back and nonchalantly wandered towards the open bedroom door to look down the long corridor. I listened for sound, movement, but there was none apart from the distant hum of a vacuum cleaner at the far end of the darkened hallway.

I slipped back inside and pushed the door shut. His eyes were fully closed, but as I approached, they flickered open. Wariness slithered through his expression.

The slow move of his hand caught my attention and I reached out, quickly knocking the call button from his hand. I took pleasure in the moment his eyes locked onto my latex-gloved hands.

Before he could react, I yanked the pillow out from behind him so his head flopped back to expose the rolls of soft, vulnerable flesh, with inflammation and a soft, soapy substance indicating intertrigo.

A small, sharp knife would have been quick and satisfying, but not so clean and way too obvious.

This way, I stood at least some chance of not being detected.

Eyes glazed with fear, he stared as I stepped behind his chair, out of harm's way as my throbbing bum reminded me how dangerous he was.

I meticulously looped the oxygen tube through the metal mechanism of his chair while that practised smile played on my lips.

'Didn't that little lady say to make you comfortable so you could have a nap before lunch? Here we go.'

I stepped back and reached for the remote control to his chair, pressing it so the back reclined, just like the assistant had instructed me to do.

'Whoops, I think she was right.' I put one finger up to my lips with an over-exaggerated moue and then pointed at the trapped tube, squashed flat between the metal mechanism of the chair.

In a panicked flurry, he attempted to twist around to see what I'd done behind him, his hand snatching at the tube to try and wrench it free. All to no avail. He simply didn't have the range of movement. I'd already assessed that ability.

Shame.

I took the damp towelling from my pocket and wiped down the back of the chair that I'd touched when I'd first come in. Before I'd realised what my mission had been. Maybe that was a lie. Before I'd acknowledged the mission in my own mind.

I slipped the cover from the pillow. The only other item I could recall touching without the latex gloves.

I bundled it up and slipped it under my elbow, not quite sure what to do with it, after all, it could contain some of my DNA. Not likely, but on the off-chance that it did, and that the little healthcare assistant remembered I'd touched it, if questions were asked, I wasn't going to risk it.

With a heart-stopping moment, my whole body jerked to attention.

Oh, my god!

I bet you thought I'd forgotten.

And I had. For a moment. But I darted back into the bathroom to snatch at another paper towel and doused it in soap and water.

I dashed back across the bedroom.

This time, when I leaned across, I made damned sure I had my hand on Mr Collington's wrist. Just in case he squeezed my tender arse again. Because if he did, I might just have been tempted to rip his arm off at the shoulder and beat him to death with it.

But he didn't. He was quite relaxed. His eyelids fluttered to show the whites of his eyes. His feet twitched a little, but nothing too dramatic. His mouth opened and closed like a landed fish. Or a rainbow fish, which made me think of Gary Philpotts. I slam that thought to the back of my mind and turn once again to Mr Collington.

There's a certain satisfaction that made me pause for just a moment to admire my handiwork, before I managed to concentrate my mind once more.

I thoroughly wiped the aluminium handle and windowsill as the man lay limp next to me. I pushed upright to wash down the arm of his chair. I washed his arm too, and his hands and in between his fingers. I'm not sure what the possibility of getting traces of my cotton underwear under his fingernails were, but I felt I may have gone far enough. Although it felt like he'd scraped my flesh raw, I don't actually think he'd achieved skin to skin abrasion. Or nail to skin.

A slight shudder of revulsion skimmed over my flesh.

Aware that if I didn't get a move on, someone might come in to check on him, I looked at my watch. It was coming up to 11 a.m., which meant they may not check until midday when lunchtime came around. Or dinner. Whatever they call that hot meal homes tend to serve in the middle of the day.

It occurred to me that if anyone checked, they would be really impressed with the cleaner in this home. Most would do a cursory wipe over. I've virtually sterilised the place.

I took one of the dryer paper towels from my pocket and wrapped it around the wet one and then shoved them all back in, hoping it didn't soak through and make me look as though I'd peed myself.

That made the whole memory circle around again.

I resisted the urge to punch him, because forensically, that would surely leave a bruise that might raise suspicion. Hopefully, this way, it would look purely like an accident.

I backed towards the door, not sure if I trusted him enough to turn my back on him, despite his apparent comatose state.

He gave a stuttering gasp, and then held his breath as I turned the door handle. A sick sense of fascination stopped me from pulling it wide just yet. He snorted like a pig and then resumed a shallow, racking breath.

'Mr Collington?'

His eyes opened a crack. I sent him a sweet smile. 'In no way can this ever make up for all those children you abused. Not in any kind of way.'

I paused to make sure he understood me. 'I hope you burn in hell.'

His eyes rolled back in his head until I could only see the whites.

With small satisfaction, I stepped into the hallway and pulled the door closed behind me.

'Waaah, waaah, waaah, waaah!'

The shrill blare of an alarm filled the silent corridor and my head shot up just as a number of pale-green scrubs-wearing people charged down the hallway towards me like a cheap version of a crash team in A & E.

I froze.
I'd been caught.

38

The thunder of footsteps peeled off to a bedroom two rooms down on the opposite side of the hallway.

My heart boomed in my chest as I looked straight ahead, slipping past the room where all the manic activity was going on. Ready to melt into a puddle of sweat and blood on the floor. But I didn't. I kept my shit together.

When I reached the full dirty laundry cart, I whipped the pillowcase from under my arm and rammed it as far as I could into the middle of the dirty linen and then passed on by, as innocent as possible.

With no one to see.

When I reached the main door, with no one on reception, I remembered to sign out, with my made-up name. Pocketing that little Bic biro smothered with my fingerprints on the way out.

The sun beat down on my head as I walked, head high, confident stride. Not too fast. I didn't want to attract attention. Although, if anyone looked closely, I'm sure they'd have wondered why there were thin streams of sweat literally running down my face.

As I sank into my car seat and fired up the engine, I scanned the street first before I peeled the sweat-soaked wig from my head and scrubbed my fingers through limp strands of hair and over my wet scalp to relieve the itchiness.

I needed to get rid of the wig, but the most pressing thing on my mind at that moment was the desperate desire for a salted caramel cream cold brew with everything, whipped cream, double espresso, a scoop of ice cream. I might throw it all up afterwards, but quite honestly, I didn't want to think of anything else.

Not that desperate, choking man. Not all the sick, sadistic things he had done. Things that could have been prevented, if only I had spoken up. The things he'd done because I didn't stop him when I could.

If only I'd spoken out.

But I hadn't. It was a vicious repeat of the last time I kept my silence.

I could have saved so many children.

So many ruined lives, because of me.

My silence had cost them all. We didn't speak up back then. We kept silent. Endured it.

It was my fault.

All my fault.

39

'What's a period?'

Coffee cake turned to ash in Bobbi's mouth, as she tried to swallow, clinging onto the self-control.

Unlike her youngest son, who snorted Coca-Cola from his nostrils to spray over the kitchen island in a brown slush.

Bobbi took a moment. While she could quite easily have snorted her own coffee out, she took a sip to wash down the dry cake, a moment ago so moist.

She leaned on the island, so her face came level with her youngest daughter's. 'What makes you ask?'

Still a little too young, she might have heard something if Shanna hadn't been diplomatic, although in that respect, her eldest daughter tended to be private in order to protect the little sister she was so proud of.

Her youngest daughter fidgeted, picked up a slice of cake and shrugged. 'I just wondered. I heard the caretaker speaking to the headmistress when I went to the toilet today.' She sent a guilty glance up at Bobbi. 'I needed a wee in lesson time.' She lifted her shoulders to her ears, holding her hands out. Going to the toilet during lesson time was frowned upon. At her age, they were considered old enough to hold it until break time, dinner time, home time. 'I was desperate.'

Bobbi raised her eyebrows. This was not something she'd dealt with before. Certainly not at this age. She was just surprised that at the age of five her daughter was already curious.

'What did you hear?'

'The caretaker.' She paused, ever one for dramatic effect. Perhaps she took after her Aunty Alexis.

'He was grumbling.' Toni leaned forward as though to take them into her confidence, lowering her voice to a mock whisper. 'He said some really naughty words.'

'Okay.' Bobbi was good at this. This was her job. She didn't normally have to deal with it on a personal basis, but five-year-old children often heard things they shouldn't, saw things not even an adult should see. 'On this occasion, you can tell me those words, but I don't want you repeating them to your friends. Do you understand?'

Toni nodded, relief creasing her brow. 'He said... he said, he didn't think he should have to clean up somebody's bloody period. He wouldn't be doing it.'

'Oh.' Bobbi raised her mug to her mouth to give herself a moment to think about what could have happened to initiate that whole conversation. 'Did somebody have an accident, do you think?'

Toni shook her head. 'No. He said someone had smeared blood up the wall. There were handprints.' Her clear eyes met Bobbi's 'Why was somebody bleeding, Mum? Were they hurt? Do periods hurt?'

Bobbi took a long, deep breath. It had come earlier than she'd wanted, but that was quite often the way with a younger child. Matthew had never noticed. She wasn't sure he had even now. He never mentioned the subject, not even to his dad. He appeared oblivious to girls.

Toni was a whole different kettle of fish and if Bobbi didn't deal with the matter to her daughter's satisfaction, she'd go elsewhere until she got the right answers.

There were things she could tell her youngest without going too deep into detail.

She raised her head, and her gaze caught her son's desperate one as he slipped from the chair, intent on slinking from the room before he was pulled into this. 'I think ...' His voice warbled the combination of deep tones together with uncontrolled squeaks that he'd had for the past year or so. 'I think I'll just...' He pointed upstairs.

Yeah. Run, boy, run.

Bobbi smothered a small stab of envy. Sometimes, she wished she could run off to her bedroom. Fat chance. She'd not done that in the past seventeen years. At least.

'Matthew.'

His eyes filled with terror as he did a slow turn on one heel.

'Before you go, just pass me the book.' She pointed at the sitting room where the 'book' resided on the top shelf of the bookcase. The one she'd read with each of her children at the appropriate time, skipping pages with a brief wash over of the subject matter until they were old enough to understand each stage.

Her son's face flushed up as he came back and passed her the book. Bobbi smiled at him. 'You can stay if you wish, there's nothing to stop you.'

Matthew's ears turned pink.

Bobbi grinned at him, knowing he would shoot off as soon as he could, but unable to resist the little tease.

Toni opened her mouth wide and took a bite of the coffee cake.

'He was shouting. I think he was really angry because he said he couldn't see why he should be made to clean up someone else's mess.'

As her son hesitated in the doorway, he looked back, a light of confusion in his eyes. Bobbi turned once again to her daughter, who shrugged.

Bobbi tried not to overreact, but her eyes widened. 'Oh, did he?'

Accidents happened. It was only a junior school, so the likelihood was the child was very young to start their periods. Possibly ten, or eleven. There was even the chance that the child had been traumatised by suddenly starting their period at school. Especially if no one had taken the time to explain it to her. Parents often didn't. Expected the school to do their job for them just because they didn't have periods for whatever reason, too old, a hysterectomy, on the pill so they never gave a thought to periods. Any excuse or reason to delay the inevitable.

The scenario played out in Bobbi's mind. It never ceased to amaze Bobbi how many parents omitted to discuss such matters with their children before the event.

Shanna hadn't started her periods until she was almost thirteen, which from a maturity point of view had made it so much simpler to explain and those explanations had been underpinned by sex ed at school. It wasn't an either-or scenario. Both needed to be involved.

'I don't understand why anybody would put their hand in their own blood, Mum, and smear it over the wall.'

'There are times when this kind of thing happens. It's normally because somebody is unwell.'

'But he said she was a dirty little bitch and needed to be taught a lesson.'

In silence, Matthew slipped the book onto the kitchen counter and dashed from the room, leaving Bobbi alone with her youngest.

Right. Bobbi had told Toni she could say anything. Bobbi hadn't quite expected that from the mouth of her five-year-old.

She looked at the clock. There was plenty of time before she needed to pick up her eldest child from football. They could take the time, just the two of them.

40

'He said what?'

Bobbi's lips tightened as she shrugged, lowering her voice so only her three sisters could hear as they grouped around the small table in the Costa coffee outlet. 'Apparently, Toni heard him call someone a dirty little bitch.'

'That's not appropriate.' Tess's face reflected the horror Bobbi felt inside.

'Go and give him a whack!'

'Sarah! You can't do things like that.'

'No. But you can have a word with the Head, surely?'

'I'm not sure. I could make the situation worse.' Bobbi picked up her millionaire's shortbread and took a bite, crumbs dropping straight onto her bosom.

'Oh, for goodness' sake. You're a social worker. You know how to deal with these things.'

Bobbi picked up her flat white, sloshing it over the edge of the cup as she caught her elbow on Alexis's arm. She sighed and put it down again as Tess handed her a thin serviette that probably didn't have the capacity to soak up the mess she'd made. Sarah handed hers over too.

She was too cramped, too warm, even with the air con blowing cooling air over the top of their heads to stir their hair in more of an irritation than a comfort.

Bobbi leaned back to give herself room to breathe and brushed the crumbs from her chest. 'The thing is, Toni technically shouldn't have been there, and if I flag it up with the Head, it might not do Toni any favours. She asked me not to say anything.' Begged, actually. A tearful plea as she went to bed.

'Perhaps it's better to say nothing at all. I'm sure it was a one-off incident,' Sarah suggested.

'I'm not so sure. I've heard a few things about him from the kids.'

Bobbi leaned back in as Tess's voice dropped lower and she looked around to make sure no one was close enough to overhear. 'Apparently, he threatened to toss one of the boys over the balcony.'

Sarah hit the table and made it wobble so Bobbi's coffee sloshed over the side again and defeated the already soaked serviettes. 'I've heard that. When I was giving swimming lessons. Apparently, he's said it to a few of the kids. They're quite scared of him. Grumpy old git.'

'Why doesn't someone do something about him?' Alexis asked.

Tess shrugged and took a delicate sip of her decaf black Americano. 'Apparently he's the Head's father-in-law. She can't do a thing about it. She can hardly sack him, can she?'

'You are joking me,' Sarah almost shouted, so Bobbi whipped a quick glance around at the other patrons, hoping no one was paying attention.

'Kidding,' Tess hissed.

'That's what I said,' Sarah replied.

'You said "joking me". That's wrong, it's "kidding me".'

'Really, Tess? Do you have to be so pedantic?'

Tess narrowed her eyes at her youngest sister. 'I'm not. I was just correcting your grammatical error.'

Bobbi sighed. 'Can we get back to the issue?'

'The issue is, someone needs to have a word with the old codger and let him know we're on to him.' Sarah slurped her decaffeinated iced mocha.

Wishing she'd never brought the subject up, Bobbi raised her hand to her forehead and blew out a breath. She'd thought to get a little support, a suggestion or two, but this was getting silly. 'He wouldn't really throw someone over the balcony, would he?' Should she make this official? It was one of those matters where she felt herself rocking from side to side on the fence she'd simply wanted to sit on.

As a social worker, it could place her in a delicate situation if she was seen to accuse the man of something he was totally innocent of.

'Of course he wouldn't.'

'But he is nasty.'

Bad tempered didn't make him a bad person. 'I overheard one of the little girls the other day say something about him always lurking around the changing rooms.'

Shocked, Bobbi snapped her head around to stare at her youngest sister. 'Oh, my god, that could be serious. Why didn't you say something?'

'Me?' Sarah's eyes opened wide. 'You're the one whose daughter just told her he called someone a dirty little bitch and you don't want to say anything about it.' Her voice rose and Tess ducked her head, looking around.

'Sshh. Sarah, keep your voice down.'

Sarah drew fingers through her still damp curly hair. 'To be honest, the girl is eleven and at the drama queen stage, and I just thought nothing much of it. She's all, you know...' Sarah wrapped one arm across her bosom and twisted from side to side in an impression of the little girl. 'Don't look at my boobies... oh, look at my boobies, they've started to grow.' She dropped her arm, resting her hand on her lap. 'Now, when you put it all together, it sounds like he's a horrible man.'

'A horrible man we can't do much about,' Alexis shot back. 'But we need to. He could do anything and then it's too late. Surely we can't keep quiet on the amount of information we have. We need to report him.'

'Not without more evidence. I mean, if you're going to complain about someone and potentially get them the sack, you can't just go on hearsay. Or unfounded comments. You know what children are like, once one kicks off, the rest of them follow. It could just be nasty rumours, getting blown out of all proportion.' Bobbi tried to calm them with the voice of reason. One she often used at work.

'Do you really believe that, Bobbi?' Alexis sat back. 'I don't have much need to go into the school, just once in a while to do a talk, and god knows I don't have any experience with kids, apart from yours, Bobbi, and Ashton, but it sounds like there are a few sources here giving out red-flag warnings.' She turned to Bobbi. 'Perhaps you should have a dig around, workwise, and see what you can unveil. Could you find out where he worked before?'

Bobbi shook her head. 'I can't see there being an issue. He's got to have been through DBS checking to even work there.'

'Maybe, but that doesn't stop him from being a grumpy old git.'

Bobbi picked up her cup and saucer, bringing them close under her chin so she could drink her coffee without it dripping down her. 'Grumpy old git doesn't make him a child abuser. I think we need to keep our ears open and listen for any other incidences. I'm going to have to take some advisement, as I'm a little close to this situation.'

Working within the same district she lived in threw up all kinds of issues. She could take a child away from a family and see the parents the next day in Aldi. She'd been subjected to under the breath cursing and the occasional hard stare, but the majority of these people knew just to step back, because it wasn't worth the backlash if one of them actually assaulted her. It also held advantages that quite often people felt she was a familiar face in the community. That they could talk to her on the same level. The advantages, Bobbi felt, far outweighed the disadvantages.

Still, this was a tricky one.

41

Heat beat down through the dressing room Velux windows as Tess slipped Graham's suit from the hanger. Normally, she'd ask the housekeeper to deal with it, but the woman seemed barely capable of keeping up with the physical housework, let alone sorting through Graham's suits and taking them to the dry cleaner's.

She reached up and pulled the black-out blinds down, plunging the room into a dim greyness only broken by the stretch of sunlight from the open door into the hallway.

Tess wrinkled her nose. She didn't want to heave the heavy suits to the cleaner's, but nor could she suffer that look from Graham when he realised three of his twelve mid-grey suits were still awaiting cleaning. She pursed her lips. That would narrow his choice.

Why financial advisers still felt the need to wear suits was beyond her. But they did. Light grey, mid-grey, dark grey. Perhaps a reflection of Graham's age that he still insisted on wearing one, but from what she'd seen from his conference photographs, age didn't matter. It was the industry he was in.

She'd phoned the dry cleaner's to come and collect. They were already in the area, they would drop by shortly.

She slipped her hand quickly inside each trouser pocket. All empty. As she'd expected from her neat-freak husband. The jacket pockets were also empty, except the last one. The one he'd been wearing the previous morning as he'd left the house but had it tossed over his arm when he arrived home, hot and sweaty and in a bad mood. One she'd chosen to avoid by pouring him a gin and tonic, herself a glass of wine and wandering out onto the patio to give him a moment to calm down.

When his phone trilled with that stupid ringtone from *The Pink Panther*, like he was a super sleuth just as he raised his glass to his mouth, he'd dashed from the house. He'd left the jacket behind and called over his shoulder for her not to wait up.

There'd probably been a dip in the market, she'd thought at the time, and one of his millionaire buddies wanted him to pacify them. Immediately. That's the way it could be, or so she thought.

Until she withdrew her hand from the pocket of the jacket she'd hung up for him, noting the thin white drip mark almost at the hemline. So unlike him to drop anything on himself. He was always so fastidious.

She dropped the jacket on top of the others and unfurled the fingers she had wrapped around a small foil blister pack.

Her trust in him splintered like a pane of thin glass. Fragile, the pieces glinted, tormenting her. The sharp shards of them stabbing through her skin to draw blood.

How had she not seen it?

Her lips turned numb.

Of course she'd seen it. She'd lived with the possibility ever since she'd stolen him from his first wife.

She stared at the four small blue pills in the palm of her hand.

Sex.

The age-old crucifier of the neglected wife.

All the signs had been there. She'd known. She'd used her own wiles all those years ago to get him for herself without a single thought to the poor woman he'd left for her. Twenty-five years they'd been married. At least his first wife hadn't had a child by him. Didn't have a family, a history. It had been the seven-year itch, he'd said.

What would he classify this as?

Was the other woman younger than Tess?

Tess closed her eyes and sank onto the wingback reading chair in the corner of the room, her fingers clutching the little packet.

Of course she was younger. The efficient thirty-something financial adviser he'd recruited before Christmas? The woman he'd been training up, apparently with a view to using her in his 'exit strategy'.

'Oh, what a fool.'

Tess came to her feet, pushed the Viagra deep into her tailored shorts pocket, swept up the suits and then paused. She dropped the suits back onto the bed and leaned over, a scowl furrowing her brow as she skimmed her fingers over the pale, chalky mark on his jacket and then scratched a long fingernail over it.

Revulsion turned her stomach sour. The dirty bastard! She might not be a DNA expert, but she was a wife and she knew dried-on semen when she saw it.

Teeth grinding, Tess scooped the suits back up and made her way downstairs.

It wasn't an exit strategy from his business he was after, but one from his marriage.

The bastard!

All these months.

Well, she wasn't going to let him get away with this. He couldn't walk out on her, leaving her alone and humiliated. She'd dedicated her whole damned life to the man. She wasn't about to let him discard her like an old rag thrown on a fire.

She wasn't going to tolerate it.

If he thought he could walk out and leave her without anything, he was in for a shock.

42

Her fingertips grazed the stem of her wine glass and then withdrew. One was enough. She needed to keep her wits about her if she was to win this game. And a game it was. A dangerous one, because if Graham found out, she had no idea what he was capable of.

What she did know was he'd lied when he divorced his previous wife and somehow managed to come out of their marriage smelling of roses. With the car, the house and the investments.

Tess had barely cared back then. She'd been in love. Not just with the man, because she had loved him back then, all those years ago when she was young and idealistic, but she'd also been in love with the idea of being a trophy wife. She had the looks, the demeanour, the willingness to learn, to be shaped.

She'd won.

The man. The lifestyle.

But she'd forever felt a trickle of wariness about Graham's dealings. A wariness that had twitched back to life recently when she caught an inkling that he'd intervened in their son's education.

Manipulative. That was the word for it.

He might just have underestimated her, though.

Her anger notched up as she opened the laptop and stared at it for long moments before she contained herself, softly closing the lid again.

She placed it back where he'd left it, tweaking it into place, just so. He was too clever by far not to notice if she'd been snooping.

Still, there were other ways.

She tapped on the HSBC app on her phone, held her thumb against the recognition button and waited for her accounts to load.

The housekeeping money was all there in her personal account. More than enough for what she really needed each month, but she'd been happy to spend it without question. After all, they'd been married long enough for her to take what came naturally. He provided. Wasn't that one of the reasons she'd married him? Financial security and a way of life she'd craved when she'd had a taste of it as his secretary.

She scrolled through her account, her stomach churning as she noticed for the first time how much money seemed to seep out. On nothing. Frivolities. Hair, nails, clothes, bags, shoes. A gym membership she barely used. A golf membership she kept going just in case. For appearances.

Was that what her life consisted of? Was this what she'd come to?

Sick anxiety churned in her stomach.

All this time, she'd felt disdainful when she compared her life to her sisters'. The money she had, the house, the lifestyle. Yes, she had actually looked down on them from her superior pedestal.

Yet it was her life that was lacking. Empty. A designer bag filled with nothing.

Sarah loved life. Alexis loved her job. Bobbi loved her kids and husband. They might, none of them, have money, but it was a rarity to have it all. Tess was beginning to believe her sisters had the better end of the deal.

She reached for her glass and took a delicate, controlled sip of the heavy red wine she'd bought from the local Co-op. The wine Bobbi bought for a fiver when it was on special offer.

Cheap and enjoyable. A rebellion against Graham's choice.

Her lips turned up in a smile and then dropped instantly as she stared at their joint savings account. The one with all their money.

None of their money.

She came to her feet in one fluid move, her hand covering her mouth as the Waterford crystal glass dropped to the floor, spilling the contents onto the cream rug to spread like a pool of blood at her feet.

Phone still grasped in her hand, she tapped on the link. Scrolled through.

The bastard.

He'd been skimming money off, transferring it to his personal account and then possibly onward to an offshore account. He was certainly the man who would know how to do that kind of thing. And stupid her, she'd not noticed. She'd had no reason to notice, to suspect. Or rather, she'd not been bothered.

It had been another of Graham's quick flings. Flings she'd chosen to turn a blind eye to long ago. Aware of the quick turnover of staff, she'd put it down to his inability to keep his lustful thoughts in his head; he must have acted upon them. No wonder they left. She'd never given it a thought before.

Too soaked in her own vat of alcohol to be bothered.

She was bothered now.

The dull thump of her own heart stuck in her throat.

What the hell should she do?

What was she supposed to do?

He was going to leave her. In the same situation he'd found her in. Destitute.

Only this time, she didn't have her good looks and slim body to barter with. Age had robbed her of those assets. What used to be slim was more stringy these days.

Panic and fury balled together.

What was she going to do?

She had no one to speak with. No one.

There was no way she could confide in her sisters. She needed time and they wouldn't allow for that. Sarah would probably punch Graham in the nose. Bobbi wouldn't be able to keep that sad look of condemnation out of her expressive eyes. She wasn't sure how Alexis would react. Alexis had never been comfortable in Graham's presence. She'd most likely stay away more than she normally did.

Tess bent and picked the glass up from where it lay on its side, undamaged from its fall onto the plush rug. She'd call in the carpet cleaners. They'd soak the red wine stain up with their expertise. It was a shame she couldn't blot the stain of her own life with such ease.

She twirled the stem of the glass between her fingers as she contemplated pouring some hot, soapy water on the mark, and her mind changed direction.

There was one person she could go to.

One person she could trust to keep quiet until she was ready to make her move.

One person whose opinion she still trusted.

43

Of all the things Bobbi had to do, this was the one that bothered her the most.

A whole day once a month dedicated to visiting Drake Hall, a closed category women's prison at Eccleshall, Staffordshire. It was only an hour's drive each way, and quite pleasant. Part M6 motorway and then onto country roads, during which time she got to turn things over in her head. Maybe that was the issue. She wasn't one for alone time. She preferred the company of her husband, four children, three sisters and work colleagues. It kept her mind occupied, her thoughts from straying.

'Hi.' She smiled through her open window at the guard on the gate. A guy so familiar, yet nameless. She waved each time she came through. He never cracked a smile, but always gave a slow nod in acknowledgement. It wasn't friendly, or unfriendly. Simply indifferent.

She parked her car in the virtually empty car park and left the engine running, window back up, air con on while she sorted herself out before the heat bouncing from the surrounding concrete walls and tarmac melted her.

Bobbi drained the last of her cold coffee from her travel mug, there was no way she was about to drink Drake Hall's offering. Even if she was offered one. She couldn't remember the last time that had happened.

She slipped her phone from her pocket and placed it into the glove compartment of her car. She brought little else on visit days. It only slowed the security process down. It was something she'd learned in her early years.

She turned off the engine and opened the door, sucking in as the heat from outside engulfed her, sending her into an instant hot flush which she knew she'd not be able to get rid of until the cool of the air conditioning inside took her temperature down a few notches.

She swiped her hair back from her instantly wet forehead and sighed. She leaned in the rear door of the car and took a small bundle of clothes from the back seat.

When she'd called ahead for her appointment time, they'd said to bring clothes. She'd brought shampoo and deodorant too.

Over the years, she'd got to know the guards. If Ralph was on shift, there would be a few moments of friendly banter while he processed her.

He wasn't.

Mike wasn't as chatty, but he was nice enough.

She placed her keys in a locker and closed it.

'You found the wand, I see.'

Mike raised the hand-held detector up like a trophy and waved it slowly around her. 'No. The Governor had to buy in three new ones. They all walked.'

'Oh, no. How does that happen?' In a place with such heavy security, it surprised her that items disappeared so easily.

He shrugged and held his hand out for her to pass through into the next room. 'I dunno. Somehow, you'd think working in a prison, there'd be honest people around. Never ceases to amaze me.'

She glanced at him, unsure if he was being funny. His face remained deadpan. The door opened and another visitor stepped inside, head down to avoid any eye contact, just as Bobbi's female escort guided her out the opposite side.

'Quiet day.' She lowered her voice out of respect. Somehow it always felt to her as though people should be considerate while walking through the long halls of the prison. It was, after all, a home to so many.

Drake Hall wasn't such a bad prison. Female prisoners weren't as raucous as their male counterparts. They tended to keep their heads down, work their sentence, get out and get on with their lives. Mental health issues were a constant battle. Women who'd left behind young children, mothers, sisters. Depression often cloaked the place in quietness. Especially on overly hot days, when all they wanted to do was sit outside on a green lawn, kids with dirty faces running in circles around them.

That was Bobbi's experience, in any case.

'Too hot for anyone to be arsed to come visit a prison. Most people have better things to do on a day like today.'

'Perhaps they need to send in an ice-cream van.'

Keys jangled on the officer's belt as she came to an abrupt stop. 'You are kidding, aren't you? You do know that's the best-known method of passing drugs.'

Bobbi flashed her a wide smile. 'Yes, I was kidding.' Of course she was. Of course she knew. She'd known the Morretti family all her life, been brought up buying ice creams from their vans since she was a kid. She'd never progressed to their drugs, but she'd known of their enterprise. Of course she'd known. The whole neighbourhood had. Buy a screwball, pass over that extra money, and you'll find that ball of chewing gum in the bottom of the conical plastic cup isn't chewing gum.

The guard led her to one of the visiting rooms and Bobbi gave her a grateful smile.

She remembered the first time she'd been sent on a prison visit. It had been a men's prison then and her visit had been official. She'd spent the entire journey wondering what the hell to say, what tone to take, what questions to ask.

In the end, it wasn't about that. She'd arrived at the prison and it suddenly became about the claustrophobia. Then, it was a full frisk, with rough, impersonal hands. Didn't matter whether you were male or female.

The biggest thing that got to her, though, was the distinctive 'clunk' of locks through each set of doors. A feeling of being led into the vaults of some kind of hell. The slide of metal against metal, clunk. The jangle of keys, clunk. The closing of another door, clunk. In reality, she'd not been taken far, but it had felt like it at the time.

Her heart had thudded. A feeling of helplessness weighing her down, pressing on her chest until she could only sip in snatches of air.

What if something happened? A prison riot. You heard about them on the news. What chance did she stand? Wasn't it always the visitors who were killed first? The guards knew their protocol. She had no idea what she was supposed to do.

That had been the first time, over twenty years ago. Things had changed drastically since then. She couldn't remember when her fear had ceased and she'd learned to put her trust in the guards who were trained to react. To protect.

Since they'd all become familiar with her, there'd been more of a relaxation of the rules. When she was led to the hall, they now allowed her the quiet corner where there was more discretion. Privacy. As private as you can get with a guard standing right there.

There was only one other visitor, who they'd placed at the opposite end.

A door opened and Bobbi's breath caught in her throat.

The woman who walked towards her held rounded shoulders hunched to her ears, so her neck almost disappeared. The age-blurred line of her jaw rested on her chest in soft wrinkles.

Oversized, washed-out grey joggers hung in folds around the woman's skinny hips and a thin grey T-shirt bearing the slogan 'In my defence, it wasn't me' clung to her chest, sweat stains spreading in darkened patches from under her arms.

At any other time, Bobbi would have snorted out her amusement at the slogan, but this wasn't the time and amusement was the furthest from her mind.

She came to her feet, scraping the chair back in her haste as the prisoner approached with a dull flat-footed scuff of her feet against the polished floor.

Bobbi's eyes pricked with tears and she squeezed out the words.

'Hello, Mum.'

44

'I thought you might turn up.'

Bobbi opened her mouth to reply but her mum held out her arms. They reached over the table, leaning in for a strong hug.

Bobbi choked back a sob tearing at her throat and clung on, her face buried in her mum's neck. It didn't matter how old she got, she was never too old to take comfort in her mum's arms.

Firm fingers dug into the flesh of her upper arms as her mum forced her away, dark eyes holding hers with gritty determination. 'Get a hold of yourself, Bobbi. We'll have none of this.'

'But...'

'No. No hanging on.' Her mum glanced over her shoulder at the guard outside the glass partition and then back again. 'It's a quick hug, them's the rules. I don't want a strip search when I go back to my cell because they think you passed me something. You should know better.'

She did. It didn't make it any easier, though. If there was one wish in her life it would be to be ten again, snuggled shoulder to shoulder on the sofa, watching TV with her mum's favourite throw over their knees. Tess upstairs, her nose in a book, and Alexis fast asleep in her cot, Sarah not even born yet.

To take the sting out of her words, her mum gave Bobbi's forearm a quick squeeze as her eyes filled with affection.

Bobbi sank onto the hard plastic seat and stared at her mum across the table.

'My twelve-year anniversary. Who'd have thought it would go so fast? I don't suppose you brought a cake?' Her mum's voice cracked with dark humour.

Bobbi lowered her head and stared at the finger she used to trace a pattern on the table-top and considered for a moment the hygiene. Who'd sat there before them? Had the table been cleaned? There was no stickiness to it. Unlike their conversation.

'I did, but they ruined it when they dug the file out.'

Her mum barked out a rough laugh.

'How are my girls?'

Bobbi raised her head and met her mum's keen gaze. 'They're well. They send their love.'

Her mum's hopeful smile faltered and then dropped away. 'Pity they couldn't bring it themselves. We could have had a celebration. Candles and all.'

Bobbi couldn't agree more. She thought that every time she came to visit. At one time, Tess would accompany her, but over the years, the visits had become less and less. Sarah sneaked in from time to time on her own and never said anything about it. The only way Bobbi found out was because her mum would mention it on occasion. Alexis refused to come. She found it all too upsetting. Too hard on her delicate feelings.

How the hell did she think their mum felt? Stuck in here, interminable days, one of her daughters couldn't even be bothered enough to visit her. She'd never been, to Bobbi's knowledge.

'I've brought you some clothes. The guards will let you have them later. They need to put them on your property card.'

Her mum hesitated for a long moment before a smile curved her lips. 'That's thoughtful.'

They sat in awkward silence for a moment before Bobbi spoke. 'I bought some Galaxy chocolate for you too.'

They didn't let visitors bring it in, just in case anything was hidden inside, but she could purchase it from the prison and they'd let her mum have it later.

'My favourite. Better than a cake and candles.'

'And some books.' They were pre-loved, but her mum wouldn't care.

'Oh?' Her mum perked up. 'What you got me, then?'

'Karin Slaughter. *False Witness*.'

Her mum raised an eyebrow. 'Sounds good.'

Bobbi smiled at her mum's interest. 'And Diane Saxon.'

'Never heard of her.'

Bobbi shrugged. 'You'll like it.'

She circled back around to the subject of clothes, just to give her longer before she said what she came for. 'I bought you a pink T-shirt.'

The other woman's mouth gave a wry twist as she smoothed a hand over her chest. 'With a slogan?'

Bobbi smiled. 'Where did that one come from?'

Her mum plucked at the figure-hugging T-shirt and shrugged. 'Apparently, all my clothes went missing in Laundry. They managed to find me some. You shouldn't waste your money buying me new stuff, you know. Just get it from the charity shop. It wouldn't matter to me.'

But Bobbi knew her mum would take pleasure in the soft fabric of the new T-shirt.

'They sometimes go missing. Even if they don't, by the time

they've been through Laundry twice, they'll look like crap. They all turn out different shades of the same colour. You should just bring me grey stuff. That's the colour it'll end up anyway.'

'I'll bring underwear next time. I just needed to know what size to get you.'

Her mum had lost a considerable amount of weight, and the last underwear Bobbi had bought her had been far too big.

Her mum smiled. 'You don't need to. I'm hoping to get out soon.'

'Oh?'

She'd heard it before, but this time there was a palpable air of excitement.

'They've been letting me out. Into the community, just for a coffee to start with. I can go for up to four hours at a time now. I've got to stay local, but all the same. Small steps. I have a Board next week.'

'You never said.'

'I thought you would have heard. Through your job...'

Bobbi shook her head. 'You're not my case, Mum, they wouldn't inform me. Data protection and all that.'

Her mum nodded. 'They reckon I have a chance.'

Bobbi sighed. 'I hope so.'

'You don't think so?'

Bobbi folded her hands in front of her. 'It's not that. You need to show remorse.'

Her mum leaned forward and snarled in an undertone, 'Remorse for killing the bastard who abused your little boy, my grandchild?'

'Mum, you didn't...'

Her mum sliced the air with her hand. 'I'll have none of it.'

'You don't have to be here...'

'What alternative do you suggest?' Her mum flung herself back in her chair and crossed her arms over her narrow chest in defiance.

Bobbi swallowed, taking a moment to compose herself as she glanced at the guard to make sure they weren't attracting any undue attention. 'Mum! All you have to do is *act* remorseful.'

Her mum's lips compressed together, but she gave a sharp nod of acknowledgement. 'I will. But given the chance, I'd not change a single thing.'

Bobbi reached across and squeezed her mum's fingers in her own. 'I appreciate that. But you could be out by now. Just do it, Mum. For me. For your grandchildren.' Grandchildren who she'd never allowed to visit her. Prison was no place for them, her mum had declared, and Bobbi was inclined to agree with her. Only Toni had come along while Bobbi was breast-feeding and couldn't leave her behind, but once she became more aware, Bobbi's mum had stopped the visits. 'You shouldn't be in here.'

Bobbi drew in a breath ready to continue and glanced at the guard, who'd turned to face them through the glass window once more.

'Quiet, now.' Her mum's voiced filled with authority. 'There's no good going over ground we've already covered. I'll be good. But he deserved to die.'

'You can't say that. Tell me you're not going to say that to the Board.'

'Your Uncle Ricky was an evil pervert. If your dad had been alive, he would have killed him, brought him back to life and killed him again for what he did to our Matty.'

Bobbi dropped her face into her open palms and scrubbed at it. The sick roll of nausea hit her, just as it did every time she remembered. Her sweet little boy. She squeezed her eyes closed but she couldn't block out the images flashing against the inside of her lids. Black and white. A steady strobe lighting effect.

Uncle Ricky. Her son on his lap in the huge wingback chair. A chair she'd set fire to in her mum's back garden. Uncle Ricky's hand down the front of Matt's shorts. And he wasn't checking to see if his nappy was wet, as he'd tried to claim. Matt had been out of nappies for some time.

Craig had been in hospital, septicaemia from a burst appendix. Uncle Ricky had offered to babysit Matt while Bobbi and her mum had gone to visit him. Josh had been in school and Shanna at nursery. It had never occurred to Bobbi that there was even a remote possibility of any issues. Her sisters were busy. It was Uncle Ricky. Family. Family didn't do that kind of thing.

Her naivety astounded her now.

In her job, she knew with certainty that it was family responsible for doing that type of thing. They were the most likely, had the easiest access. Yet it had never occurred to her that her Uncle Ricky couldn't be trusted. This was how these things happened.

If Craig hadn't been asleep all the time they'd been there. If they hadn't returned unexpectedly early.

The touch of her mum's fingers on the back of her hands had her snapping her head back up. 'Oh, Mum...'

Her mum ran a hand over Bobbi's head and cupped her cheek before dropping it back down to the table and glancing at the guard. 'How is he? How's my Matty?'

Bobbi nodded, dragging a little composure back. It was always this way. Unable to fully express themselves, there was so much left unsaid, so many blurred lines. 'He's doing brilliantly.' She shook her head. 'We know what happened, Mum, but Matt has no idea. He was far too young to realise. We got there just in time. I don't think he even thinks about it. It could have been so much worse if...'

'It was bad enough.'

'It was all my fault.'

'Well, it taught us all a life-long lesson.' Her eyes turned bleak. 'None of us had any idea, my love. How were we supposed to know? When your dad was alive, we all got along. They weren't very close, but when we saw him, there was never any inkling of him being a bad one.'

'He never touched any of us when we were little.'

'None of you were boys.'

Bobbi shook her head. 'Perhaps none of us were left alone with him.'

'I can't ever remember. There was never a need. It was a different era when you were little girls. Safer. You girls could run wild and free without us having to track your every move. The world has changed. Become evil.'

Bobbi held still. Forced herself not to cry out. The world hadn't changed. There had always been monsters. They'd just hidden themselves better before the internet, before awareness, before the innocence was lost and society realised they existed. Exposed them. No longer turned a blind eye.

She wanted to say, 'Look what happened to Alexis. Don't you remember that? How could you forget?'

Only, sometimes it was better to let the past die.

For their own self-preservation.

Sometimes secrets still existed. Monsters were still in hiding.

There would be no gain reminding her mum of something she didn't need to think about. It would simply be another torture to a woman who lived with remorse every day of her life. Who unfairly took the blame for not recognising the monster that had lived among them.

45

Guilt snapped at her heels as Bobbi dashed through the corridors, barely pausing to snatch her keys from the locker. Tears blurred her vision of the prison officer and stung her eyes as she stumbled out into the bright, searing sunlight.

God, she had to get away. She'd not been able to stand a moment longer in the claustrophobic atmosphere pretending that nothing was amiss when everything was. Cooler than outside, it didn't matter. She had to get out, needed the open space. Miles of pure blue, cloudless sky to make her feel alive again.

How her mum survived in that place, that prison, was beyond Bobbi. She couldn't do it. Couldn't spend her life locked inside. She'd lose her mind.

She opened her car door and let the air escape in a ball of heat. The seat was going to singe her backside when she slid in and the sun would be scorching the steering wheel. She should have put the windscreen protector up, but she'd not given it a thought as she arrived.

She slipped inside and turned on the engine, leaving the car door open while the air con rattled on.

She should be delighted that her mum might qualify for release. Delighted.

How the hell was it all going to work out?

Would her mum expect to come and live with them? They barely had enough room for the six of them without trying to squeeze in a virtual stranger who would need her own bedroom. The kids didn't even know her, and they certainly needed their own space as they grew. The two boys shared a room already. It would be Shanna and Toni who would need to make a sacrifice, if anyone. And that wasn't going to go down well. It wasn't appropriate with their age difference. Shanna needed her privacy.

The council house her mum and dad lived in had long since gone to someone else. There was nowhere for her to go. She'd be discharged. A handful of cash and her few paltry possessions.

Tess's prick of a husband wouldn't offer for her to live with them, even as a temporary measure. On the contrary, he'd probably fight tooth and nail to keep a convicted murderer from his door. They weren't even allowed to speak about their mum in front of him. On the rare occasions Tess had visited in the past, she'd never let him know.

It was no use Alexis putting her up, despite having a two-bedroomed flat. The pair of them had always rubbed each other up the wrong way. They'd probably have another murder on their hands. Bobbi's lips twitched in spite of herself. Mum and Alexis. The perfect storm.

It wasn't fair to expect Sarah to have her either. Her flat was only one-bedroom.

Bobbi suspected there would be changes there, too. If ever she got her youngest sister alone, she'd pin her down and see what was going on, but other things had taken priority.

What a mess!

She should be delighted to have her mum out of prison.

Coming up to twelve long years and the woman stood a genuine chance of getting out and all Bobbi could think was how awkward it was going to be. How embarrassing.

The kids barely knew their own grandma. Matthew had been almost three, Shanna almost four, Josh just turned six. Bobbi had been expecting at the time. Almost six months pregnant. She barely remembered that time. The trauma had brought Bobbi's labour on early. The baby had gone into foetal distress. The miscarriage had been a crippling blow.

In hospital along with her husband, there was no bigger horror than having lost her baby to then turn her other children over to her youngest sister, who'd only been twenty-three at the time.

Sarah had rallied. Excelled herself. Stepped in and smoothed everything over while their mum was tried and convicted of murder.

A murder she'd confessed to willingly.

46

It's not easy to get into a school. But it's not impossible.

You just find a good enough reason. And I found one.

Deliver contributions to the summer fête when the PTA have arranged to meet there.

Do they let you roam around unaccompanied?

Certainly not. Not in the everyday, run-of-the-mill kind of way.

No.

But they do allow you certain freedoms when you have an enhanced DBS check. Which all of us do. All four sisters, because we like to do our bit. And when most the PTA are congregating to finalise the arrangements for the summer fête, then mostly you go unnoticed once you've signed in.

I wasn't quite sure exactly what it was I was about to do when I juggled my way through the main doors, arms full of boxes. Not just the face paints. I had the balloons and balloon pump, together with a small gas cylinder which I was dropping off.

Then there was my dilemma. I mean, should I speak with the headmistress about the caretaker's inappropriateness and her very possible lack of action? Was it my place to do so? Whether or not he was aware he'd made those remarks in the presence of a student. A child. Wasn't it still inappropriate? And the other rumours about his behaviour. Unacceptable behaviour.

Should I take it into my own hands? Was it my place to do so?

I push through the doorway into the stairwell that leads to his office. Strictly speaking, it's his cleaning cupboard, but everyone knows he has a chair in there. No window.

I hesitate.

Should I go straight to the Head's office? This is serious. Perhaps I need to get a grip, not start shouting at the caretaker. Not that I intended to shout. After all, if he's not had the error of his ways pointed out to him, how is he supposed to understand?

I'm halfway up the stairs and I pause on the first landing before I take the next flight up to the first floor.

He should damn well understand. He's an adult. Adults in positions of authority involving children should conduct themselves with a certain decorum. But what's the best way to tackle this? Through official channels, or just a quiet word?

I balance the boxes on the stair rail and use the heel of my hand against my cheek to wipe away the itchy coating of sweat and grime from the sand that's blown in from the Sahara Desert. No wonder it's so hot. This isn't climate change, but the whole Earth is being plunged into the depths of hell. This heat hasn't let up for the past six weeks, I swear. Only another week and the school will break up for the summer holidays.

I hesitate, still leaning on the banister, and listen to the empty echo of children's voices distant in their classrooms, barely audible unless I strain to hear.

What the hell am I doing here?

Haven't I learned my lesson by now? I can't interfere. It's not my business.

Mind made up, I pause on the stairs.

I'll take the face paints and balloons up, see if there's anything else the volunteer group needs and leave.

This situation has nothing to do with me. I have to let it go.

The long strap of my handbag slides from my shoulder to catch at my elbow and leave my small bag to swing at my feet as I push away from the railing.

The door above me slams open, a lone man's voice rebounds down the stairwell.

'Fucking little whores.'

I blink and step back against the wall so I can't be seen. A frisson of shock rippling through me. I don't want to be seen.

The anger vibrating through that voice was unreasonable. I don't need to meet someone like that. Don't need to feel that anger. I haven't a clue who he is talking about. It might be one of the teachers, the Head. It may be one of the children. Whoever it is, it's none of my business and I don't want to know.

I take a cautious step down so I don't have to pass him on the stairs and readjust my boxes as the strap of my bag slips from elbow to wrist until the bag rests on the step above my foot, strap dangling.

Awkward now, as I can't move in case I trip.

There's nothing I can do about it unless I put the boxes down on the stairs and readjust everything.

The caretaker comes into sight, running down the stairs with a strange sideways gait, his right foot taking the lead down each step in an awkward bounce as though he has a problem with his hip.

There's a slight hesitation as he sees me, and then he continues down onto the landing three steps above me.

'Hi,' I say, because I decide I don't want any friction. I don't want a confrontation with this man, whose gaze pierces through me.

Heavy grey eyebrows dip low and he holds my eyes with aggression and challenge as though I might rebuke him about his language.

I don't want to take that responsibility on.

I'll speak with the Head instead.

He doesn't respond, doesn't answer me. As though I hadn't spoken. I don't exist. I'm not important enough for him to acknowledge, or I'm wearing my invisibility cloak.

I shift. Hitch the boxes again, ready to move on past. My little bag swings.

His right foot, the lead one, gets caught in the dangling loop as I grab at the overbalancing boxes.

'Stupid fucking bitch!'

Our eyes lock over them and shock hits me. 'Don't speak to me like that. Don't speak to anyone like that.'

His face turns thunderous and it all happens in an instant.

He's slightly off balance. His back to the handrail.

I twist, snatching my hand up, and the leather strap whips further over his foot.

Shock widens his eyes and in the final moment, I see understanding because my gaze is as hard as stone as I give a firm, unapologetic yank.

The boxes explode from my hold.

His arms flail out too late as his right leg does a 90-degree angle and his whole body flips.

He bounces down the stairs, headfirst, skull cracking like a gunshot on the hard stone flooring. The sound echoes up the stairwell.

Why they haven't thought to make stairs in schools more child friendly, I'll never know. That's not my job. Then again, it could be argued that this wasn't my job either.

A spurt of blood sprays up the wall as the man continues down, head over tail until he reaches the ground-floor landing. My handbag strap still wrapped around his ankle. My bag under his foot. Three boxes on the landing next to him.

Panic grabs me.

I fly down the stairs, all the time assessing the damage to him.

Is he okay?

What should I do?

Blood seeps from his head and his right leg lies at a sickening angle, a jagged bloodied bone poking through the material of his cheap cargo trousers. Almost too obscene for me to look at. Then again, too fascinating for me to take my gaze away.

I hesitate as I reach the bottom, careful to avoid putting my footprints in the smudges of blood, almost tiptoeing.

My heart sings. My breath chokes in my throat.

I'm so divided on this one.

Does he deserve to die? Really? A grumpy old sod who makes disgusting remarks about children?

I reach his body and snatch the leather strap from around his foot, yanking at it so the strange angle of his leg grows even more peculiar and the jagged bone juts out, white and stark, the sharp point of it protruding, covered in blood.

A dull groan stretches out as his eyes crack open just a slit so I can see the faded blue. 'Help me.'

Blood oozes from his head in small pulsing gushes.

My stomach contracts and threatens to spill the entire contents on the foul little man at my feet.

'Help me.'

I loop the strap of my handbag over my head so it lies crossbody and snatch the boxes up, holding them tight against my stomach, checking them over for signs of blood splatter. Nothing. Or at least nothing I can see from this angle. I hug them to me, tiptoe around the caretaker and reach for the door.

I check both ways before I slip into the main hallway and make my way to reception before I stop halfway along. No, that would be the most stupid move I could make to leave just as soon as I arrive. That would be a dead giveaway.

Instead, I take the disabled lift up to the first floor, making sure I leave my prints all over the door and button to prove the route I've taken, if proof is required, before I step out onto the empty landing and walk along to the classroom the volunteers are using while Year Four are on a school trip.

After all, I've come here to help, haven't I?

47

Tess tapped her foot as she waited for Bobbi. Really, she worked far too hard. There was so much pressure on Craig to be there for the kids. Although surely the big ones were old enough to look after Toni? Weren't they?

A distant memory since Ashton was little, he seemed to have been so independent, or was it just that the childminder Graham had employed had taken up more of her little boy's early years than she remembered? She had no memory of when she'd first allowed him to stay home alone, let alone go out with the local teenagers to wreak havoc on the estate. Not their gated community, that wouldn't have done. Besides, most of his friends had been at the private school, not local.

By the time he reached the age of eighteen, they were done with each other. Not in a bad way. They hadn't argued or fallen out, Ashton simply no longer needed her. Or anyone.

Now she watched Bobbi's children.

'Aunty Tess?'

Jerked from her reverie, Tess looked up into the beautiful, wide-spaced hazel eyes of her eldest niece. Long black lashes framed them, so like her dad's. The polar opposite of the Wilson family. All four of them had long eyelashes, but they were blonde. Tess had hers dyed every eight weeks, along with eyebrow tint and wax.

'Shanna.' A smile spread across Tess's face. Now her niece was older, she had a soft spot for her.

It would have been nice to have had a girl. Her name was beautiful too. Exotic. Named after the heroine in a Kathleen Woodiwiss novel. Bobbi was such a romantic. Who would have thought they came from the same family? Apart from their looks, which only consisted of their colouring, hair and eyes, but not their shape and height, they were so different.

'Dad says would you like a drink?'

Her taste buds quickened as she flicked a brief look at the time on her iPhone. Too early yet.

'That would be lovely, darling. A glass of water would be great.'

'Dad, Aunty Tess says yes, please,' Shanna yelled over Tess's head, almost blowing out her eardrums.

Graham would never put up with that kind of behaviour. Young, loud, frivolous. Tess loved it. There was a comfort in the madness of Bobbi's house.

Craig seemed to revel in it too as he lumbered across the kitchen, Toni wrapped around him, feet on top of his as tuneless music blared. She swore she heard the 'F' bomb in a long string of almost indecipherable hip-hop.

Tess glanced at the time again and wished she'd asked for a glass of gin and tonic. It might only be 5.15 p.m., but it was hot, and she longed for the slide of alcohol to take the sharp edges off life.

Shanna leaned over the top of Tess and an icy drip of water landed on the top of Tess's nose as she looked up.

'Whoops!' Without thought, Shanna swiped it off with an equally icy forefinger, her long manicured nail scraping the top of Tess's make-up off, she imagined.

She pulled off a weak smile that spread wide as Shanna offered her a flute of something fizzy and alcoholic.

'Can I have one?' Shanna called, again over the top of her head to her dad.

The volume of the music dipped suddenly to almost off, so it sounded more like an irritating tick in the background instead of a boom.

'Nice try, but not on your life. Or my life, if your mother ever caught me giving you wine.' Craig flopped into the armchair opposite and raised a frosted glass of beer to Tess.

Tess took a sip and let the cool liquid slide down a throat she'd not realised was parched. 'A little early for me.'

'It's Friday. It's hot. What better excuse is there for a cool drink? Except you.' He pointed a finger at his eldest daughter, who held a can of Appletiser in her hand and the expression of a deprived teenager on her face. 'It's not often I get the weekend off, but I do this weekend. I'm going to have a beer and just kick back.'

'I thought you were going to take me to football, Dad.'

A startled look raced over Craig's face. 'Not tonight, Matthew. I'm sure there's none tonight.'

'No!' Matthew flung himself on the floor as Shanna perched on the arm of the settee, so close Tess could smell the fresh apple scent of shampoo from hair that appeared damp. 'Tomorrow morning, Dad, but it's early.'

Craig yawned and stretched. 'Isn't it your mum's turn?'

The grumble from his son wasn't so much an argument as a protest. 'Daaad.'

Craig grinned across at Tess as she took a sip of the wine and tried not to pull a face as the saccharine sweetness hit the back of her throat. Oh, god. It was that low-alcohol crap. She curved her lips, aware he was watching with perceptive eyes. Despite his laid-back attitude, she'd never underestimated Craig. He was far more intelligent than he portrayed.

She took another sip to show she enjoyed it. The strain was going to kill her.

She wasn't sure if the teasing twinkle that entered Craig's eye was meant for her or his son. 'He only wants me to take him because he knows I'm up for it when it comes to grabbing a McDonald's afterwards.' He leaned forward and knuckled his son's head. 'Your mum's not such a pushover, is she?'

The front door banged open, and Craig swivelled in his seat. 'Talk of the devil, here she comes. I'd say she's early but I've no idea what time she started this morning.'

He got to his feet and let out a soft grunt as he turned, straightening his back and walking stiff-legged over to his wife.

'Bobbi, Tess is here.'

She wondered if he did that to warn Bobbi, or was she reading too much into it?

She didn't bother getting to her feet as Bobbi slumped onto the settee beside her and rested her head on Tess's shoulder. 'To what do we owe this honour?'

Tess drew a glance around the room. How to explain? I'm lonely. I wanted company.

'I was just passing by on my way back from the gym, and I thought I'd pop in and say hi.'

'Hi.' Bobbi grinned and reached for the flute of wine Tess had barely touched. She took a quick drink, tipping her head back. As she straightened up, she pulled a face. 'Shanna, go and get your Aunty Tess a proper glass of wine. She won't appreciate this stuff. Come to think of it, neither do I. Who buys low-alcohol? All the calories, none of the taste. Yuk.'

Tess opened her mouth to object.

'I told Dad.' Shanna pushed up from the arm of the sofa and reached out for the now half-empty glass.

Bobbi pulled it away, an astute frown flickering over her brow before she handed it over, after all, it was low-alcohol if Shanna did decide to sneak a sip. It might put her off for life. 'There's a bottle in the wine rack in the bottom of the fridge. A blue label. Aunty Tess's favourite. Bring the bottle and a couple of glasses.' She turned to Tess. 'Are you staying for dinner?'

'No, I...' She'd love to, but how could she impose? She'd not intended to stay. Just have a chat, feel less unsettled and then go home. If she'd intended staying, she would have brought a bottle of wine with her. She normally did, but that was usually by invitation. It was unlike her to drop by unannounced.

'Nonsense.' Craig smiled at her. 'We're having Bolognese. My speciality.' He was handy in the kitchen. It was a shame Graham never even tried to cook. Mostly, he ate at lunchtime with a client or a rep. 'There's plenty to go around. I always make enough in case the kids bring someone home.'

She used to love cooking, but there was never anyone around to appreciate it these days. She felt like a fraud turning up on their doorstep, but what else was she supposed to do? She didn't want to pace around an empty house, considering her next move. She wanted time to not think because her mind was spinning.

'But I'm in my car. I parked it further up the street.' It was a weak protest, one she felt they must see straight through. Pathetic, really, as she wanted to stay, wanted the company, so why the pretence?

'You can leave it where it is. It's fine parked there,' Bobbi replied. 'Craig will walk you home later and you can fetch it in the morning, or I'll drive it around to yours. It's such lovely weather, we're going to sit outside to eat.' She smiled and scrubbed a hand through her hair. 'Thank god it's Friday. I deserve this.' She raised her glass in a salute before she took a sip.

The door clattered open again and Alexis swept inside, with Sarah close behind her. She extended her right arm and circled round a pointing finger.

'You are not going to...' she cast a quick glance around at the kids and Tess suspected changed the wording of what was about to come from her mouth '...freaking believe this!'

48

Sometimes Bobbi just wanted to put her head in her hands and weep.

Alexis's face was animated, eyes sparkling. Bobbi just knew she wasn't going to be able to stop the verbal diarrhoea which was about to explode from her sister's lips and which predictably shouldn't be said in front of the children. At least, not Toni. The others probably heard far worse from their school pals.

Sarah and Alexis seemed to lack that certain ability to hold their tongues. Was it because neither of them had children of their own, which made you stop and consider what comes out of your mouth?

Craig stood. 'I'll add some mushrooms to the pot.'

Did they even have mushrooms? He'd probably sneak some carrot in there too, and an extra tin of tomatoes if he could get away with it. It was going to really have to stretch. At least they had lots of pasta.

Bobbi could kiss him. He would just fade into the background without a care. She really did love her husband. His no-nonsense, no-fuss personality.

They'd hoped for a quiet evening, just the three of them. Bobbi, Craig and Toni. After dinner, the older ones would slink off out until curfew which with the long days had been extended to 10 p.m. on a Friday night. In all honesty, as long as Josh kept in contact, he no longer had a curfew. Almost a man, he'd always be her baby.

She smiled at him now as he tucked his hands into his denim short pockets and shuffled off after his dad. Most likely to see if he could persuade him to let him have one of those small bottles of beer that seemed to be all the rage.

Alexis threw herself into the seat Craig had vacated, shuffling over to let Sarah squeeze in beside her.

'Guess what?'

Shanna glided back into the room and handed her Aunty Tess a glass of wine, a bottle in her other hand.

She held out an empty glass to her mum and Bobbi held it while Shanna poured. As she stopped, Bobbi wiggled her glass to encourage her daughter to pour more. She ignored her daughter's raised brow. She had a feeling she was going to need all the help she could get. She could just tell. Alexis was on a high, rather than a low, so it was safe to drink.

'What now?'

'Haven't you heard?'

Tess raised her glass and almost drained it in one go. Possibly afraid if she didn't get her share of a decent one, it would run out and they'd have to revert to the low-alcohol crap.

There was plenty of the good stuff. Craig had paid Tesco a visit to take advantage of their 25 per cent off wine offer. Tess's favourite just happened to be reduced already, making it a bargain to sweep up six of those at a time. They were well stocked, but Bobbi hoped no one let on that they had another five. Her sister would be there all night.

'If we'd heard, I'm sure we'd be as excited as you are.' She touched her daughter's hand as Shanna put the bottle down on the side table and gave a quick nod to her younger sisters. Nothing more was needed, Shanna knew to fetch drinks for them too.

'Mr Dent fell down the stairwell at the school. His head busted wide open.' Alexis splayed her fingers in an imitation of an exploding... head.

Toni gasped.

Bobbi took a gulp of her wine. 'That's terrible, Alexis.' She tried to impress upon her younger sister the inappropriateness of the subject, but Toni lapped up anything her gruesome Aunty Alexis offered up. Bobbi considered her daughter would become one of two things. Either a doctor, or a serial killer. Her taste for the gory details was insatiable.

Sarah leaned forward and tapped Alexis on the knee. 'Tell them what happened.'

'I just did.'

'No, tell them everything.'

'Well...' She reached up a hand and accepted the bottle of beer from Josh. 'Thanks, bab.'

Bobbi pursed her lips but said nothing. She'd given up trying to persuade Alexis to use a glass instead of drinking straight from the bottle. She didn't want to preach, though.

Josh reached over with an orange juice for Sarah. Bobbi frowned. Her sister caught the look and raised the glass in a salute. 'I'm driving. Apparently, Alexis needs to get bladdered.'

There goes any benefit to the discount they'd gained, because Alexis would abandon the beer once they started to eat.

'Oy.' Alexis elbowed Sarah in the ribs and Bobbi caught the quick wince but let it pass.

She needed to have a word with her little sister. Now wasn't the time. Let Alexis get it all out.

'What happened, Aunty Alexis?' Toni jigged up and down on the spot. 'Tell us.'

'Well, we were called to the school late this afternoon. Apparently, the end of school bell sounded, the kids all crowded into the stairwell, and there is poor old Mr Dent. Blood sprayed up the walls and pooled around his head.'

'I never heard, I never heard.' Toni perched on the arm of the chair so they were all squashed together.

'Didn't Daddy pick you up from your netball match today at Redman Junior School?'

Toni put her forefinger right in the centre of the dimple on her left cheek, her perfect mouth forming a pout. 'Oh, yes. I forgot.' She rolled her eyes for dramatic effect.

'Poor man.'

'As well as a caved-in head and a compound fracture to his leg, the poor guy almost got trampled.'

Bobbi watched as Tess screwed up her face in distaste.

'Is he dead?'

Alexis shook her head. 'On life support, last I heard. Cracked skull. Lost a few pints of blood. They have no idea how long he'd been lying there. It could have been anytime from afternoon recess onwards. He'd got hypothermia and they've put him into an induced coma.'

'That's horrific.'

'I thought you only got hypothermia from the cold.'

'Shock, blood loss. Any of those. The air may be hot, but lying on those cold stone tiles in the stairwell wouldn't have kept him warm. It's such an old building those walls are probably made of stone, not brick. Also, his age is against him, the older you are the more likely to go into shock after a fall like that.'

'Kids!' Craig's voice echoed from the kitchen. 'Whose turn is it to set the table?'

Toni and Shanna both pointed at each other.

'You can both do it,' Craig called. 'We're eating outside.'

The girls both raced to help out. Eating outside was so much more fun. And serviettes, they got to put out serviettes. The pretty ones with butterflies Craig had let Toni choose last time they were in Tesco.

'Josh, Matthew. Come and deal with the drinks.'

With a small groan, the boys ambled through with less enthusiasm than the girls. It was hardly a big ask, most of them already had theirs.

Alexis beckoned them all closer, leaning into the circle as she lowered her voice.

'Don't you think it's odd?'

'Odd?' Sarah squinted at her.

'What?' Tess took a sip of wine.

'What's odd?' Bobbi cradled her glass. She'd savour the next few mouthfuls, not rushing it before they ate. She needed to keep her head at the moment.

'That's two people now that something bad has happened to.' Alexis looked over her shoulder and watched as the kids all moved from the kitchen into the garden. She turned back around and studied each one of her sisters in turn. 'Two people who have recently come to a messy ending who we know. Who we don't like. Don't you think that's odd?'

Sarah jiggled her leg up and down. 'I heard Mr Collington died too.'

'Mr Collington?' Bobbi squinted at her sister. What had he got to do with this? How could Sarah possibly see a connection?

'Yeah, remember the old school headmaster?' Sarah leaned forward and rested her forearms on her smooth, tanned legs.

'I do. Dirty old goat, wasn't he?' Alexis dipped the neck of her bottle as though she was pointing at them.

'Dirtier and older when I was there,' Sarah said.

'Are you trying to tell me I'm old?' Tess gave her youngest sister a light shove.

Sarah snorted. 'No, but Mr Collington was. I hear there's an enquiry.'

'An enquiry into what? Mr Collington?' Bobbi dragged in a breath as the hot flush started in her ankles and skittered up the back of her knees. In a moment, she'd lose her mind and that all-encompassing fog brain would descend. She was going to go insane.

'Not into him, although there probably should have been years ago. Slimy sod. Into his death. Apparently, he had some sort of breathing difficulties and was on an oxygen machine. The oxygen tube got strangled on his electric chair and...' Sarah made a slashing motion with her finger across her throat.

'Couldn't happen to a nicer guy.'

'Tess!'

All three of them turned shocked eyes onto their eldest sister.

'Well...' Tess didn't have the grace to look abashed. 'He was a real perv.' She looked around at her sisters, keeping her voice low. 'Can't you remember? Didn't any of you think so?'

Bobbi placed her glass on the small wooden coffee table. She raised her hands and scraped fingers through a scalp that had turned wet. 'Yeah. I remember. We used to be sent to him for reading improvement.'

'I'm not sure what it was supposed to improve, but he made me stutter when he slipped his hand up the back of my thigh,' Tess said and then fell silent, her head dropping. 'Sorry, Alexis. Some things are far worse.'

Silence hung.

'He touched my breast once.' Alexis's voice had taken on a quiet tone. 'I told my teacher and she said he'd probably done it by accident, that he'd most likely been reaching for something.' She looked around, encompassing them all with her gaze. 'I said, yeah – my tit!'

Bobbi gasped, hung onto it and then burst out laughing as Alexis grinned. It was her way of letting them know it wasn't the time or the place to get into the dark, serious stuff.

'You did not!'

'I did! She never sent me to him again. Said my reading had improved sufficiently.' She craned her neck to look into the back garden and then turned around again.

Sarah reached around to smooth her fingers over Alexis's arm in a conscious comfort and sign that they all understood. They all stood by her, no matter what. 'Anyhow. What are we saying about these three men, Alexis?'

'I don't understand.' Tess drained her glass and looked around for somewhere to put it, or maybe she was looking for the bottle that Shanna had taken away with her to put on the table.

'I can't see it personally. There's no connection.' Bobbi shook her head and then dabbed the back of her hand over her top lip as the flush subsided.

'No way.'

'Dinner's ready.' Craig's voice boomed from the kitchen.

Alexis squinted at them all as they came to their feet in unison. 'You're not telling me you can't see a connection? Each one of them, we personally know. There's got to be something. It can't be a bloody coincidence that these three...' she almost whispered, 'perverted bastards don't have something in common?'

'Well, that's not true. Poor Mr Dent...'

'Poor Mr Dent, my eye! Look what he called that little girl. Look what he threatened to do to those other children.'

'It doesn't make him a pervert, Alexis. And apart from that, it's all hearsay,' Bobbi insisted.

'I don't think so. It makes him pretty horrible. I heard he threatened to throw one of the boys over the school balcony because he'd trailed yoghurt all down the stairwell last week. Poor lad never realised it was leaking out of the bottom of his backpack.' Alexis was quite insistent.

'Maybe that's what he slipped on,' Bobbi offered up and the others sniggered. 'Maybe the little boy got his own back.'

They laughed louder as they moved out of the lounge through the dining room and kitchen to the open patio doors.

'I don't think he did.' Alexis tossed her empty bottle into the bin as she passed by, opened the fridge and reached in for another. 'But I wouldn't be surprised if someone did. He wasn't a popular man. Nor were the others.'

'Are you saying these deaths... accidents are connected, and the connection is us?' Horrified, Bobbi stared at Alexis, conscious that the whole family were steps away waiting for them to move outside.

'Why not?' Alexis met each of their gazes in turn. 'Perhaps we've found a fairy godmother.'

Bobbi frowned. 'Or they've found us.'

49

Alexis gave a small shudder and peered up the dusky empty stairwell to her flat.

In giving voice to her own thoughts, she'd scared herself. More than usual. She'd always been scared, it was more a matter of on a scale of one to ten, how scared was she today, this very moment?

Right now, she was an eight. Still in control. Not quite hyperventilating, but not far off. Aware of her own breathing, she climbed the stairs.

Pippa wouldn't be there tonight. A thirteen-hour night shift. On for three days. Alexis wouldn't get to see her until the end of next week as their shifts clashed so badly. Pippa would go back to her own place and crash so she didn't disturb Alexis.

Alexis poked the key in the front door and held still, breath frozen in her throat.

Something rattled on the other side of the closed door.

Fear curdled in her stomach.

She took her hand slowly from the door, leaving her keys and key ring dangling from the door, a hushed ting, ting, ting as metal bounced on metal.

What should she do? What if it was true and there really was someone killing off people they knew and disliked from their past? Maybe they weren't just killing off the bad ones. She'd not heard of any other suspicious deaths, but what if they were all connected in some way?

She glanced along the short hallway to her neighbours' doors. There were three other flats on this level.

She didn't even know her neighbours. Never saw any of them with the shifts she worked. It wasn't as though she had a garden like Bobbi and Tess where they spent their evenings and weekends digging and planting and speaking with neighbours as they passed by. Not that Tess lifted a finger in her own garden, that's what the gardener was for. But she spent time out there, inspecting the borders, monitoring progress.

Alexis slipped her hand into the neat little leather bag she'd crossed over her body and pulled out her phone, ready to dial 999.

A muffled bump came from inside her flat and she hit the first nine.

From experience, she knew that once you hit the second nine, it's already starting to dial.

Sweat trickled down her spine and pooled at the base until her T-shirt clung, limp and damp.

Her fingers holding the phone shook.

'Stop it,' she murmured. 'You're not a child.' She felt she still was inside; deep inside, that little girl still cried in the dark, the monsters still lurked under her bed. Reality was worse than monsters. They were pure imagination, but people were real.

Mum had always said, 'It's not the dead you need to fear, it's the living.'

Another bump sounded.

Alexis's jaw clenched. 'Come on!'

She raised her free hand, turned the key and flung the door

wide so it slammed against the inner wall. With one hand bunched into a fist, the other ready to stab another nine on the dial pad, she marched into the hallway.

The iPhone slipped from limp fingers as she stared at the figure silhouetted by the dusky light from the living room window.

50

'Mum!' Alexis wilted against the wall of the entrance to her flat. Hand pressed hard against her chest, the sound of her pounding heart thundered through her ears. 'What the f...'

A wild-eyed woman she barely recognised spun around at the gunshot sound of the door slamming open. Her scrawny frame squeezed into a pair of garish purple leggings. A limp T-shirt clung to her sagging breasts with the logo 'run wild, run free' emblazoned in a greyish-green across the front.

'Alexis!'

Weak-kneed, Alexis reached out and gave a listless push to the door, watching it swing closed with a soft click.

'I nearly called the bloody police.' She bent and picked up the iPhone, still with only two nines on the display.

The whites of her mum's eyes showed as she reared her head back, terror lining her pale face. 'Don't do that! They'll give me another ten years.'

'Mum.' Alexis stepped forward, hand held out to take her mum's frail ones in hers. 'What are you doing here?' Had her seventy-year-old mum done a jailbreak?

Her mum's guilty gaze bounced away, refusing to meet Alexis's, making her believe her outrageous assumption might just be right. Had she escaped from prison?

'I told Bobbi. They've been letting me out on day release.'

Bobbi hadn't said a word. Then again, Alexis never asked. Never wanted to know. By the time her mum had been sentenced, Alexis's nerves had been in shreds. Her counsellor had said the incident had broken open Pandora's box and all the terrors of the world had come down on Alexis's head. Her past had reared up and threatened to consume her. History repeating itself.

With little thought of her mum, she'd had to nurse her own mental health back. Self-preservation had kept her away.

Her mum had understood. Said she'd understood, in any case.

Looking at the aged woman in front of her, Alexis wondered if she'd been right. Twelve years, yet her mum looked older than she should have. Withered and wizened.

Not knowing what to do with herself, Alexis tucked her phone into her pocket and rubbed damp palms on the front of her T-shirt.

'How did you get in?'

Her mum gave an awkward jiggle of her shoulders, a shrug of sorts, not something Alexis recognised as a natural move her mum would have made in the past. It looked painful, jerky.

'I had a bunch of keys in my lockbox. They let me have them.'

'Did they?' Alexis was surprised at that.

Her mum's shoulders moved again. 'Not really. I managed to palm them. They never noticed.'

Alexis said nothing. How had her mum still had keys to Alexis's flat after twelve years? What if she'd moved? If some stranger had arrived home from work and walked into their own flat to find this strange, wild-looking woman there.

Her mum plunged her hand into her pocket, pulled out the set of keys and jiggled them. 'I went to my house.' A sadness settled over her face. 'There're new people living there now. They look like a really happy little family.'

Alexis didn't know what to say to this stranger standing in her flat. One she barely recognised.

Pain of sweet memories deepened the wrinkles on her mum's face. 'Like we used to be.' Wistfulness threaded through her voice. 'A happy family.'

Alexis didn't remember it that way, she couldn't remember ever seeing it that way, not after Gary had done what he had. She kept quiet, not wishing to upset her mum further. There was no need to dredge up a past that was best buried.

'Fancy a cup of tea?'

Her mum sent a guilty look at the kettle. 'I already had two.'

Alexis's heart dropped like a stone. 'Oh, Mum, how long have you been here?'

Her mum offered up a weak smile. 'I thought you were never coming. I was just about to leave. I've gotta get back, you see. I'm only on day release.'

Alexis glanced at her watch: 8.18 p.m. 'What time are you supposed to be back?'

Her mum looked uncomfortable. 'I think it was 7 p.m. Could have been 6 p.m. I forget.'

Alexis suspected she hadn't forgotten. She was almost two and half hours late. Terror rose in her throat as she pictured police officers with battering rams at her door. She had a great relationship with the police, on a professional basis, when they all pitched in on a job together, protecting lives, saving lives.

This was different. Her mum was effectively a fugitive.

'Oh, my god. Mum.' Panic sent a tremble through her nerve endings. 'Hold on. Let's phone them. Do you have a number?'

Her mum dipped her hand into her pocket and brought out a rumpled slip of paper. 'They said to phone it if I got into trouble

I'm not in trouble, am I?' Eyes huge in a gaunt face pleaded with her.

'You might well be.' She didn't want to scare her mum, but there was an urgency. Words from her past and her own mum's lips echoed in her reply. 'We'll see what we can do about it.'

She turned her back on her mum and wandered through to the open window, just to catch a hint of a breeze on the evening air. Grateful that her mum had opened it, she dialled the number and waited.

Breathless by the time the prison answered, words rushed from Alexis's mouth. 'Hi. I'm calling on behalf of my mum, she's with me. She should be back with you, but she got all turned about and now she's late and we're worried she's going to be in trouble. Is she in trouble? I can't put her on a train. I'll have to drive her there.' She thought of the three beers she'd had at Bobbi's house. Calculated how much that must have been. They'd been small bottles. A pint? Maybe a pint and a half. That would be offset by the large helping of spaghetti Bolognese which sat like a lead weight in her stomach along with the slosh of cheap vanilla ice cream. She'd not had any of the wine when she noted how fast Tess was putting it away.

She stopped gabbling and waited a beat.

The male voice on the other end of the line soothed with a calm deliberateness. 'What is your mum's name?'

What an idiot. She'd never even said who her mum was. But in all truth, she'd thought they'd be on high alert, waiting for word of her missing mum. How many prisoners on day release went missing, for heaven's sake?

Her breath stuck and she let out a strangled noise before she uttered her mum's name, aware of the tears now filling her eyes. 'Tina. Tina Wilson.'

'Okay.'

'Is she in trouble?'

The beat of silence told her she would be.

'Is your mum with you now?'

'Yes.'

'Is she okay?'

Alexis made a slow turn and inspected her mum from head to toe. Was she okay? This woman she'd not seen in almost twelve years? To Alexis, there was nothing left of the vibrant, energetic woman her mum had once been. Before her stooped a desiccated wheatsheaf resembling nothing she ever remembered.

'Yes. I think so.'

'Is she in a safe place?'

'Yes. She's with me in my flat. She came to me.' Her bottom lip quivered. Her mum had come to her. Not Tess, or Bobbi, or Sarah. But her.

Alexis was the one who'd hurt her the most. She'd sent birthday and Christmas cards, but after the first three years, she'd stopped sending parcels. She'd put her own mum to the back of her mind. Self-preservation, her counsellor had advised her. Selfishness, she realised now, in a wash of shame.

'Okay. What time do you think you can you get her back to us?' His voice was a calm reassurance that they weren't about to jail her for harbouring a fugitive.

Alexis glanced at the time on her phone. She'd never been to the prison. Bobbi said it was roughly an hour. She blew out a breath. 'Nine-thirty.'

'Make sure she's here by ten.'

'Is she in trouble?'

'She's not in trouble. Not yet. We just need to get her returned as soon as possible.'

'Thank you.' Tears ran freely down her face now. 'Thank you so much.' A sob escaped.

'Miss?'

'Yes?'

'Give yourself a few minutes to calm down. You don't want to get in your car like that. I'll put down that you'll be here by 10 p.m. We'll be waiting. Go and see to your mum.'

The phone went silent. Alexis held it in her hand, tears dripping onto the screen.

When she raised her head, her mum stood in front of her, anxiously stepping from foot to foot. 'I'm sorry, Alexis. I didn't mean to upset you. I just wanted to see you. To hold you. It's been so long, and I worry about you every day knowing I'm not there for you.'

Tears streamed down Alexis's face as her mum held her arms wide open but never made the move forward. That was for Alexis to do.

A choking sob escaped, and she flung herself into her mum's arms, hugging her with bone-breaking fierceness.

'I'm sorry, Mum. I'm so sorry.'

51

There's something pleasingly delicious about following another person. I mean, the whole prospect of being spotted or being found out just builds an inner excitement, so my insides quiver with anticipation.

I've never, ever thought of myself as an adrenaline junkie. People would laugh at the mere thought.

This is certainly the closest I imagine I've ever come to that feeling people describe when they jump out of a plane, when they leap from the side of a cliff into pure nothingness. It's the exhilaration, the fear. A deep-down primal lust for life.

I wouldn't class myself as a stalker, either. That would be wrong on so many levels, but as I mentioned before, I'd kept a close eye on Gary Philpotts. I pretty much knew his bus routes, his habits. Where he ate. Mainly at that awful greasy café at the bottom of Junction Road. It was a wonder his heart hadn't given out long before I punctured his lung for him.

This was different, though. This held a special importance and relevance. If I was caught doing this, there would be a fallout of epic proportions.

I wouldn't just be questioned as to my reasoning. I'd never be trusted by my own family again. That can't happen. I can't allow it.

I keep my distance. Three cars behind, I promised myself, but it's not so very easy to do when the streets aren't that busy. I've never tailed anyone before. It's not like on TV.

I bite the fingernails on one hand until I get that metallic taste of blood in my mouth.

Graham is too self-absorbed for his own good as he parallel parks that monstrosity of a car between two others, but I don't underestimate him. I'd hate for him to see me. I'm not in my own car, but still. He may just notice me. I consider too late that I should have used my wig.

I flip the visor down as the sun strikes me in the eyes, almost blinding me.

I drive past and pull into the next side road.

I literally leap out of the car and dash around the corner, skidding to a halt as Graham only just gets out of his car. What the hell could he have been doing? I thought he'd be halfway down the street with his back to me, and I'd be following him at a discreet distance.

Instead, he's actually facing my way, which makes my feet stumble to an ungainly halt. I drop down on one knee, head bowed, and untie and re-tie the laces on my trainers, not daring to glance up.

Had he been checking his hair out before he got out of his car?

I sneak a look as he starts to turn away.

He's holding one of those expensive bottles of white wine in his left hand and he tucks his car keys into the right back pocket of his overly tight jeans, leaving them to jangle half out as he approaches the blue painted front door of a Victorian house.

Jeans?

I've never seen Graham in jeans. It throws me for a minute, and

I stagger as I get to my feet all too quickly. He's wearing a casual shirt too, the type I've never seen him wear either. Collarless. Cool, rather than slick.

I come to a standstill, peering through a narrow gap in the hedgerow as the resident opens the door and embraces Graham in a passionate hug before pulling him in for deep soulful kiss.

I don't just mean a 'Hi, it's good to see you' kind of kiss. I mean a full-on 'I'm going to strip your body naked in twenty seconds flat' kind of kiss.

My breath is literally sucked from my lungs.

I couldn't see that bottle of wine being opened in any kind of a hurry. Possibly, it would be warm before it was consumed. Then again, room temperature is best as Graham always insists.

You could have knocked me off my feet. I know I was expecting it, but to witness that kind of full-on, no-holds-barred lust gave me an unexpected jolt. Who knew Graham was capable of such passion?

I can't take my eyes from the pair of them.

I run my fingers through hair sticky with sweat. When would this weather let up?

Just in case either of them looks over, I duck my head and slink away as fast as I can.

This is not good. Not good at all.

52

Tess fumbled with the small package Graham placed in front of her, his hand resting heavily on her shoulder as he leaned over to watch her open it.

Her perfect pink fingernails tugged on the golden ribbon and then peeled back the thick embossed paper, a sense of foreboding heavy in her chest.

She opened the white leather box, and her heart sank.

Inside, nestled on a puffy white cushion, lay a garish ring, semi-precious stones sparkling in a myriad of colours. Nothing she'd ever choose for herself. Nothing her husband would ever buy for her. Normally. Previous to his infatuation with a much younger woman. One on whom the ring would look fabulous, no doubt.

Tess preferred the simple. The wide band of her platinum wedding ring was plain. The two-carat diamond engagement ring nestled against it, designed to fit together in elegant understatement. Until you noted that the diamond was flawless. When Graham had bought it for her, it had cost almost as much as Bobbi's house back then. Tess had never given it a second thought. But she did now.

She stared at the cheap, nasty ring in the white box and forced a smile as she raised her head.

'Did you keep the receipt?'

Unable to suppress his startled surprise, his mouth dropped open. Never in their married life had Tess ever questioned him. She'd bowed to his superior knowledge and obvious experience. She was experienced enough now to know he'd not applied his superior knowledge in this case but asked his secretary to choose something for his wife. This little piece of jewellery screamed 'younger, cheaper woman'. Even when Tess had been younger, she'd had expensive taste.

Resisting the urge to snap it shut, Tess closed the lid on the box, slow and controlled, and slid it into the middle of the kitchen island. 'Perhaps you can return it and I can choose something else for myself.'

Cool feathered across her shoulder from where he'd removed his hand and taken a step back. Stiff disapproval vibrated through his silence.

'I thought you'd like it.'

She pushed her hands against the counter, so the tall stool swivelled around until she faced him.

'Graham, I haven't worn rings other than my engagement and wedding ones for the past ten years, my love. I would hate to think it's going to sit in my jewellery box, unworn.' She gave a little sniff. 'Perhaps I'll get that puppy I've been thinking about.'

'Puppy? Puppy?' Horror streaked across his face as though she'd asked him to slaughter an animal and hang it from the ceiling.

'Yes, Graham. You asked me what I'd like for my birthday a couple of months ago, and I told you I'd like a dog.'

'I thought you were joking!'

She stared at him for a full minute before she replied, her voice low and controlled. 'Why would I joke about wanting a dog? I have nothing else in my life. Why wouldn't I want a dog?'

Confusion stole across his face and then slid off, giving way to anger. 'Why would you want a puppy? Just to have it piss up the furniture and shit on the carpets?' He slashed both hands out to indicate the room, the house. 'You have everything you could ever want. You need for nothing.' He brought his head in close to hers and she narrowed her eyes. 'I've worked incessantly to provide for you. You've never lifted a finger to contribute to this house, your car, your clothes, your jewellery. This marriage! What more do you want, woman?'

Her heart thundered. Graham's tongue could cut her to the bone, but she had never felt in peril of a physical confrontation. Not until now.

His muscles vibrated with fury. His hands balled into fists at his side.

Determined not to be intimidated, Tess pushed aside her fear and slipped to her feet from the stool, bringing her almost eye level with him. She placed her hand on his chest and gave a firm push as she brought her head up.

'A puppy.'

She stepped past him and glided from the room.

53

Bobbi held her arms wide and enveloped her older sister in a hard squeeze. Tension vibrated through Tess's willowy body as Bobbi kissed her on the side of her neck and then on her cheek.

'Happy birthday, Tess. Fifty! Fifty! And you look fabulous.'

She passed her sister on to her husband so he could treat her to one of his bear hugs.

'You don't look a day over forty-nine.'

Tess let out a strained laugh. 'I knew I could always rely on you to make me feel good.'

Craig looked over her head as she disengaged herself. 'Where's Graham?'

Tess waved a casual hand over shoulders stiff with annoyance. 'He's parking the car. He couldn't find a space.'

Craig frowned, oblivious to the nervous friction pulsing off his sister-in-law. 'Parking? Haven't you walked so you can both have a drink? It's a special occasion, after all. You're almost over the hill and far away.'

Tess's eyes flooded with tears, and she shook her head. 'He's not staying. He's got an important client visit, he says.'

Bobbi leaned in close and hissed in Tess's ear, 'But it's your birthday. Your fiftieth. This has been planned for the last fifty years. Surely he's told his bloody important client that?'

Alexis stormed into the kitchen, pointing behind her. 'I've just told him he's a twat!'

Bobbi blinked at her younger sister as Tess streaked a finger under her eyes, a bubble of laughter bursting from her slick, glossed lips.

'Graham says he's not staying! Twat!' Alexis spat out again.

'Alexis.' Bobbi did a slight head jerk in the direction of the open patio doors where the children played in their pocket handkerchief garden. 'Don't let the kids hear you. I don't need that word coming out of Toni's mouth.'

Alexis slammed her arms around her chest, making her bosom almost bounce out of the strappy T-shirt. 'Well, he is a...'

'Alexis.' Bobbi lowered her tone to serious as she glanced at Tess's eyes, filling with tears once again.

Alexis unravelled her arms and grabbed her big sister almost in a headlock. 'Someone had to tell the twat,' she whispered against Tess's hair. 'I told him he had to come in and at least have the decency to have a cup of tea while we gave you your surprise weekend away with the girls present.'

'Alexis!' Bobbi's shock made her grind her teeth.

'What? Are you saying she doesn't know?'

Bobbi's mouth fell open. Guaranteed that if anyone was going to spoil the surprise, it would be Alexis. 'She does now.'

Tess's lips twitched before they broke into a wobbly smile. She pinched them between her thumb and forefinger in a 'my lips are sealed' action and then sprang her fingers apart, just as a commotion had them all turning in the direction of the door. 'No one will ever know I know,' she whispered, just loud enough for Bobbi to pick up the words.

Craig had his meaty hand wrapped around the back of Graham's neck, a wild grin on his face as he powered both of them through the door. 'Put the kettle on, love. He'll be staying for half an hour. Enough time to give our gorgeous Tess her presents.'

Bobbi opened her mouth, then closed it again as she turned to pick up the kettle and fill it from the gushing tap. Craig loved Tess like a sister, but she'd never known him tackle Graham head on before. Served the selfish git right.

She looked over her shoulder. 'Craig, get Tess and Alexis a drink and everyone go into the garden. I'll be out in a minute.'

Alexis hovered behind as they made their way through the patio doors into the back garden. 'Sarah not here yet?'

'No, I...'

'Bloody typical.'

'No, it's my fault. I sent her to pick up the helium balloons.' Bobbi snapped on the kettle and turned to the cupboard to lift down a short, squat mug. She knew Graham preferred his bone china, but he could go and sing for that today. Inconsiderate little man.

She dropped a teabag into the mug. Not the stupidly expensive stuff he liked, but a good proper old-fashioned tea.

She turned to her sister. 'She should be back any minute.'

Alexis's jaw flexed. 'Are you making excuses for her?'

Bobbi swallowed. She didn't want an argument, today of all days. But then again, Alexis always chose family gatherings to kick off. It was her thing. Attention seeker that she was. 'No, it's genuine.'

The door gusted open, and Sarah's bright smile glowed with triumph as she wrestled fifty rose-gold, pink and metallic white confetti balloons through the door.

Alexis's mouth popped open. 'Jesus Christ. Isn't that overkill?'

Bobbi grinned. 'It's fifty balloons.'

'Did we need fifty, really?' She flung her arm out to encompass her younger sister and the balloons almost engulfing her. 'Am I paying towards these, they must have cost a bloody fortune? Couldn't you have got them from Amazon?' Alexis moaned.

'And blow them up ourselves? Who has the time?' Sarah glared at her sister. 'A friend of mine did them. She has a party shop.' Forced to defend herself, she held out her hands. 'She gave me a discount.'

Bobbi turned her back on her sisters as she poured boiling water into the mug, treating herself to a silent eye roll. She kept the frustration from her voice as she glanced out of the window at everyone. Her own children, scrubbed clean and turned out in shorts and T-shirts. Even Matthew, despite his attempt to skip out by claiming to have a football match. A claim his dad quite easily negated.

Only five more days starting tomorrow before they broke up for the summer holidays and she had a well-earned rest too. A fortnight off work. She'd never looked forward to a summer holiday quite as much as she did this year.

'How about we light the candles and take the balloons and cake out at the same time? That means Graham gets to join in that bit before he goes to work.'

'You're shitting me.'

Bobbi dunked the teabag several times and squished it against the side of the mug with the back of a teaspoon, her back still to them as she replied to Sarah's question. 'Nope.'

'Graham's going to work? It's his wife's bloody birthday. Does he know what an effort we've made on his behalf, so he didn't have this lot in his impeccable back garden? Has anyone 'ad him? I'll 'ave him.'

Bobbi pressed her lips together, trying not to say anything while she concentrated on stirring sugar into the tea. Round and round with the teaspoon. A distraction from the whole situation.

Sarah's biggest effort was collecting the balloons. Alexis turned up with two bottles of wine and a crate of beer. Everything else, Bobbi had arranged. All the effort had been hers. She ground her teeth.

Today wasn't going to be good. This celebration she'd spent months arranging. Not a surprise party. Tess would never have thanked her for that. She hated surprises. She needed to know something was arranged. But it was her actual birthday today and Tess was miserable because her thoughtless idiot of a husband thought it was okay to go into work. On a Sunday.

That was the sure sign of a marriage in its dying throes and yet Tess hadn't even spoken to them about it.

Perhaps there'd been too much going on for her to feel as though she could confide in everyone. Or was she too proud to admit there was a problem?

Bobbi stared at her out of the window, bright sunlight glinting off Tess's pale blonde hair as she stooped to sweep Toni up in her arms, her face tucked into the child's neck for a long moment. Was that to hide her upset from Toni?

Bobbi reached for the milk Craig had pushed to one side earlier when he'd made his tea just as everyone arrived. He was up early again in the morning, so he'd maybe have a beer, but no more. Perhaps they'd let Tess get legless and then he could walk her home later.

Bobbi was going to make the party work. They would have fun. Possibly more once grumpy old git had gone.

With a smile firmly plastered on her face, she turned and handed the mug of steaming tea to Alexis. 'Here, pass this to Graham and give me a couple of minutes to light the candles, then we'll follow you out.'

'You'll need more than a couple of minutes if you're going to light fifty bloody candles as well,' Alexis grumbled.

'You're going to melt the icing if you light that many.' It was more of an evil snicker from their youngest sister.

'The icing's going to melt in this heat anyway as soon as we take it into the sun,' Alexis quipped back at her.

Bobbi gave her sisters a moment to bitch while she slid the cake from the bottom cupboard she'd had to clear just to get it inside. It was a lead weight. She'd never made a cake quite like it. She loved to bake, but she didn't claim to be any kind of expert. This had been a challenge that had kept her up until 1.30 a.m. Pink and purple piped flowers swirled all over the top of vanilla icing on the outside. The inside was seven layers of sponge, all the colours of the rainbow stacked on top of one another, glued together with the same fondant icing. She'd not wanted Toni to see it, so she'd waited until her daughter had gone to bed before she'd started. She soon regretted that move once she realised how much work was involved and how long the sponges took to cool in the July heat.

She clicked the lighter four times before a barely visible flame danced from the end. 'You can give them the nod and Sarah and I will bring out the cake and balloons.'

Alexis's lips turned down at the edges and Bobbi whipped the beautiful gold bottle of Prosecco from the bottle bag on the bench and thrust it at her sister, anticipating the whine rising because she wanted something to carry too. It was always the way of things.

'Give that to Graham to open for his wife.' She almost bared her teeth as she grinned at her sister. This day was going to go down fine. She'd spent a fortune on food she could ill afford and presents that were ephemeral.

She handed Alexis the matching golden envelope with details of their girly weekend spa printed on thick, expensive card with gold calligraphy. She couldn't bloody afford that either, but Craig had insisted.

It was Tess's day, and nothing was going to go wrong.

As Alexis left the room, Bobbi touched the flame to the wick, first on the number five candle and then on the zero and watched them take light.

It was going to be a good day.

She'd make sure of that.

54

'Bobbi! Bobbi! Come here.'

Alexis grabbed her older sister and dragged her into the downstairs toilet, which was barely big enough to hold both of them. She slapped the bolt across and opened her mouth to speak just as someone knocked on the door.

'Bloody hell! Do you never get a moment to yourself?'

Bobbi grinned and slid the bolt back over. 'Never.' She swung the door open and Sarah hovered outside, a glass of something pink and fizzy in her hand. Probably Ribena and lemonade because they didn't have rosé today. It was all about the Prosecco.

At least they had beer.

'What's going on?' Sarah demanded.

'What?' Bobbi stepped back into the toilet.

'Nothing,' Alexis insisted, although she should have just told her to bog off.

'So, why are you hiding in the loo?'

'We're not.' There was no way Alexis could pacify their little sister. She hadn't even had a chance yet to have a quiet word with Bobbi before Sarah nosed her way in. 'I just wanted...'

'A poo? With your sister in attendance?' Sarah crossed her arms over a bosom which seemed to have expanded recently. Alexis was going to have to speak with Bobbi about her shortly because this was getting silly, but perhaps today wasn't the day.

Sarah balanced the glass on her forearm.

'What's happening? Do I have any more surprises?' Tess stuck her head around the open doorway and gave a sloppy, inebriated grin.

'Jesus H!'

Alexis closed her eyes. Did it really matter if they were all there? She'd wanted a quiet word with Bobbi, a couple of things she wanted to discuss with her in private. But like flies to ointment, the rest of them had swarmed around. Alexis pushed forward and stepped out of the toilet so she could look up and down the short hallway for anyone else lurking.

Shrieks of laughter came from outside, where Craig entertained the kids with swing ball and a hosepipe that was supposed to be filling the small paddling pool they'd bought for Toni's birthday two months previously.

She could tell them one thing, but the other would have to keep. There was no rush on that. She didn't need them all to know about Pippa yet. Introducing her to her whole family at once would be a mistake. Alexis knew that from previous history. Twice she'd introduced boyfriends to them at family functions. Twice she'd never got another date.

She turned to face Bobbi. 'How long have you known Mum was being allowed out on day release?'

Bobbi's face went blank. Poker face blank. Totally wrong for her.

Sarah gasped, but Tess swayed and leaned against the opposite wall, unable to hide anything.

'You knew?' she asked Tess.

Tess nodded. 'Bobbi told me.'

Bobbi sighed. 'Thanks, Tess.'

'Well, we shouldn't have secrets between us. We need to talk about things.'

Bobbi did a slow rise of her eyebrows and Alexis wondered if she'd lose her temper. It was a rare thing, but beautiful to see when she did.

'I agree. I wasn't keeping a secret.'

'No one told me.'

Bobbi closed her eyes, obviously hanging on to the last vestige of her control. When she opened them again, she stepped out of the toilet and closed the door, leaning against it with her arms crossed under her bosom in an exact imitation of Sarah.

'Okay. Here's the skinny...'

'You know that's not what people say these days, don't you?' Sarah asked. 'It just shows your age.'

Bobbi gave their youngest sister the dead-eye. 'Do you want to hear this?' The laughter died down outside. 'Before the horde come running in to find us?'

Sarah just smiled, knowing her little dig had struck home. Bobbi wouldn't use that phrase again.

'Mum has been let out of prison recently on day release. It's a gentle introduction back into the community. They give her some money, let her go out for a couple of hours into the local town for a cup of coffee and wander around. Then she returns. It's a sink or swim scenario.'

'Well, she didn't bloody return the other night.' Alexis hadn't quite meant it to come out like that, but the frustration had been left to fester over the past few days while her shifts hadn't allowed her breathing space to come around and see Bobbi.

Bobbi frowned. 'What do you mean?'

'Shit,' Sarah said.

Tess stood in silence.

'When I got home from here the other night, Mum was in my flat.' She hung on to her composure, knowing if she burst into tears in front of them all, she'd never properly get the story out.

She rubbed her hand over her churning stomach. 'She looked so old.'

'How did she get in?' Bobbi's face had gone blank again. She was probably trying her best not to say that the difference in their mum wouldn't be as unnerving if Alexis had bothered to be around as she grew old.

'She, umm, had the key to my flat. They let her take a couple of things from her lockbox at the prison. She took my key. Palmed it, apparently.'

Bobbi nodded. 'She probably has keys to all our houses.'

'Not mine,' Tess moved. 'She never had any reason to have my keys.'

Sarah mumbled something under her breath and Alexis, who was the closest to their younger sister, could have sworn she said, 'Graham wouldn't have her over the threshold.'

Before Tess responded, Sarah spoke up. 'She won't have keys to mine any more, I moved over six years ago now.' She grimaced. 'I hope she doesn't use them, someone's going to get a hell of a fright if she lets herself in their flat.'

'You'll have to have a word with her,' Bobbi said.

'Me?' Sarah's eyes shot wide.

'Yes, you. It's your flat.'

'But I thought...'

Alexis stepped in, after all, this wasn't about them, it was about her. 'Anyway. Mum was in my flat when I arrived home the other night.'

Sarah clamped her lips closed.

Bobbi dropped her hands from hugging her middle as her face turned scarlet.

'She'd been there for hours.'

'Why?' Bobbi queried. 'Why wouldn't she come here?' Insult laced her voice and not surprisingly. After all, it had been Bobbi who'd kept up contact all these years, visited their mum in prison, despite having four children. She'd even gone while she was carrying Toni, taken her with her when she was an infant. That had stopped once there was a hint that Toni would start to remember things.

A stir of guilt wound its way through Alexis's conscience.

'She wanted to see me. Alone. I'm not sure she could cope with everyone in one go.' Alexis blew out a breath and pushed off the wall to pace down the hallway. She brushed a lock of hair back from her face as she turned to look at them again. 'It was so sad. She's quite frail, really. Compared to...'

She expected Bobbi to make a snide remark about Alexis not seeing their mum, but she didn't.

'She's not the same woman. She's lost so much of her vitality. Her energy.' Bobbi gave them a sad smile. 'I know it happens anyway as we get older. I think sometimes our bright colours just fade to grey.'

'Oh, god. Thanks, Bobbi,' said Tess. 'Now I'm depressed. I'm fifty! I've got another twenty years and I'll be a sad silhouette of my former glory.'

'Eh, look on the bright side, you could be run over by a bus.'

'Sarah!' the other three chimed in, like it was a practised line every time Sarah blurted out some inappropriateness.

'Anyway.' Alexis spoke with some irritation as their attention turned away from her. 'I had to take her back.'

'To prison?' Sarah asked, not quite suitably abashed. There was bound to be another quip in her arsenal.

'Yes. I had to feed her first. She hadn't eaten all day.' Alexis felt the hard pressure in her chest as she thought about it. 'She said she'd had two cups of tea, but when I asked her, she said she'd looked in my fridge, but she didn't want to deprive me of anything.'

Alexis's sisters all raised their hands to cover their mouths, eyes filled with sympathy for their mum's predicament.

'So you fed her?' Bobbi asked.

'I sent her for a shower while I made her something.'

'What did you give her?'

Really? Did it matter? She'd fed their mum, hadn't she? Why did they have to query it? Sarah looked at her as though she didn't know how to cook. Well, Pippa did, and there'd been leftovers in the fridge that she'd heated up for her mum. The rich food had made her mum fart all the way to the prison in Alexis's car, but she wasn't going to mention that. It was between her and Mum.

Moroccan lamb tagine. She knew there'd be more questions if she said that. 'Lamb stew.'

Tess's perfectly waxed and tinted eyebrows raised in any case. 'Nice.'

'What was she wearing?'

Alexis puffed out a disgusted breath. 'You don't want to know. I gave her a pair of my cream shorts and a plain navy top.' She looked at the others, anticipating what they were about to say. 'No. They weren't too big for her. I kept them for when I lose this two stone.'

Bobbi went blank-faced. Her favourite expression, it appeared, today.

Tess pressed her lips together but couldn't help cruising her gaze over Alexis's robust figure.

Sarah grinned.

'So you took her back. Was everything okay?' Bobbi squinted at her.

'Yeah. She was late but I smoothed that out. She looked exhausted.' Shrivelled, she wanted to say. Lifeless. 'But she's fine. The guard on the phone was nice. I suspect he didn't want me to delay getting her back. But they took it really seriously. They said they'd have to review the surrounding circumstances, but because of her age, and possible confusion, it might not delay the process.'

'For what?' Sarah asked.

'For life on the outside.'

'Jesus. When?' Tess flopped back against the wall, her head making a soft thunk.

Alexis looked at Bobbi for confirmation and raised a brow.

'Six weeks.'

'You're kidding!' Sarah's mouth fell open. 'Why don't I know this?'

Bobbi shrugged. 'I thought we'd deal with Tess's birthday first.'

'Get it over with.' Sourness crept into Tess's voice.

'No.' Bobbi was firm with her older sister. 'Not spoil or detract from it. I have it in hand. I have a one-bedroom flat lined up for her, if all goes well. One of the council places. I managed to pull a few strings. It's not far from here. She can have her independence, but we can all keep a watch on her.'

'Does she need to be watched?'

'Duh! She killed a man.'

'Sarah!'

Sarah spread her hands. 'She did. She murdered Uncle Ricky.'

They all fell silent for a moment while Alexis clenched her jaw to stop her from blurting out that she might have killed him too, if she'd witnessed what he did to Josh.

Instead, she let her mind take a different route that only just sneaked through her consciousness. Her mouth dropped open as she studied the others.

'How often has Mum been allowed out for these coffee and cake in the community trips?'

Bobbi turned to her, a thoughtful frown creasing her brow. 'She only told me about them the other day, but I'm not sure. Three. Maybe four times.'

'Three. Maybe four.' Alexis ran a tongue over her teeth as she watched the other three closely.

'You don't think those three, maybe four times might have coincided with, let's say, those three deaths, do you?'

55

'Do you think she's sunburnt?' Bobbi leaned over the sink so she could peer out of the kitchen window at Tess. Her fair skin had brightened to pink across the top of her nose, her cheekbones and hairline. Her head lolled to the side over the back of the deck chair, so Bobbi had no doubt Tess would wake with a crick in her neck. Her lips were parted to show her newly whitened teeth.

Still, the woman managed to look elegant in her state of stupor, her long, shapely legs draped over the footstool Craig had taken out to her earlier.

If that was Bobbi, she'd have dribbled down her chin and trifle would be splattered over her bosom.

Bobbi glanced down. Trifle was splattered over her bosom and she wasn't even drunk.

'Yep.' Craig dried up yet another glass while the dishwasher chugged away with the second load they'd just filled it with. 'Toni dabbed sun cream on her face earlier, but I'm not sure she got it all.'

'We'll just finish these and I'd better wake her. I'll walk her home before it's too late. You get yourself to bed, you're up at 4.30 in the morning.'

'That's okay, I'll walk her home.'

She'd love him to, really. Her feet throbbed like a bitch from standing most of the day on the kitchen tiles, not to mention the night before while she made the cake and prepared food. Exhaustion layered over the wild turbulence of the day.

She loved her family. Loved having them around. Sometimes, she loved to see the back of them too. They seemed to have almost taken up residence in her home lately. Why hers? Why did they always make a beeline for her house, her food, her wine?

That was a little unfair, as Alexis and Sarah had contributed food-wise, in a fashion, and Graham had dropped off a mixed case of wines, albeit only to smooth over Tess's upset and gloss over his guilt.

'It's fine. I can do it. I'll take my phone with me. I haven't had very much to drink at all. Besides, I want to check on her, just me and her alone. I'm worried about her, Craig.'

He rubbed, one handed, across her shoulders and she let out a small groan as the sting of her own sunburn made itself known.

Alexis and Sarah had already gone and the kids were upstairs, Toni in bed. They'd let Tess sleep it off for a while, but the sun was starting to set and they all had work in the morning.

Craig's fingernails glinted Barbie-pink as he reached for his mug of tea.

Bobbi nodded at them. 'I don't have any nail varnish remover. How are you going to get that off before tomorrow?'

He slanted a narrow-eyed stare at her. 'I hope you're kidding.'

She broke into a grin and leaned into him, head swirling just a little with the three glasses of wine she'd consumed throughout the afternoon. She was such a lightweight. 'I'm joking. I knew Toni would want to put nail varnish on someone. Tess wasn't about to let her ruin her manicure. Alexis doesn't have the tolerance to sit still, and Sarah preferred the dark red. Toni always wants to do pink.'

Craig dropped the tea-towel and wrapped his arms around her, resting his chin on the top of her head. 'She's had a good day. All things considered.'

'Who, Tess?' She had her doubts. Her older sister had been full of gracious appreciation and, true to her word, she'd acted surprised with her present. But that's what it was. An act.

'No, Toni. She had fun. Your sisters are great with her.'

'They are, aren't they?' She smoothed a hand over his garish Hawaiian shirt. 'It turned out so much better than I'd imagined.'

He pressed another kiss above her ear and whispered, 'It helps when the prick isn't here.'

Bobbi laughed and made to pull away, but he hauled her back into his arms. 'Don't get chatting and stay all night. I'll wait up until you get back.'

She patted his chest and moved away. If she wanted to get back, she needed to get going. 'Hopefully, Graham will be back home and I can pass her over to him.'

Strained lines creased Craig's face. 'Don't count on it.'

'Sorry?'

He was serious.

'What do you mean?'

'You must know he's having an affair.'

She took a step back, her hand going to the throb at the base of her neck. 'Graham? He's not.' She wanted Craig to deny it.

'Bobbi, bab, all the signs are there. He's lost weight, been working out. I haven't seen him look that fit for the past twenty years. He had that shiny stuff you women like to put on your face.'

'Moisturiser?' Her response was automatic, but her lips were frozen as she whispered the word. Craig was right, Graham's face had been shiny and pretty smooth for a man of his age.

'Perhaps it was just sun cream.'

'Sun cream. Right. Because a man in his position puts sun

cream on to go to a meeting, with a freshly laundered shirt, a pink tie and suit trousers. Mark my words, if he's not having an affair, bab, then I'm Santa Claus.'

Bobbi dropped her face into her hands and shook her head. 'Oh, no. How's she going to handle this?'

56

Arm in arm, Tess and Bobbi weaved their way along to Tess's house, Bobbi mainly just propping her sister up as they talked in hushed voices.

'Will Graham be home by now?' She bloody well hoped so. If not, they were going to be having words. It wasn't good enough. She should have let Sarah have at it before. She wanted to. She was gutsy enough to.

There was something slightly off-kilter with her younger sister, though, and she'd seemed more emotional than her normal warrior-like self. Bobbi hadn't wanted her to wade in, in case she got hurt in the fallout.

'Who knows?'

'You do have a door key, just in case? Don't you?'

Her sister stumbled to a halt, almost dragging Bobbi over. Didn't you bring yours?'

She stared at Tess in disbelief. 'Mine? Why would I bring mine? It's your house.'

Tess pulled her arm away from Bobbi and gave a small stagger on heels that were way too high for a garden party. Ones she'd kicked off for most of the day. 'We'll have to go back and get your key.' Her words ran into each other.

Bobbi snatched at her to stop her from stumbling. 'We're almost there, Tess. Let's check if he's home first.'

'He's not going to be there.' Tess's words tumbled slurred from her lips. 'I just know it.'

'Shall we wait and see?'

Knowing Tess was incapable of inputting the code into the security gate, Bobbi did it for her.

She guided her along the path, their feet slowing as they approached Tess's house and the police car parked outside under the pale glow of the streetlight.

They both stuttered to a halt as two police officers stepped from the car.

'Mrs Leaming?'

Wordless, Tess dropped her hand from Bobbi's arm and stepped forward, her hands twisting together, anxiety pulsing from her as she nodded.

A heavy pressure settled on Bobbi's chest so the air she pulled in was strained and thick with an unknown fear.

'Mrs Leaming. I'm PC Darren Sutton, and this is PC Julie Hardiman.' He glanced around at the empty twilit street. 'Can we go inside, please?'

'Inside?' Tess raised her hand to a forehead wrinkled with confusion. 'I haven't got my key.'

Bobbi stepped forward and pushed aside the growing fear as she pulled together her knowledge and experience of working with the police on all levels. 'Hi, I'm Bobbi Channing. I'm Tess's sister. It's Tess's special birthday today and we've been celebrating.' The officers' faces dropped, and the sense of foreboding grew. 'Tess is a little the worse for wear. We've not got the house key, but I'm sure Graham, her husband, is home and he'll let us in.'

She was already convinced he wasn't from the absence of his large, vulgar, overpriced car.

'I'm afraid that's not possible.' PC Hardiman stepped closer and touched a hand to Tess's elbow. 'Mrs Leaming. Tess. Would you like to come and sit in the police car?'

'I haven't done anything.' The words burst from her sister's lips, but she didn't pull away.

Bobbi anticipated her sister's next move and grabbed her arm as Tess's legs started to give way.

Between herself and the officer, they half-lifted Tess the few steps to the open door of the police vehicle and lowered her onto the front seat.

With weak knees of her own, Bobbi slumped against the back door of the car. 'What's happened?'

The question came from her, but PC Hardiman never took her attention from Tess as she crouched down in front of her. 'I'm very sorry to tell you that your husband, Graham Leaming, has been involved in a car crash.'

Tess's hand went to her mouth. 'Oh, oh, no.'

Bobbi pushed away from the car and circled around to face the PC. 'Is he okay? Where is he?'

The PC's complete stillness flagged up that Graham wasn't okay. Bobbi's stomach churned and she glanced at her sister. Her pale face glowed in the lamplight.

A sickening tickle started in the back of Bobbi's knees and crawled up her legs as a cold sweat broke out across her forehead and heat rushed up her neck, sending her mind into a complete fugue. She pressed the back of her hand against her mouth and nose and took in long, slow breaths as her knees buckled and she let herself slide down the side of the car until she rested on her haunches.

'I'm sorry to tell you, Mrs Leaming. Your husband is dead.'

A thin lamenting wail slipped from Tess's lips, and she fell forward from the car as Bobbi twisted and caught her in her arms. She hugged Tess's slender body tight against hers as her backside hit the rough tarmac and Tess fell on top of her.

Tess pushed away, but the scalding wet splatter of vomit hit Bobbi's white linen trousers as her sister's body purged itself of two bottles of Prosecco, three gin and tonics, barbecued chicken, burgers, chilli con carne and trifle.

Bobbi's own stomach rebelled but she held on as she rolled away and to her knees and then pushed to her feet.

'Oh, Bobbi, Bobbi. I'm so sorry.' With tears and desperation, her sister's voice warbled out as she stood, swaying as sick dribbled in a string from her lips.

Without thought for herself, or the sanctity of her clothes, Bobbi took Tess into her grip again. This time not as tight. She rubbed her hand over Tess's back and soothed her, like a mother with a hurt child. 'Shh, it's okay, don't worry. It's okay.'

57

If she closed her eyes, the world swirled with gathering clouds of black thunder. Despite puking her guts up all over her younger sister, the alcohol still swam through her veins with barbed fins.

She removed the cool flannel from her forehead and blinked her eyes into focus.

They thought she hadn't taken in what they'd told her, but she had.

He was dead. Her husband, Graham Leaming. Dead.

Shock had rendered her motionless. She barely remembered them ushering her into the police car and bringing her back to Bobbi's house. She did remember Bobbi insisting she, herself, was going to walk home, the sour smell of sick clinging to her.

By the time the police had navigated the road system and Bobbi had used the slip through, they arrived at her house at almost the same time, with Craig standing in the open doorway waiting to let them in, having obviously been told by Bobbi over the phone as she walked home.

Bobbi sat opposite her now on the small footstool Tess had propped her feet on all afternoon, a thin grey dressing-gown wrapped around her. Her hair still wet from the shower she'd taken as Tess had sat with the police officers in silence.

Craig leaned forward in his armchair, his elbows on his knees, his hands dangling between them, fingers linked. He'd dragged on the shorts he'd been wearing earlier, together with the incongruous Hawaiian shirt, so out of place now.

She didn't care.

She was numb. From the tips of her fingers clutching the shredded tissue, all the way through to her ice-cold heart.

'I was so angry with him.'

PC Sutton rolled his shoulders forward. 'Angry?'

Tess caught the warning look from her sister, but it didn't make any difference. Graham had been in an accident. She had nothing to do with it. Her guilt for all the savage thoughts she'd had about him deserting her on her special day wanted to spew from her lips, just as her vomit had earlier. A savage, hot frothing torrent of fury.

'It's my fiftieth birthday today and Graham decided he was going to work.'

PC Hardiman nodded, compassion softening her features as she shuffled into a more comfortable position on Bobbi's sagging sofa. 'It's quite natural to feel this way under the circumstances. Does he normally work on a Sunday?'

Tess lowered her head, refusing to meet her sister's stare. There were things sometimes you didn't even share with your sister. 'He's been very busy lately. Working late. Working weekends. Staying away overnight. Trying to catch up with things. I think he has an important client he's trying to impress.'

Fleeting doubt flickered over their faces. She caught it before it was gone. Satisfied she'd got her point over without having to ram it home. Because that would never do.

The crash was an accident. She didn't need to cast any kind of suspicion on herself by raising the issue of her knowledge of his affair. That might rattle cages. For all they knew, Tess had no knowledge of another woman. That's the way she wanted it to stay. She may be drunk, but she wasn't unaware. She wasn't stupid either.

She stretched forward and picked up her mug, the black coffee sloshing over the sides onto Bobbi's patterned carpet. She rubbed it in with the sole of her stupidly high, toe-pinching sandal that she'd worn just to impress her husband because he'd always liked her ankles. It wouldn't matter. Bobbi wouldn't care. The kids made a bad enough mess of her carpets. One more splash wouldn't matter. Craig would use the carpet cleaner on it, once again.

She held onto the mug with both hands and raised it to her lips, hesitating for just a moment. 'How did you say it happened?'

Her brain might be fuzzy, but she was pretty sure of what they'd told her earlier. It didn't harm to have it confirmed again.

'Your husband's car seems to have left the road at speed and crashed straight into a lime tree.'

Tess wondered at the relevance of the type of tree. Did it make a difference? Was the trunk of a lime tree less yielding than say an oak, or a willow?

'Didn't his airbags go off?'

PC Sutton nodded, his tone bleak. 'I'm afraid in certain cases, it doesn't make a difference and we don't want to make any assumptions at this stage, not until the coroner gives us the right information.'

She rattled the mug back onto the table and rubbed the flannel over the back of her neck. 'Was anyone else involved?'

What she really wanted to ask was 'Was his little slut in the car with him? Had she survived, or was she dead too?' She held back. Let them come forward with any information they had. She was admitting to nothing. Whatever had happened, it had nothing to do with her and she refused to become embroiled. After all, she didn't want her name dragged through mud if it came to light that her husband had been having an affair.

'No. It appears not. His car just left the road, of its own volition. He was driving along Pensnett Road. It doesn't appear as though any other vehicle was involved. The road was very quiet.'

Bobbi's face screwed up and she leaned forward into their circle. 'I thought he was going to meet someone at work. That's the wrong direction from here to his office. What was he doing in Pensnett Road?'

Her sister turned a confused face to her, and Tess's blood ran cold. For god's sake. Don't interfere, Bobbi. Keep your big, enquiring, social worker mouth shut.

Tess let out a guttural howl and buried her face in her hands, letting the tears come naturally. It wasn't an act. She was devastated. Her husband of the past twenty-eight years was dead.

'I don't know. I don't know what he was doing there.' She raised her head and peered through her tears at the others. 'I don't understand. Maybe he was meeting them at their house.' She turned to the officers. 'He's a... he was a wealth manager. It wouldn't have been unusual for him to go to someone's house. I don't know...' She paused, her shaking fingers touching her lips. 'Does it matter?'

'Probably not.' PC Hardiman's voice soothed over her hysteria. 'Tess, you say that it was your special birthday. Was your husband drinking before he left?'

Tess snorted. He'd barely let his backside touch the garden chair before he was up and off. He only drank his tea and ate a small slice of that beautiful rainbow cake because Sarah had given him the stink eye.

'No.' She shook her head. 'He had a cup of tea, and then left. He'd not had any alcohol. Not when he left here. What time did it... what time was the accident?'

'Umm...' PC Hardiman looked down at her notes. 'We were called just after 3 p.m.'

'Oh.' Tess flopped back in her chair. 'Well, he'd barely even left here. How far along Pensnett Road was he?' Instead of waiting for the officer to answer, Tess turned to her sister and brother-in-law, who sat in silence now. 'We must have made him late for his appointment. He was in a panic, I could tell from the way he kept tugging at his collar.'

It was a bloody hot day and the foolish man still insisted on wearing a suit and tie. Typical wealth manager. All about the presentation.

It could have been more to do with the way Sarah kept piercing him with an evil look.

'Oh, no. He wasn't speeding, was he?' She knew he did all too frequently, just stepped on the accelerator and flew ten miles over the speed limit. She'd often pulled him up on it.

PC Hardiman tucked her chin down and gave her a sympathetic look from under lowered brows. 'Tess...' She noticed how the officer kept repeating her name to keep her grounded, she assumed. 'It's natural to ask questions at a time like this. However, we'll obviously be undertaking an investigation and until such a time as the post-mortem has been carried out and we have more information, we can tell you very little.'

PC Hardiman leaned forward and touched her on her knee. 'I am so sorry for your loss, Tess. If there's anything we can do for you, any questions you have over the next few days, please call us.'

Tess let the tremors shudder on because right now, she wasn't upset, she wasn't devastated.

She was seething.

58

Oh gosh, oh gosh, oh gosh, oh gosh, oh gosh! I hadn't meant for it to happen that way. I never thought through for one moment the consequences of my actions.

Was it, in fact, my actions that were the cause of Graham's death? Or was it because he was simply driving too fast and hit a tree?

I scrunch my eyes shut, not wanting to think about that.

I'm twisting my fingers together, literally wringing my hands. What the hell had possessed me to do such a thing? Like everything I've done so far, it hadn't been planned. Not to the nth degree. It had been a knee-jerk reaction to his refusal to stay for the party. The inconsiderate bastard.

I've started to recognise that red haze that comes down, understand what's going to happen when my fury takes over. It doesn't give me any more control over it. Not before and not on this occasion either.

What a let-down for everyone. There wasn't a single person there unaffected by his insensitive decision and action. Even the children were confused, asking questions. Why wasn't Uncle Graham staying? I mean, really, the disappointment on their faces. They'd already accepted that their cousin, who they all look up to as he's the eldest, wasn't going to make it. Another thoughtless being. Like father, like son. He'd put his own desires first. Never mind that his mum would be celebrating her fiftieth.

In a way, though, he could be forgiven for his youth and impetuosity.

Not so his dad, who should know better.

There's a line you draw in the sand for these kinds of things. I've never trusted the man. I mean, if he could destroy one wife, he'd not think twice about tearing down another. They weren't precious to him, merely a commodity who, once they outlived their youth and attraction, were a disposable asset.

All the same, I'm now regretting what I did.

The one saving grace was that he never hurt anyone else when he drove his car off the road and straight into that tree. And that's really set me back a moment because, until now, I never considered that in taking Graham out, I would endanger anybody else's life.

That can't happen again. I'm not a cold-blooded murderer. I just want to keep people safe.

Children safe, to be more specific.

Not that Graham had been a threat to children. He didn't even particularly like them.

Unlike the rash of paedophiles I've recently dispatched.

Graham was different from the others. Not necessarily evil in the same sense of the word, but the harm he was about to wreak was inconceivable. I'd just needed to get rid of him in the best, most economical way before he destroyed everything.

You wouldn't know it, but I've never really liked him. As a rule, I wouldn't wish any ill on him, not until I understood the full extent of what he was about to do. Family are the one thing. Protect them on all counts.

Don't mess with mine.

Normally I wouldn't kill for it. But on this occasion, with this man, I made an exception.

59

Bobbi closed her eyes and rested her head on the back of the sofa. Exhaustion had her head spinning. By the time the police had left and she'd consoled her sister and then the children had woken, she'd not even had the chance to put her head on the pillow.

She considered whether to go and join Tess where she'd tucked her into her bed, but the moment she went up there, one of the kids was bound to want her attention. She'd fed them all at lunchtime, but their appetites were insatiable. They'd probably all be back shortly for more food.

She didn't have the heart to send Tess back to her own empty house. How could she?

They'd not managed to get hold of Tess's son. Until he checked in with them, he was out of range.

Her head pounded. She was dizzy with tiredness.

She'd stumbled on through the day, sending Josh out in charge of a McDonald's breakfast, guilt gnawing at her as she was torn between looking after Tess who'd turned into a strand of over-cooked spaghetti and seemed to flop, lifeless, onto the bed.

It was strange how resilient children were. They were shocked, moved to tears. They treated their Aunty Tess with such gentle reverence. But in the short-lived memory of children, life went on. Energy needed to be expended, food consumed.

Perhaps she should have sent them all to school, but under the circumstances, they'd be better at home. At least for today.

Bobbi had no appetite. She hadn't the least interest in eating.

She could do with losing a stone in weight, but this wasn't about to do it for her. She pretty much knew that once everyone went to bed tonight, she'd raid the cupboards for that giant bag of crisps she'd stowed away where no one could find it. In the slow cooker she only used in the winter. It was the one place she could guarantee the kids wouldn't look. She'd have to pull the stool out so she could reach into the top cupboard above the oven.

Craig knew where her hidey-hole was, but he wouldn't dream of taking her emergency supply of comfort food. They both pretended it didn't exist. Just like she pretended not to know Craig still sneaked the occasional cigarette when he was stressed. He'd given them up over ten years ago, but from time to time, the stale scent of them clung to his clothes. She knew it wasn't regular. She could almost pinpoint the exact moment he would light up. When his truck was delayed at the port, when he'd stood for an hour or so in the rain waiting for one of the boys to finish their football match. When his brother-in-law had just died.

The numbness from the shock had worn off to the extent that she'd started to think of practicalities.

She probably needed to go back to work tomorrow. Her team had been sympathetic as she doled out her workload, but they'd be swamped all week and she needed to set in place a care order for a three-year-old and six-year-old.

The Anslow court case, where the stepfather had abused the children, needed to be prepped and she was the only one who could do it. She was the one who'd carried out all the interviews

Her stomach had churned at the obscene things those children had been subjected to, so by the end, she'd not wanted to be in the same room as him. Pure evil.

She could only hope that justice would be served.

The flutter of her heart roused her and she opened her eyes as heat filled her core and spread like a wildfire, shooting through her veins and exploding from her hairline. Dear god, she hated this whole menopause lark. She needed to do something about it because it was driving her insane.

Her mind clutched onto sanity, fingernails scratching at raw nerves as she surged to her feet.

The forgotten cold mug of coffee she'd cradled on her lap hit the carpet to join the dried splashes from Tess's coffee the night before.

She needed to get the carpet cleaned while the weather was so fantastic, but for the life of her, she really couldn't be arsed.

A small groan slipped from her lips as she bent to retrieve the mug and a wash of dizziness swept over her, almost sending her crashing headfirst into that coffee-stained carpet.

She staggered a little, righted herself and then wandered to the open sliding patio doors to lean on them and stare at their pathetic excuse for a garden. Wiping the sweat from her forehead, she contemplated how much time she had before the children came crashing back in.

Shanna had taken Toni with her.

Silence hung like a white shroud.

The bright peal of the front doorbell almost shot Bobbi through the ceiling.

'Christ!'

It wouldn't be the kids, they'd have just charged in around the back. She'd hear them coming from a mile off.

Delivery people didn't ring the doorbell any more. They simply dumped and ran.

The dark shadows of two people wavered through the frosted glass of the front door.

Bobbi swung it wide, surprise popping wide weary eyes.

'Hi.'

Nerves jumped at the sight of their serious faces. She placed her hand over her thrumming heart.

'PC Hardiman, PC Sutton. I wasn't expecting you.'

PC Hardiman stepped forward. 'Is Tess here, Bobbi?'

With a self-conscious upward flick of her eyes, Bobbi nodded. 'She's still in bed.'

PC Hardiman sent her a tight smile. 'Can we come in?'

As though coming out of a coma herself, Bobbi jumped. 'Of course, of course.' She stepped back to allow them through.

Both officers stepped inside, PC Sutton closing the door behind him.

In the tight squeeze of the darkened hallway, claustrophobia tightened a fist around Bobbi's throat and another hot flush rode the waves, crawling just beneath her skin.

She turned on her heel and made her way through to the living room and the open patio doors. She needed air, she needed to breathe. She'd rather mask how panic-stricken their unexpected visit had made her.

In the open doorway, she turned, dabbing the back of her hand over a sweat-beaded upper lip.

'If you wouldn't mind, could you go and wake Tess? We need to talk with her.' The officer's voice was gentle, but firm.

'Do I have to disturb her?' Bobbi glanced at the wall clock. It was almost 4 p.m. Good god, where had the time gone? Evaporated. She must have been asleep for almost an hour and a half herself. No wonder the coffee had turned cold. Her limbs turned sluggish.

'We would appreciate it if you would.'

'Isn't there something I can help you with? She really needs to rest. The stress has knocked her completely off her feet.'

'Bobbi.' PC Hardiman stepped forward and touched a hand to Bobbi's overheated bare arm. 'We need you to get Tess for us, now.' Her voice strengthened, became more forceful. 'We've had the report back from the post-mortem. The toxicology report, too. We have questions only she can answer.'

60

'An overdose? Of Viagra?'

Tess wilted into the overstuffed armchair Craig usually inhabited. Wrinkles normally smoothed over with heavy moisturiser and good make-up wreaked havoc across a forehead still bearing yesterday's make-up.

'I'm sorry.' PC Hardiman took a seat on the settee while PC Sutton stood by the open doorway, perhaps also trying to catch a rare waft of cooling air.

Bobbi had managed to quickly splash icy water over a puffy face in the upstairs bathroom while waiting for Tess to rouse herself. She didn't dare apply moisturiser herself, that would look too obvious and shallow. It wasn't about outward presentations. Was it?

Was it better to look cool, calm and collected? Or was it preferable to fall apart and let the cracks show? On a professional level, Bobbi presented herself with quiet authority. Right now, her insides were shaking apart and the reflection of that had to show on her face.

Tess's features had crumpled with confusion. 'I don't understand. Why was there Viagra in his bloodstream?' She darted her gaze first at Bobbi and then between the two police officers. Her voice dropped to an embarrassed whisper. 'He doesn't take Viagra.'

A wash of scarlet flooded her face and neck and Tess dragged in laboured breath after breath, in peril of hyperventilating. The choking sounds coming from her warned Bobbi that her sister was in the middle of a meltdown.

Helpless to do anything about it, Bobbi slipped onto the chair arm and rubbed her sister's back in soft circular motions. 'It's okay, Tess. Breathe in, slowly. Slow down.'

'I'm going to faint. I'm going to faint.'

'Head between your knees.' Bobbi guided her sister's head down, feeling the resistance in the steel of her sister's spine. 'You're not going to faint. Just hold on. Breathe nice and slow for me.'

She glanced up at PC Sutton. 'Would you mind grabbing a glass of water for her?' She almost asked for one for herself, too, but decided that wouldn't be right. She could hang on. She'd make them all a cup of tea in a minute when she got her own shock under control.

PC Sutton returned and pressed the glass of water into Tess's shaking hand as she came upright. Her face florid and strained, her hair a wild mess.

Bobbi had never seen her sister like this. Even when she went into labour with her son, Tess had seemed to keep her composure, only letting the F-bomb slip once. The air had been blue when Bobbi gave birth. Well, when she gave birth to Toni. She'd been the most challenging. And one other time.

PC Sutton looked around for somewhere to sit and Bobbi leaned forward to drag the footstool out. He perched on the edge. Legs too long came almost up to his ears. Under any other circumstances, Bobbi would have laughed. Felt the need to now but recognised it as hysteria.

She kept her hand on Tess's back. The mere contact comforted her and, from the slowing down of Tess's breathing, seemed to be working for her sister too.

Instead of waiting for Tess to ask the questions, Bobbi surged forward. She wanted to know what had happened.

'So, what exactly are you telling us?'

PC Hardiman leaned forward in her seat, intense eyes searching Tess's face. 'According to the coroner, your husband had a considerable quantity of phosphodiesterase in his bloodstream. Well above the normal level for this drug.' She nodded her head from side to side, as though she was waiting for something. An answer. A response. 'Viagra.'

Tess cupped the glass of water in both hands and took a sip. As she lowered it, she cast Bobbi a quick sideways glance before she spoke. 'I don't understand. Viagra.' It stuck on her tongue as though she had no idea what it was. But she did. Everyone had heard of Viagra, hadn't they? Even if they didn't use it. Inappropriately, it was plastered on adverts on the TV at what seemed like any given hour of the day.

Tess scooted forward to the edge of the chair and Bobbi's hand fell away. 'I don't understand why my husband would have Viagra in his system.'

Bobbi recognised this woman. Here she was. Her big sister, composure slipping back in place like a close-fitting glove. She ran a hand through her hair, smoothing it into place as could only be done with a perfect haircut. She sat taller in her seat.

'PC Hardiman. PC... Sutton.' She pursed her lips before she continued. 'Never has my husband taken or required Viagra in the whole of our married life.'

The slow smoulder of anger in Tess's voice resonated through her voice as she stared at one then the other of them, including Bobbi.

Aware that Tess might be embarrassed at the personal informa tion about a sex life they'd never discussed, Bobbi wriggled on the armchair next to her. She didn't want to know about her sister's sex life. She did know Tess didn't sleep in the same room as her deceased husband. Hadn't for several years. It was nothing to do with Bobbi. The fact that Craig and Bobbi still slept in the same bed and had regular sex, albeit muted because of the children, had nothing to do with anyone else either. Craig didn't need Viagra. Just a wink of her eye, a tilt of her head and he was up for it.

'Why would my husband take Viagra if he was on his way to an important client meeting?'

Tess dropped her hands and the glass of water hit the carpet with the rest of the liquid that had been poured over that spot during the last sixteen hours.

She surged to her feet, clapping both hands over her mouth. The high colour of a moment ago seeped from her skin to leave a grey mask in place. 'Oh, no! No, no, no. He was not having an affair. Tell me he was not!' She turned stricken eyes on the police officers.

A little too stricken.

Don't overdo it, Tess, Bobbi thought.

PC Hardiman stood up and wrapped a gentle hand around Tess's arm. 'I'm really sorry, Tess, we don't know that information at this stage. What we do know is that according to his secretary, there were no appointments in his diary for yesterday.'

Tess turned. Her face roiled with confusion and anger. 'I don't understand.'

'Tess... your husband had around four times the normal amount of this drug in his system. I have no idea whether he took it recreationally, but what I have been told by the coroner is that this was the likely cause of his death. It appears he had a heart attack and that's the reason his car careered off the road and into that tree.' She smoothed her hand over Tess's arm as Bobbi sat in shocked silence.

What a way to find out your husband was having an affair.

How humiliating.

What would they tell everyone?

Tess's face had set. Bobbi imagined it was as numb as hers felt. She cleared her throat. 'Why would he take so many?'

Tess shook her head. 'He wouldn't. Graham had a heart condition.'

Bobbi's brows shot up. Surprise rippled through her and set off another hot flush so her brain fog thickened. 'I didn't know that.' She stared at her sister. 'I'm sure you haven't mentioned it.' She couldn't keep the inflection of insult from her voice. Tess told her everything, didn't she? Apart from her sex life, which Bobbi didn't want to know about. But who knew Graham had a heart condition?

Tess shook her head as she circled around and walked towards the patio doors. She wrapped her arms around herself and spoke over her shoulder.

'He'd been diagnosed with tachycardia a few months ago. He was due to have an operation in a few months once the rhythm had become stable.' She turned from the doorway. 'What a stupid man. Why would he deliberately take Viagra? Surely that can't be healthy for a man with a dodgy heart?'

'Not in that quantity,' PC Hardiman replied.

Bobbi pushed herself up and swayed a little. She shoved back on the tiredness as she faced the police officer who continued speaking. 'I'm no expert on the drug, but I certainly know the coroner believes that the amount taken played a major part in Mr Leaming's death.'

Tess turned from the window. 'Then did someone kill him?'

61

Tess took a sip of Graham's single-malt whisky. The one he'd paid a fortune for and refused to open. Well, she'd opened it now. There was no one to stop her.

All three of her sisters sat nursing their own tipple of whisky in Tess's house. Bobbi wouldn't drink hers. She didn't like whisky. Alexis would down hers in one go, just to get rid of the stuff, and Sarah... Sarah would take a sip and put it to one side, because Sarah still nursed her secret.

Tess knew what it would be. Sarah was obviously pregnant. Yesterday she didn't want to steal Tess's birthday thunder. Today, she didn't want Graham's untimely and inconsiderate death to overshadow her exciting news.

Sarah had always put her own news on the backburner, used to being second fiddle to Alexis, who overshadowed every happy moment the youngest of them had.

Inconsiderate had always been the description for that man. He'd overshadowed her even more.

Alexis's glass clinked against the glass-topped table and made them all wince. There was something about Alexis. Ham-handed, their mum used to call her when they were little. Now it would be considered a lack of spatial awareness. Downright clumsy was the truth.

Tess wasn't like Bobbi. Tolerant and so very PC. That's the kind of continuing education Bobbi had in the social services. She wasn't so much the job, the job was her. She'd drifted her way into it after having Josh, when she'd found it so difficult to breastfeed. Thinking initially she must be abnormal. There was something wrong with her. There was nothing wrong. Women have difficulties. Women suffer guilt. Bobbi had been stronger than that. She'd taken matters into her own hands and formed a group for women having difficulties. She'd received and given guidance. She'd ended up going to university to get her degree in social work. She'd be finished with her Master's soon, too. How the hell she managed to fit it all in, Tess would never know.

Tess stared at her sister. Bobbi wasn't perfect by any means, but Tess envied her the family she had, the husband she'd married. If not for Craig's continual support, Bobbi would still be working in Tesco. She was intelligent enough to have made it to manager by now, possibly shifting over to HR as her personality would have suited that. It suited social worker even more.

Alexis shifted again. Uncomfortable in the silence that had formed. Out of respect? Discomfort?

'So.' Tess decided the time was right. 'You all know now. As much as the police told Bobbi and me, at least. Graham had a heart attack caused by an overdose of Viagra and crashed his car into a tree. He would possibly have been okay. The airbags all deployed, but a tree is, by the police account, very unforgiving.'

'An overdose even more so.' Alexis leaned forward and scooped the glass from Bobbi's hand, downing her drink too. 'What?' She addressed them all, hands wide. 'She wasn't going to drink it. If you want us to enjoy a drink, at least get the good stuff out.'

'It's £300 a bottle.'

Sarah's eyes went wide and she handed hers to Alexis. 'I don't want it.'

Alexis swigged that too, screwing up her face. 'Just shows, shit is shit, no matter how much it cost.'

'Alexis.' The reproach in Bobbi's voice had Alexis shooting Tess an apologetic look.

'Sorry.' She placed the glass on the table next to the other two while Tess sipped at hers, holding the heat on her tongue and letting the flames lick up her nose. She liked it. Always had. The soft tones of this one would ensure oblivion later, without the hangover in the morning. She wanted oblivion, just for tonight. Then she needed to get her shit together, because there was no way she was about to take the blame for her husband's mistake.

'Why would he take so many pills? Was it deliberate or did he make a mistake?' Sarah turned confused eyes onto Tess.

About to answer, Tess started to shrug, but Alexis cut in. 'No way would he do that deliberately. The tablets in his system shouldn't be taken until you actually need them. They give you an instant hard-on.'

'Alexis.'

'Well, for god's sake, Bobbi. It's true. I had a boyfriend once.'

'Many,' muttered Sarah under her breath.

Alexis coughed. 'He needed a little assistance in that area, you know.'

Tess put her hand to her forehead. 'Too much information.'

'No. Listen. I'm just trying to clear something up, here. If we wanted sex, he popped a pill and hey presto. Immediate reaction. Different ones respond differently, but from what you say, he had those instant reacting ones you pop under your tongue and bingo!'

'Sounds like he had a full house.'

'Sarah!'

Her sisters were getting out of hand. It wasn't funny. But then again, how else were they supposed to react?

It was surreal.

'Why would he take them? He was supposed to be visiting a client,' Tess appealed to her sisters.

Sarah bit her lip as though holding back another quip.

They all fell silent, a mutual sympathy riding their emotions.

She knew why. She knew about his mistress, but she wasn't about to admit that to anyone, including her sisters. Tell no one. Trust no one. She was not going to risk ending up in prison like her mum. The whole family were going to be labelled jailbirds at this rate.

'The police think he may have been going to an assignation.' Bobbi's quiet voice broke the silence. 'Tess had no idea.'

'I didn't know he was having an affair. I thought he was going to a business appointment.' She breathed out through her nose, the heat of the whisky stinging her nostrils and bringing tears unbidden to her eyes, though they served their purpose.

'Was he definitely having an affair?'

'Why else would you take Viagra?'

'Well, did he take them by mistake? Think they were something else?' Sarah looked around at the rest of them. 'Sweeties. Did he pick them up at your house, Bobbi, thinking they were sweets?'

Affronted, Bobbi rounded on her sister. 'He certainly did not. Apart from the fact that we don't need any help on that front,' she glared at Alexis as she snickered, 'I wouldn't dream of leaving any medication lying around. We keep ours in a locked medicine cabinet. We are responsible adults!'

'Of course you do. Of course you are,' Tess felt the need to intercede. Although why she felt the need to defend anyone was beyond her. She was simply weary and now, ready for them all to go. Go, so she could be left alone with her own thoughts. 'I'm sure Sarah didn't mean it that way.'

'Then what way?' Bobbi snapped, and then instantly looked contrite. 'Oh, I'm sorry, Tess. We're trying to help, but I think we may be making the situation worse.'

'How much worse can it be? My husband is dead. My son hasn't contacted me in the last four days and I've just found out that Graham may well have been having an affair. The police are looking into that, and there's definite finger-pointing going on that he either took an overdose or someone slipped him a Mickey Finn. I don't think anything any of you can say will make matters worse than they already are.'

Exhausted by her own outburst, Tess slumped back and slugged her drink down, regretting it immediately as the blaze hit her lungs. She sat forward, spluttering, and instantly her three sisters crowded around patting her head, her shoulders, her back as hot tears streamed down her cheeks and deep gulping sobs tore from her throat.

'Graham, oh, Graham. Why?' She shrugged off the hands and leaped to her feet. 'Why would he do that to me? Humiliate me. Make people believe I'm a lesser wife, that he had to find another avenue of satisfaction. I hate him.' Her voice strangled from her throat and she launched the heavy Waterford crystal glass into the fireplace.

It exploded in a shatter of sparkling glass at the same time her temper did.

'Bastard!'

62

I've often wondered why you would ever trust anyone with your deepest, darkest secret.

I mean, let's face it. Can you trust anyone with absolute authority other than yourself?

Mum always ingrained in us, 'Never put anything in writing; Never tell anyone where you hid the body.'

Isn't that the best advice ever?

I mean, really!

I thought it was a joke. Seems I was wrong.

For a time, I thought I could trust my sisters. I thought I'd be able to call them and say, 'Hey, I've accidentally killed someone,' and they'd reply, 'I'll bring a shovel.'

Turns out, that was a misconception. Much as I adore each one of them with their flaws and idiosyncrasies, I know now I cannot trust them with my secret.

Take Mum as testimony to that theory. Would any of them have lied on her behalf? No, they didn't.

I did.

Then again, she didn't give me any choice in the matter. She took me to one side on that horrific night and told me I was never to breathe a word to anyone. Not one single person.

Here's the thing, though. When I'm entrusted with a secret, I'm going to take it to the grave with me. Yep. All the way.

But that doesn't mean to say I'm not going to action it. Because, let's face it, there's a reason my mum told me her latest secret. She wanted me to do something with that information, because she's not willing or capable of taking action herself.

It doesn't make her a weak person. She's incarcerated.

It makes me strong.

No one wants to know what I did with that secret. They never will.

It's done. I'm sure, in the long run, the benefits will show. Right now, maybe not so much. Although, I do believe with Graham being in wealth management, he was extremely well insured. Why wouldn't he be?

I'm quite sure matters will work themselves out.

We'll wait and see.

63

Sarah stood on the doorstep, a hand softly cradling the underside of her belly, her eyes filled with pain.

'I have something to tell you.'

Bobbi opened her arms wide and took her youngest sister in for a gentle cuddle, her hands rubbing soft circles over Sarah's back. 'Congratulations. What took you so long to tell me?' she whispered into her ear and gave her a kiss.

Sarah pulled back and gave her a quizzical stare. 'How did you know?'

Bobbi wondered what answer she had to that. There were so many. Numerous giveaways. 'I've had four – five,' she said remembering the precious one she had lost, 'babies of my own. You're my sister. I think it would be very remiss of me if I missed the fact that you've changed in little ways over the past few weeks.' She pulled back and cupped her sister's face in her hands. 'Are you coming in?'

Sarah made a quick glance up at the bedroom windows. 'Nah, they're all in bed and you need to get off too.'

'It's okay.' Bobbi reached for Sarah's hand.

From the shadows, two dark figures emerged.

Bobbi gripped her sister's hand, ready to yank her inside away from the imminent threat.

'Hi.'

Bobbi blew out a breath as Alexis slipped into the glow of the porch light, a tall, slender black woman by her side. Hands linked.

Alexis gave a quivering smile. 'I thought I'd catch you alone, but seeing as you're here too... what better time.' She cast her gaze at Sarah. 'I've got something to tell you.'

64

Bobbi let out a wide yawn and screwed up her face as she reached for her cup of tea.

Craig looked over from where he stood in front of the dish washer, putting the last of the clean dishes away in the cupboards.

'It's been a long day.'

'It's been a long month.'

Concern wreathed his face. 'Do you think you might be over doing it?'

Bobbi picked up her pen and tapped it on the paperwork she' piled at the side of her laptop.

'I don't know. I feel... exhausted. Stressed.'

Craig turned his back on the kitchen counter. Folding his arms he frowned at her and made her realise that she never showed he weaknesses. Never asked for help. Not from anyone. Not even he own husband.

They worked as a team, the cogs turned, not always smoothl They had a few bumps along the way, but never had she confesse to feeling stressed.

In all truth, she'd never felt like this before.

She rubbed the back of her neck. 'Tess told me to make an appointment to see the doctor. She reckons my hormones are going stir-crazy.'

Craig lifted an eyebrow. 'I think having your mum come out of prison, your brother-in-law die and your workload might have more to do with your stress.'

It sounded like he understood. He certainly was understanding.

How did she explain it to him? When people termed it 'going through the change', she'd never thought it actually meant that. Change. Turmoil, they should call it. Going through turmoil. Because she'd never felt so out of control, like a rollercoaster ride that just wouldn't stop doing loop-the-loops.

'I know. Tess has this expensive gel stuff she reckons made her feel better.'

Craig pushed away from the counter and came over. He pulled out the chair next to hers and sat on it, leaning his forearms on the kitchen table. 'You feel bad?'

Tears welled up in her and she couldn't believe how close she was to crying. 'I feel horrid, Craig. Like I'm not in control.'

He reached out, cupped one of her hands in his, but the terror on his face spoke volumes. He had no idea what to do to help her. He'd never had to help her before. She was the strong one. The kingpin. She was the one who kept the entire family together, not only their own children on the straight and narrow, but her sisters too, ever since their mum had been sent to prison. Despite losing her precious baby, she'd never lost the plot. Not then. Her control had been rigid.

She conjured up a weak smile that wobbled and faded. 'I'm slowing down.' She placed her hand on the pile of files to her right. 'Do you know, I don't tear through the work any more. It seems to have more meaning. I'm getting too involved. That's not healthy.'

'Have you spoken with your manager?'

She snorted. 'I speak with her and she goes off sick for another week. She can't stand the pressure.'

'They should promote you.'

'I don't think I could stand any more stress. Besides, I love what I do. The hands-on side of things. I wouldn't want to do admin all day long. No wonder Esther is going crazy.'

She fell silent for a long moment, holding on to him with fingers that were already starting to sweat. 'I sometimes feel I'm going crazy. I think I will see the doctor. Tess said HRT saved her sanity.'

'Really? She's crazy as a box of frogs.'

Bobbi laughed. 'Not as crazy as the rest of us.'

'I might just agree with you. What will she do, now, without Graham?'

'Have a nice life.'

'I know you shouldn't speak ill of the dead, but he was a twonker. Fancy overdosing on Viagra when you have a heart problem.'

'Poor man. I wonder what made him take so many.'

Craig laughed. 'Lust. A desperate desire to satisfy that younger woman he had on the go.'

'How do you know it was a younger woman?'

'Of course it was. It had to be. No other reason for all that late-night working, nights away and Viagra. I'm surprised you'd be so naïve.' He nodded at the files. 'Especially when you deal with family issues every day. There must be a great deal of that type of thing goes on with the families you deal with.'

She shrugged. 'Sometimes I hear too much.'

'Your older sister is going to be a rich widow. Perhaps I should run off with her.'

Bobbi smiled again. He'd washed over her weakness, not let it become a fear for either of them. Made her smile.

'Well, you won't be running off with Alexis. Not now, anyhow.'

'Who would have thought she'd change sides like that? Become a lesbian.'

Bobbi looked at him from under lowered brows. 'You do know you don't just "become" a lesbian, don't you?'

'Really?'

Bobbi hummed in the back of her throat.

'Did you know?' he asked her now.

Bobbi shrugged. 'Not really, but it wasn't a shock either. She's always had such tumultuous relationships with men. They never work out.'

'This one might not.'

'Possibly. Then again, I don't think I've ever seen Alexis so calm. I think Pippa may be good for her.' She looked at her husband. 'I liked her.'

He nodded. 'Me too.'

Craig reached out for her hand and gave it a light squeeze before he pushed away from the table and came to his feet. 'Interesting times ahead. For your whole family. All your sisters' lives are changing. I wonder how Sarah will cope with being a single mum.'

A small flutter of something akin to envy stirred in her. Not because she wanted another child, but perhaps she craved the time when her children were young. 'It was a brave decision for her to make, to go ahead with her pregnancy without involving anyone else.'

'Does she know who the father is?'

Bobbi sent him a long stare. Didn't he know? Hadn't they mentioned it in front of him?

'She went to a sperm bank.'

His mouth dropped open. Evidently, they hadn't told him.

'I'm so pleased. Our kids are going to have a cousin.'

'Another girl,' he grumbled. 'Outnumbered every bloody time.

Now there are only three males. There's going to be eight females. How will I cope?'

She grinned and picked up her almost tepid cup of tea. 'Like you always do.' She took a sip. 'You'll hide in the kitchen and cook for everyone. And there won't be eight, there'll be nine soon.'

'Your mum. Is she going to be here all the time?'

'I don't think so. She has her own flat. I suspect she's going to want some alone time.' She paused for a moment and slid in something she'd been meaning to say for a while. 'We need to furnish the flat for her before she moves in.'

'It's unfurnished?' His mouth dropped open.

'Well, yeah. It's cheaper that way. I said we would sort it.'

'And your sisters?'

'They're all contributing. She needs a new bed. Everything else, I think we can get off the marketplace on Facebook, or from the local charity shops. I think she'll be grateful for anything.'

He pulled a face. 'Anything you need, bab. Let me know.'

'I've been keeping an eye out for stuff. Can't get anything until we get the keys. They're going to let me have them tomorrow.'

'No wonder you're exhausted. Talking of being exhausted, I'd better get off, I've got an early pick-up tomorrow, and a long day.' He stood, pushed his chair under the table and then stepped around it to reach out and stroke a rough hand over her hair. 'Are you coming up, bab?'

turn my head and smile up at Craig as he cups my face with his
wide, rough palm. I love this man with a passion I could never
explain. He gave me my children. We raise them together. I would
die for them, kill for them. I already have.

I caress the back of his hand. 'You go to bed, you've got to be up
early. I'm just going to sit here a while and unwind.'

He leans forward and kisses me on the top of my head. A soft
affection as he scoffs. 'Unwind. You're going to read another file,
aren't you?'

I smile because he understands me so well. As well as anyone
can understand another human. Which is not necessarily as well as
we like to think.

With one last stroke of my cheek, he drops his hand and moves
away. 'Don't be late. You're overdoing it. Burning the candle at both
ends.'

'There's only one end to my candle.'

He lets out a low chuckle. 'I think there are a myriad of ends to
your candle, bab. You put your whole heart into your work, our
kids, your sisters...'

'You.'

'Me.' He smiles and bends forward to touch his lips to mine. 'Goodnight. Put your files away, now.'

'Just one more. Then I'll be up. Goodnight, love.'

I come to my feet as he disappears up the stairs and swipe up the glass of red wine still sitting on the kitchen table. There's a cool breeze wafting in from the Fens tonight and as I stand at the patio doors and sip my drink I feel my temperature come down a notch or two.

I've dotted little solar lights through the garden, highlighting my favourite bits. Though there aren't many well-tended parts in our little garden, the rockery at the bottom has done well this year. Plants that like dry arid earth normally struggle in our heavy clay based soil, but this year they've thrived. Campanula tumbles over the rocks and has started to creep its way across the small metal birdbath I brought home with me that night.

Funny how not one of them has commented on my acquisition. It's as though that little birdbath has always been there. Just a sweet little bowl, really. A little rusted and placed strategically on the ground to hide the fact that it has no base. No spike to drive into the ground. The solar light beside it casts a long shadow of the little metal bird on top across the lawn. A finger pointing at me.

There's no regret. That was a good day's work for me.

Messy. I wouldn't really want it that way again.

If I'd been brave enough to speak out all those years ago when he touched me, Alexis would never have been raped by that monster.

I would never have had to live my whole life with crippling guilt.

The guilt is still there, coating my existence, but so too is the satisfaction that I took action. Eventually.

You'd think it was my first time.

It wasn't.

Uncle Ricky was my first time.

That night when Mum and I arrived back home and there he was, his hand down my son's shorts.

It was the first time I saw red. I don't mean blood. I mean a red haze of absolute, utter fury.

I snatched my son from his arms and handed him to Mum. Before she was even halfway up the stairs, Uncle Ricky had the blade of her cheap twelve-inch kitchen knife firmly embedded in his chest, the shaft giving a lazy to and fro. Almost like a cartoon. Boing, boing.

He'd not even risen from the chair he'd been sitting in. He never rose again.

Mum is the only person alive who knows my secret. Our secret. We are forever bonded by it, and that was her doing, not mine.

At almost six months pregnant, I could barely function. My hormones raged. I simply agreed with everything she told me I had to do.

When she confessed, I nodded.

When they cross-examined me, I miscarried my beautiful little girl. Samantha we were going to call her.

The shock, they said.

Convenience, I later thought as the devastation ripped me apart.

She took the rap for me. Never let me speak about it from that very moment. Not even in private am I allowed to mention it. Maybe that time will come when she gets out of prison.

I don't let her into any of my other secrets. But she told me one of hers. Well, that's not strictly true.

She told me Tess's secret.

You see, Tess went to see Mum without telling anyone. Although if any of us cared to check, I'm sure it would be on the prison visitor record. None of us did. None of us would. Why would we?

So, Tess never told me Graham was having an affair. No. She didn't need to.

She told Mum.

It wasn't that difficult to find out about the Viagra, either. After she'd told Mum about it. Tess hadn't hidden them. She'd put them in her dressing-gown pocket. Four of those little blue suckers, all in a neat little packet. Apparently.

She didn't know what to do with them. Should she confront him? Should she just dispose of them? But she'd kept them there. Typical of her to be so indecisive.

I thought she'd have confided in us, but maybe she was trying to get her ducks in line before saying something. Sad, really. If only she'd spoken out on this occasion. She would have had all our support.

It wasn't difficult to obtain the Viagra. I just checked in her dressing-gown pocket when I popped her home one night, helped her to bed. She was asleep before her head touched the pillow.

When I stirred them into his tea at her birthday party, I had no idea how much it would take for them to dissolve. After all, I've never had reason to research these things, and I certainly am too astute to have looked at anything like that on my computer, either at home or work. After all, we don't want to risk the police looking at my search history, do we? Luckily, it didn't come to that. If it had, I don't think they'd have just looked at me.

Sarah was the key here. Champing at the bit for a fight on the day of Tess's birthday, Graham hadn't dared refuse that cup of tea she handed him. She'd have ripped his throat out and he knew it. He couldn't afford to get into a fight as that would have made him even later than he was already. Late for his assignation. And holy cow, when I found out it was with a man...

So, Graham got all he deserved, and more.

And Tess got what she deserved too. Who'd have known a wealth manager would have been so highly insured? Well, me, of course. He'd confided in me a few years ago. Boasting, showing off his position, his wealth. His superiority. Lording it over me and my poorly paid husband.

I've always thought it doesn't take money to make you happy.

Craig and I couldn't be happier, and we live pretty much pay cheque to pay cheque.

I'm sure Tess will realise that when Ashton arrives home. She has the money, but that's not what will make her happy.

It had taken so long to get hold of her son. Turns out he'd made his way to Cambodia. Now he's making his way back and will be home tomorrow. It'll be good to see him. Ashton is a lovely young man. Perhaps, without his father's entitled encouragement, he'll do well.

Tess certainly has since Graham's accident. I haven't seen her drink once. I'll keep an eye on that, in case she relapses, but I think she's going to be just fine. Especially when she gets that Golden Labrador puppy she's reserved. Two more weeks, and he'll be hers. She needs the company.

I smile into the glass as I take another sip. Only one glass of wine. That's my limit. That's my control. Any more and I might possibly wrong-step. But I won't.

I never did with Mr Collington. When he'd asked about the children in our household, I'd lied. We hadn't four children at that time, but I'd been so proud, I'd raised my head and grinned at him, knowing that a baby was swelling my mum's belly right at that moment. A pride he'd squelched without thought.

That one was easier. Less mess. There hadn't even been a sniff of a suggestion that there was something amiss. An accident, I'm sure. With no family to protest, to object, it would be dropped.

Some care worker would get their wrist slapped and a new policy would be written.

I'd like to think no one lost their job over it.

It had to be done, though. Vile man that he was. Sadistic.

I'd pushed him to the back of my mind, but I'd never forgotten him.

My forefinger naturally goes to stroke the thin white scar on my upper lip. This was the permanent reminder of what he did to me that day. Worse still, in my mind was that he caused me to pee myself in front of the whole class. I've never recovered from that humiliation.

Still, I heard it wasn't as bad as what he'd done to Carol all those years ago. Poor Carol, the first girl to develop in our class. He ruined her life.

I wish she'd spoken out.

I wish I'd spoken out.

My guilt cripples me.

I have certain regrets about the caretaker. He was the one who wrong-stepped there. Straight down those stairs. Unfortunate he didn't die straight off. It would have been kinder. He has care workers in to help him, though. Brain damaged. He can't help himself. Never will be able to. Poor man. I think perhaps I acted a little impulsively there, never checked my facts thoroughly, which isn't like me.

I should have waited longer, spoken to the Head, but when the opportunity presented itself, I took the step I believed was right to protect my youngest. There was no way I was about to risk something bad happening to Toni.

She did the right thing. She spoke out. I took action. Threat removed.

I wander away from the door, the breeze cooling my over-hot skin.

Still. I have more to do.

Perhaps I will take Tess's advice and look at HRT. I've got an appointment in a couple of weeks to see my GP.

I think my hormones are raging. Lack of sleep certainly can affect a person's viewpoint.

I slip back into the dining room chair and flip open the file I'd been reading.

That cooled skin flashes to hot again as I stare at the photograph on the file. Into the eyes of the woman who got away with torturing those children. The Anslow case. Don't ask me how. She managed to pile it all onto him, but I know her intent was just as vil. I know she had more involvement than she'd admit to.

I tried every which way I could, but the woman managed to wriggle herself out of prosecution.

It doesn't mean she can writhe her way out of justice, though.

I stare at her new address, committing it to memory, and then lose the file and rest my hand on it for a moment.

It's just a matter of time.

People like her can't expect to get away with atrocities against children.

I won't let them.

Justice will be served.

ACKNOWLEDGMENTS

It seems the more I write, the more I owe thanks to the people around me, and that circle has certainly widened of late.

It was while writing *My Little Brother* that certain memories erupted from my childhood. A near miss, incidents that my older sister seemed to rescue me from. No damage was done, but memories surfaced, and as always, I asked the question 'what could have happened...?'

I owe a great deal of thanks to Ross Greenwood for all the encouragement, critiques, 'nudges', and humour.

To Margaret, as always and from the very beginning.

My beta readers who between them helped me to give this book more focus: Andi Miller, Sarah Oakes, Margaret Palmer, Andy Parkes.

To my wonderful editor Caroline Ridding who makes me rip the guts out and re-write a much stronger version every time.

To all of those who champion my work.

MORE FROM DIANE SAXON

We hope you enjoyed reading *My Sister's Secret*. If you did, please leave a review.

If you'd like to gift a copy, this book is also available as an ebook, digital audio download and audiobook CD.

Sign up to Diane Saxon's mailing list for news, competitions and updates on future books.

http://bit.ly/DianeSaxonNewsletter

Discover more gripping thrillers from Diane Saxon.

ABOUT THE AUTHOR

Diane Saxon previously wrote romantic fiction for the US market but has now turned to writing psychological crime. *Find Her Alive* was her first novel in this genre and introduced series character DS Jenna Morgan. Diane is married to a retired policeman and lives in Shropshire.

Visit Diane's website: http://dianesaxon.com/

Follow Diane on social media:

facebook.com/dianesaxonauthor

twitter.com/Diane_Saxon

instagram.com/DianeSaxonAuthor

bookbub.com/authors/diane-saxon

Boldwood

Boldwood Books is an award-winning fiction publishing company seeking out the best stories from around the world.

Find out more at www.boldwoodbooks.com

Join our reader community for brilliant books, competitions and offers!

Follow us

@BoldwoodBooks

@BookandTonic

Sign up to our weekly deals newsletter

https://bit.ly/BoldwoodBNewsletter

THE

Murder

LIST

**THE MURDER LIST IS A NEWSLETTER
DEDICATED TO SPINE-CHILLING FICTION
AND GRIPPING PAGE-TURNERS!**

**SIGN UP TO MAKE SURE YOU'RE ON OUR
HIT LIST FOR EXCLUSIVE DEALS, AUTHOR
CONTENT, AND COMPETITIONS.**

SIGN UP TO OUR
NEWSLETTER

BIT.LY/THEMURDERLISTNEWS

Printed in Great Britain
by Amazon

19440816R10200